*Charmed, Texas, is everything the name impiies ~ q...,
and as small-town friendly as they come. And when it comes to romance,
there's no place quite as enchanting . . .*

Lanie Barrett didn't mean to *lie*. Spinning a story of a joyous marriage to make a dying woman happy is forgivable, isn't it? Lanie thinks so, especially since her beloved Aunt Ruby would have been heartbroken to know the truth of her niece's sadly loveless, short-of-sparkling existence. Trouble is, according to the will, Ruby didn't quite buy Lanie's tale. And to inherit the only house Lanie ever really considered a home, she'll have to bring her "husband" back to Charmed for three whole months—or watch Aunt Ruby's cozy nest go to her weasel cousin, who will sell it to a condo developer.

Nick McKane is out of work, out of luck, and the spitting image of the man Lanie described. He needs money for his daughter's art school tuition, and Lanie needs a convenient spouse. It's a match made . . . well, not quite in heaven, but for a temporary arrangement, it couldn't be better. Except the longer Lanie and Nick spend as husband and wife, the more the connection between them begins to seem real. Maybe this modern fairy tale really could come true . . .

Books by Sharla Lovelace

Charmed in Texas
A Charmed Little Lie

Published by Kensington Publishing Corporation

A Charmed Little Lie

Charmed in Texas

Sharla Lovelace

LYRICAL SHINE
Kensington Publishing Corp.
www.kensingtonbooks.com

To the weird ones, the introverts, the misfits and those hiding in plain sight. . . High five, my loves. You are me and I am you. You are my tribe. ;)

Acknowledgements

A quick note to all my wonderful readers. . . I am so over the moon excited to bring this new series to you! I fell in love with Charmed from the moment the idea wiggled its way in, and I hope you will, too. Lanie and Nick have a special place in my heart, kicking things off with A Charmed Little Lie, and I can honestly say this is one of my favorite books to write so far. I hope you will love them like I do—and Ralph of course. Because who couldn't love Ralph?

Everyone knows I thank and love them, I couldn't do this writing thing without my husband's support and all my coworkers at my day job when I'm on deadline and having to think about numbers and I'm walking around in a wide-eyed frenzy like, "But I need the words!" Thank you all.

And oh—as usual, there's a recipe waiting for you, so get you some!

May you be drizzled in honey... ;)

xoxo
Sharla

Chapter One

"Take caution when unwrapping blessings, my girl. They're sometimes dipped in poop first."

In retrospect, I should have known the day was off. From the wee hours of the morning when I awoke to find Ralph—my neighbor's ninety-pound Rottweiler—in bed with me and hiking his leg, to waking up the second time on my crappy uncomfortable couch with a hitch in my hip. Then the coffeemaker mishap and realizing I was out of toothpaste. Pretty much all the markers were there. Aunt Ruby would have thumped me in the head and asked me where my Barrett intuition was.

But I never had her kind of intuition.

And Aunt Ruby wasn't around to thump me. Not anymore. Not even long distance.

"Ow! Shit!" I yelped as my phone rang, making me sling pancake batter across the kitchen as I burned my finger on the griddle.

I'm coordinated like that.

Cursing my way to the phone, I hit speaker when I saw the name of said neighbor.

"Hey, Tilly."

"How's my sweet boy?" she crooned.

I glared at Ralph. "He's got bladder denial," I said. "Possibly separation anxiety. Mommy issues."

"Uh-oh, why?" she asked.

"He marked three pieces of furniture, and me," I said, hearing her gasp. "While I was in the bed. With him."

"Ralph was in the bed?" Tilly asked.

"*That* was the part that caught your attention?"

"Well, I just don't allow him up there."

"It wasn't by invitation," I said. "I woke up to him staring down at me and then he let it rip."

I liked my neighbor, Tilly. She was from two apartments down, was sweet, kinda goofy, and was always making new desserts she liked to try out on me. So when she suddenly had to bail for some family emergency with her mom and couldn't take her dog, I decided to take a page from her book and be a *giver*. Offer to dog-sit Ralph while she was gone for a few days.

"Oh wow, I'm so sorry, Lanie," she said.

"Not a problem," I lied. I'm not really cut out to be a giver. "We're bonding."

"How's he eating?" Tilly asked. "Sometimes he's shy about eating around other people."

I glanced over to see Ralph lick pancake batter off the cabinet, then sit back on his haunches and lick himself.

"I think he's doing all right."

Tilly sighed on the other end. "Thank you so much for this," she said. "It takes a load off my mind to know he's taken care of."

Something in that sentence or in her voice sounded weird.

"So, how long are you going to be gone again?" I asked.

"Um, well," she began. "Things are a little complicated, so it may be a little bit."

A little bit. My weird radar perked up.

"Yeah?" I prompted. "Like—a week? What are we talking?"

"Well, I'll call you in a couple of days when I know more," she said. "It's—you know, my dad is really sick, and family just gets so—"

"Your dad?" I asked. "I thought it was your mom."

"Oh yeah," she said. "That's what I meant. Sorry, I'm just a little scattered right now." She laughed. "I'm buzzing on too much coffee, probably."

Too much something.

Ralphed belched.

"Hey, remember," Tilly continued. "When you put him outside to leave for work, talk sweet to him so he doesn't think it's a punishment."

"Heaven forbid."

"Seriously, Lanie."

"He peed on me!" I exclaimed. "His fragile ego isn't my biggest concern right now."

"I know, I'm sorry," she said. "I'll send you some money to clean your mattress. I actually kind of hoped he'd cheer you up."

What? "Cheer me up?"

"You've been so—I don't know—forlorn?" she asked. "Since your aunt died, it's like you lost your energy source."

Damn, that was freakishly observant of her. Maybe *she* got the Barrett intuition. She nailed it in one sentence. Aunt Ruby *was* my energy source. Even from the next state over, the woman that raised me kept me buzzing with her unstoppable magical spirit. When her eyes went, the other senses jumped to the fight. When her life went, it was like someone turned out the lights. All the way to Louisiana.

Honestly, I had this thought. That I'd feel her more after she passed. After all, she'd been the one with all the *intuition*. A rumor that had wagged tongues in Charmed, Texas my whole young life. Something I'd thought was cool when I was little, spent most of my teenage years denying, and mostly forgot as an adult—living hundreds of miles away. Forgot until I'd go for a visit, anyway. One step inside that old house left little question.

There hadn't been any *intuition* my way, however. No feelings. No aromas of baked apples or orange peels. No sudden penchant for raw honey or the color blue or the new ability to sew. No Aunt Ruby.

Well, maybe the honey part, but that was just me. You can't grow up in a bee-farming community and not have strong feelings about honey. You either love it or despise it.

I was truly alone and on my own. Realizing that at thirty-three was sobering. Realizing Aunt Ruby now knew I'd lied about everything was mortifying. Maybe that's why she was staying otherwise occupied out there in the afterlife.

Then again, *lying* was maybe too strong a word. Was there another word? Maybe a whole turn of phrase would be better. Something like *coloring the story to make an old woman happy.*

Yeah.

Coloring with crayons that turned into shovels.

No one knew the extent of the ridiculous hole I had dug myself into. The one that involved my hometown of Charmed, Texas believing I was married and successful, living with my husband in sunny California and absorbing the good life. Why California? Because it sounded more exciting than Louisiana. And a fantasy-worthy advertising job I submitted an online resume for *a year ago* was located there. That's about all the sane thought that went into that.

The tale was spun at first for Aunt Ruby when she got sick, diabetes taking her down quickly, with her eyesight being the first victim. I regaled her on my short visits home with funny stories from my quickie wedding in Vegas (I did go to Vegas with a guy I was sort of seeing), my successful career in advertising (I hadn't made it past promotional copy), and my hot, doting, super gorgeous husband named Michael who traveled a lot for work and therefore was never with me. You'd think I'd need pictures for that part, right? Even for a mostly blind woman? Yeah. I did.

I showed her pictures of a smoking hot, dark and dangerous looking guy I flirted with one night at Caesar's Palace while my boyfriend was flirting with a waitress. A guy who, incidentally, was named—Michael.

I know.

I rot.

But it made her happy to know I was happy and taken care of, when all that mattered in her entire wacky world was that I find love and *be taken care of.* That I not end up alone, with my ovaries withering in a dusty desert. Did I know that she would then relay all that information on to every mouthpiece in Charmed? Bragging about how well her Lanie had done? How I'd lived up to the Most-Likely-To-Set-The-World-On-Fire vote I'd received senior year. Including the visuals I'd sent her of me and Michael-the-Smoking-Hottie.

So later on, in Aunt Ruby's last days, when said boyfriend—a very fair, blond-haired GQ-style guy named Benjamin—wanted to come with me to meet the woman that raised me, and be with me at the sparse little funeral, I couldn't do that. Not when Lanie Barrett's *husband* was dark-haired, tall and blue-collar sexy Michael. Which would have come as somewhat of a surprise to Benjamin.

"I know, Tilly," I said, pulling my thoughts back to her as Ralph finished up cleaning the cabinets and had come nosing around the counter to find the source. "I probably have been in a funk. Just—nothing's been the same."

"Well, and Benjamin," she said, and I could hear the nod.

Damn, I really needed to stop talking to people so much about my personal life. I forgot I'd told her about my boyfriend.

"Benjamin was a douche," I said, feeding Ralph a burned pancake. Maybe he'd be less likely to pee on me tonight.

Benjamin *was* a douche. He called me cute.

He didn't understand the insult, but it was really the whole disclaimer phrase that went with it that got my goat. The words still echoed in my head.

I've always wanted that average, girl-next-door, dependable girlfriend. The one that isn't too sparkly. Cute but not gorgeous.

I wanted to throw up just thinking about it. Nothing in my entire life had made me feel more mediocre than that. Whether it was true or not, your man shouldn't be the one to say it. Not that I was looking for undying love. I didn't do love. But I was certainly looking for unbridled lust with someone who thought me *above average*.

My phone beeped in my ear, announcing another call, from an unknown number. Unknown to the phone, maybe, but as of late I'd come to recognize it.

"Hey, Till," I said, finger hovering over the button. "The lawyer is calling. I should probably see if there's any news on the will."

"Go ahead," she said. "I'll call you in a few days and see how my Ralph is doing."

So, not coming back in a few days.

"Sounds good," I said, clicking over. "Hey, Carmen."

"Hey yourself," she said, her voice friendly but smooth and full of that lawyer professionalism they must inject them with in law school. She warmed it up for an old best friend, but it wasn't the same tone that used to prank call boys in junior high or howl at the top of her lungs as we sped drunk down Dreary Road senior year.

This Carmen Frost was polished. I saw that at the funeral. Still Carmen, but edited and Photoshopped. Even when I met her for drinks afterward and we drove over to the house to reminisce.

This Carmen felt different from the childhood best buddy that had slept in many a blanket fort in our living room. Strung of course with Christmas lights in July and blessed with incense from Aunt Ruby. That Carmen was the only person I truly let into my odd little family circle. She never made fun of Aunt Ruby or perpetuated the gossip. Coming from a single mom household where her mother had to work late often, she enjoyed the warm weirdness at our house. It wasn't uncommon for her to join us to spontaneously have dinner in the backyard under the stars or dress up in homemade togas (sheets) to celebrate Julius Caesar's birthday.

Returning for the funeral and walking into that house for the first time without Aunt Ruby in it broke me. It was full of her. She was in every cushion. Every bookcase. Every oddball knickknack. Her scent was in the curtains that had been recently washed and ironed, as if she'd known the end was near and had someone come clean the house. Couldn't leave it untidy on her exit to heaven for people to talk.

We sat in Aunt Ruby's living room and cried a little and told a few nostalgic stories, trying to bring back the old banter, but it was as if Carmen had forgotten how to relax. She was wound up on a spool of bungee rope and someone had tied the ends down. Tight and unable to yield.

Still, we had history. At one time, she was family. Which is why Aunt Ruby hired her to handle her will and estate.

A word that seemed so silly on my tongue, as I would have never associated *estate* with my aunt or her property. But that was the word Carmen used again and again when we talked. Her *estate* involved the house and some money (she didn't elaborate), but it had to be probated and there were complications due to medical bills that had to be paid first.

Which made sense. It had taken almost two months, and I had almost written off hearing anything. Not that I was holding my breath on the money part. I was pretty sure whatever dollars there were would be used up with the medical bills, and that just left the house. I figured that would probably be left to me. I was really her only family after my mom died young. Well, except for some cousins that I barely knew from her brother she rarely talked to, but I couldn't imagine them keeping up with her enough to even know that she died.

I didn't know what on earth I'd do with the house. It was old and creaky and probably full of problems—one being it was in Charmed and I was not. But it was home. And it had character and memories and laughter soaked into the walls. Aunt Ruby was there. I felt it. If that was intuition, then okay. I felt it *there*. But only there.

So I'd probably keep it as a place to get away, and spend the next several months going back and forth on the weekends like I had right after she passed, cleaning out the fridge and things that were crucial. Mentally, I ticked off a list of the work that was about to begin. That was okay. Aunt Ruby was worth it.

"How's it going over there?" I asked.

"Good, good," Carmen said. "How's California?"

Oh yeah.

"Fine," I said. "You know. Sunshine and pretty people. All that."

I closed my eyes and shook my head. Where did I get this shit?

"Sounds wonderful," she said. "It's been raining and muggy here for three days."

"Yeah," I said, just to say something.

"So the will has been probated," Carmen said. "Everything's ready to be read. I wanted to see when you'd be able to make it back to Charmed for that?"

"Oh," I said, slightly surprised. "I have to come in person?"

"For the reading, yes," she said. "You have to sign some paperwork and so do the other parties."

"Other parties?"

"Yes—well, normally I don't disclose that but you're you, so…" she said on a chuckle. "The Clarks?" she said, her tone ending in question.

"As in my cousins?" Really?

"I was surprised too," she said. "I don't remember ever even hearing about them."

"Because I maybe saw them three times in my whole life," I said. "They live in Denning. Or they did. I don't think you ever met them."

"Hmm, okay." Her tone sounded like she was checking off a list. "And you'll need to bring some things with you."

"Things?"

"Two, actually," Carmen said, laughing. "Just like your aunt to make a will reading quirky. But they are easy. Just your marriage certificate—"

"My what?"

Carmen chuckled again, and I was feeling a little something in my throat too. Probably not of the same variety.

"I know," she said. "Goofy request, but I see some doozies all the time. Had a client once insist that his dog be present at the reading of the will. He left him almost everything. Knowing Aunt Ruby, there is some cosmic reason."

Uh-huh. She was messing with me.

I swallowed hard, my mind reeling and already trying to figure out how I could fake a marriage certificate.

"And the second thing?" I managed to push past the lump in my throat.

"Easy peasy," she said. "Your husband, of course."

Chapter Two

"Men are like icing, Lanie. Sweet and tasty and good to look at, but kind of unnecessary without your favorite cake. Wait for the cake."

The paralysis that afflicted my vocal chords had a similar effect on my feet. I stopped dead in my tracks halfway around the counter, wet rag in hand to clean up where Ralph had left off.

Bring my husband?

Think fast.

Laugh.

I started chuckling, and it sounded something like gargling plastic so I stopped, then flipped my hair, which Carmen couldn't see but it gave me the nonchalant *I'm not lying* air I needed.

"Bring my husband?" I said, laughing again. "That's crazy. He's working."

"We didn't decide on when," Carmen said.

"He's always working."

"Wow, that can't be an easy life," Carmen said. "What does he do?"

Right now, he was making me sweat. "He, um, well, he—" My gaze darted wildly for inspiration. Landed on a chair, a towel, a dark spot on the rug—ugh, *focus, Lanie!* Coming back to the kitchen, they stopped on pancakes. "He cooks!" I blurted.

"Oh, he's a chef?"

"Yes! Well, no," I amended, realizing I should make it more generic and less able to prove. "Not a chef, but he's working on that. In a major restaurant."

"Really? Which one?"

"It's local."

Oh God, please end this.

"So—he travels for a local restaurant?" Carmen asked, and I nearly groaned out loud.

"No, the travel is because—" Why? He's a banker? Corporate lawyer? *Snooze*. Something hotter. Something— "He works construction."

So much more logical.

"Oh!" Carmen said. I could hear the what-the-fucks ticking in her brain.

"I mean, not just works construction," I said, wondering when my mouth would surrender and stop digging this giant hole. Maybe I could get my cooking-construction-working husband to fill it in. "He has a team that he runs. They're all over the place. All the time."

"I see," Carmen said.

"And I don't know if I can take off any more time right now," I said. "Maybe you can mail me the doc—"

"Oh, it can be on a weekend," she said quickly. "But no, unfortunately, it has to be in person. The pesky legal process."

"Yeah," I said, staring at Ralph. Who stared back, his ears stuck out to the sides all Yoda-like. *Give me some wisdom, Yoda.* "So what would happen if I came alone?"

"Well," Carmen began. "Your part of the will would become null and void, I'm afraid.

Sweating again. "What?"

"I know," she said. "It's crazy, but some wills are just—unique like this."

"Unique?" I said. "Requiring my husband to be with me or nothing? That's not unique. That's bullshit."

"Actually, it's your husband and the marriage decree," Carmen reminded. And all the dots lit up and connected.

"She didn't believe me," I said softly.

"I'm sorry?" Carmen asked.

"Aunt Ruby," I said, clearing my throat. "She wants proof that I'm really married."

I heard a sigh. "Something like that."

"Or what?" I asked, the panic melting away as I unraveled my aunt's diabolical plan. Unbelievable. I bit off a piece of pancake and proceeded to talk around it. "The house becomes a museum? Goes to charity? New library-slash-coffeehouse?"

There was a pause that I distinctly felt my old friend enter. And another sigh. That was probably good.

"I could so get disbarred for telling you this ahead of time," she said, lowering her voice.

"What?" I whispered, hunching my shoulders like a spy receiving a government secret.

"If you can't produce the proof," Carmen said. "Then the house and the money go to the Clarks."

"Seriously?" I exclaimed, standing fully upright again.

"Afraid so."

"Why?" I demanded. "What was her reason? What would *they* do with it?"

"I—" Another sigh. "I don't know, Lanie. I just do what I'm paid to do. She didn't confide in me."

I slapped a hand over my eyes. I wasn't worried about money. Let them have whatever pennies were jingling around. But the thought of strangers—no, not real strangers because oddly that would be better—but these people, who claimed to be family and yet never showed their faces when Aunt Ruby got sick. Never stepped up to help me out paying for nurses and hospice and all the other expenses.

Hell, if they even knew. Honestly, I never asked because they never crossed my mind. They weren't part of our lives. Were they even at the funeral? I couldn't remember. And probably wouldn't recognize them now if they had been.

So why would she leave them our home?

Our home.

That was the kick of it.

"I've—kind of heard a rumor," Carmen said, almost on a whisper. "But dear God, Lanie, you can't say anything. Shit, I shouldn't even—"

"Tell me!" I yelled. Maybe too loudly. I cleared my throat. "I mean, come on, you can trust me."

She paused. "I don't know if this has any merit, but I did hear some noise about a condo deal," she said. "The older brother has connections or something. And he's on his phone a lot."

"A condo—" My tongue stopped working and I had to stop and take a deep breath. "A condo deal? Like as in tear everything down?"

"I don't know," she said. "I swear that's all I heard. I don't even know if it's about the same thing."

Oh, it was about the same thing. Bryce Clark struck me as a weasel back in the day, and I was willing to bet he still slithered. *Condos. Seriously.* Over my dead body.

"How's this Saturday?" I said, tossing the remainder of my pancake to Ralph, who caught it in midair.

"As in day after tomorrow?" Carmen asked, sounding surprised.

"Very same."

There was the sound of a page turning. "Do you—don't you need to check flights?"

Oh yeah.

"Yes. Let's pencil in late afternoon, but I'll confirm."

"Sounds good," she said. "Let me know when, and I'll pick y'all up at the airport."

Jesus.

"Nah, we'll get a car," I said. "We'll want to wander around later."

"What about your husband's work schedule?" Carmen asked. "Michael, is it?"

"I'll figure it out," I said.

The first true thing I'd said to her since *hello.*

I *would* figure it out. I wouldn't lose my childhood home to Aunt Ruby's little shenanigans. I just had to find a husband.

* * *

Benjamin—scratch.

Neighbor guy—scratch. Freaky homicidal girlfriend.

Dark-haired IT guy at work—scratch, scratch. No coworkers in this sketchy plan.

Friend of Tilly's? Maybe.

He was brunette. Dark eyes. Tall. Nose a little big, and a little skinny for my taste, but I wasn't *actually* marrying the guy. Just borrowing him. And he agreed for a measly fifty bucks, and he owned a suit. We had a plan for meeting up early Saturday morning so I could give him the scoop and we'd hit the road for the seven-hour drive. In a rental car. Ugh, this lie was getting expensive.

So there I sat in the parking lot of Dollar General at seven-fifteen in the morning, with Ralph in my back seat (didn't tell the rental place about him). Dressed in a black pencil skirt and my favorite blue silk blouse. Aunt Ruby always liked me in blue. Which felt ridiculous, like I was winning her over so she'd pick me. Really? Why on earth was I having to fight for my own home, and keep the walls that I knew Aunt Ruby still resided in? I wouldn't have thought that to be a hard sell. But hey, that's just me. There was an envelope lying neatly in my bag, containing what I prayed was the world's best fake marriage license, printed out in color and copied over a few times like most people have to do when they don't want to bring the original. A document bonding Michael McKnight and me forever in holy fraudulent matrimony.

I was going to hell.

When my phone rang, I knew without looking that he wasn't coming. Why did I trust this flaky girl?

"Hey, Tilly," I said, closing my eyes.

"I'm. So. So. Sorry," she said.

I just nodded. "I know."

"He—"

"It doesn't matter," I said, mentally waving good-bye to the house and wishing I could throw something at Aunt Ruby. "It's not on you, Tilly, you tried. Thanks, anyway."

"So, how's Ralph?"

I could throw something at her too.

"He's fine," I said. "He's all seat-belted in, with a sippy cup."

There was the hair's width of a pause. "Really?"

"No, not really, dork," I said. "He's back there on a towel—" I turned to look. "Licking himself right now. I brought his leash and a bowl. I'll stop every hour or so and give him some water and a pee break."

"Thank you," she said. "Sorry you're having to do this alone."

I stared at the open highway in the distance as we hung up and then down at what had become the first descent into deception. The sparkly CZ "wedding" ring I'd bought to show Aunt Ruby. Her old eyes might have been going at the time, but she sure managed to notice that my left hand wasn't in a state of bling.

"Okay, Ralph, you up for this?" I threw over my shoulder.

I got a snort. Well, that was more than my AWOL husband had to say.

* * *

Four pee stops later, and finally in Texas, I needed one myself. Hobbling over gravel and cigarette-butt-loaded pit stops in heels (should have thought out the shoe situation better) had my hair tumbling loose from its bun and the rest of me feeling very un-fresh. And hungry.

A diner sporting a "We Dare You To Eat It All, Y'all!" sign looked like just the ticket. Ralph's nose went to twitching.

"I'll crack the window, and get it to go, okay?" Glancing around the car for the dog abuse police. "I'm not leaving you in the car longer than fifteen minutes."

I opened my door and pointed a finger back at him. "Don't pee on anything."

Okay, I was maybe a bit overdressed for this place. I realized that. But everyone stopping mid-chew to turn around and stare me down was a bit much. It wasn't like I had Ralph with me. My heels clicked loudly on the sticky floor as I made my way up to the counter.

"Can I see a menu?" I asked a blond ponytailed woman that rushed by. She pointed at a chalkboard behind her and kept going.

"Okie-dokie," I said under my breath, perusing the colored chalked choices.

Chopped beef. Pulled pork. Grilled chicken. Cheeseburgers. Any variety of the above served fried or barbecued, and slathered in your choice of sauce. Another sign above that one offered a ten-pound burger for free for anyone who could eat it all on the spot.

"Can I get it to go, do you know?" I asked a man on a stool.

He was devouring a barbecued chopped beef sandwich and fries like it was his last meal. Sauce was everywhere.

"I assume so," he said, wiping his mouth. "I never have, but I would think."

"Ma'am?" I called out as the busy waitress hurried by, yelling at the cook in the window to speed it up. "Can I order something to go?"

The woman leaned over while never missing a step and pulled out a Styrofoam container. "With you in a sec!"

"I recommend the barbecue," the man next to me said around another bite. "Outta this world."

It did look and smell good, as long as I didn't look too closely at the mangled mess rolling around his mouth. One look down at my silk blouse, however, told me I'd be wearing it, and blue didn't go with reddish brown.

"Nick!" yelled the woman again, making me jump. "This isn't the Ritz, come on already. I need these orders!"

"Quit your damn yelling at me!" Nick called back through the window. "You want super speed, go to McDonalds. You want good? You can wait an extra damn thirty seconds."

The dark head poking through the window with the impossibly dark eyes and chiseled everything certainly convinced me. The slight Cajun lilt to his words didn't hurt, either. Extra thirty seconds? I was good with that. Ralph was good. If I could just maybe get it started.

"Can I—" I held out a hand.

"What?" Blondie said, turning on me.

"Um," I stammered, a little taken aback. "To go order?"

"I gathered," she said, holding up the Styrofoam container.

"Jesus, Brenda," the guy in the window presumably named Nick muttered. "Screaming at me, rude to customers—"

"You don't talk to her that way," growled another older-sounding guy out of sight, somewhere behind Nick. "You're expendable, you know."

"Of course I know, you never stop telling me," Nick said, putting the most beautiful burger I'd ever seen in the window, perfectly framed by sizzling golden crisp tater tots.

He hit the bell and my mouth watered on command.

"I want that," I said, pointing. "Just like that."

The waitress rolled her eyes. "Another solid cow all the way with tots. To go."

"Solid cow?" I said. "*Burger* was too simple?"

An icy pair of overworked blue eyes locked on mine.

"That'll be five-fifty," she said.

I smiled and pulled out a ten. "Keep the change."

Nick's eyes landed on me, and I could swear there was appreciation there. Or amusement.

"Restrooms?"

She pointed again, this time to a sign over a hall off to the side.

I nodded. "Thanks," I whispered.

She did a fluttery thing with her overdone eyelashes again, and huffed as she turned around.

"Do me a favor and make sure she doesn't spit in my food while I'm gone," I said under my breath to barbecue-guy.

"You got it," he said.

I'd barely gotten my skirt hiked up, however, before I heard all hell break loose. There was a loud growling yell—had to be Gripey-Older-Guy. Blond Brenda's voice went on high-pitched bitch mode at chipmunk speed. And tone-ala-Nick was interspersed in clips among all of it. I couldn't make out the words, but it didn't sound good. And by the time I made it back out, Brenda was flinging her arms around, Older Guy was slamming something metal around, and Nick was storming out the door.

"Wait!" I exclaimed, my head on a swivel between retreating Nick and really ugly sweating Older Guy now taking up bulk space in the window. "What about my order?"

"Not my problem," Nick said, giving me a what-the-fuck look.

Which was technically true, but I'd seen that other burger and I *wanted* it. "Hang—" I began, but he was already out the door. Damn it. "Balls."

My feet had me out the door after him. To what? Make him fry me a burger on the hood of my car? What was I doing?

"Lady, he'll make your burger," Nick said, slinging a backpack into the bed of an old truck. "It'll taste like shit and be soggy with grease but it'll be there. God, what a prick." He opened his door with a creak. "Good luck."

"But—"

"Seriously?" he said. "There's a *but* in this conversation?" He propped an arm on his door. "I have to find another job. Like today."

And angels sang.

Tall, dark hair, dark brooding eyes, body that looked like it could feasibly work construction, and he could cook. Looked delicious in jeans and a white T-shirt. And—needed a job.

Probably a better paying one than me.

But—

"Do you have a suit?" I blurted out.

Those eyes looked at me like I was crazy. Yeah, I might be. "What?"

"I have fifty bucks and I need a guy that looks like you."

Chapter Three

"Three things to keep in your purse at all times. Bag of peanuts, pack of tissues, and a tampon. You can survive any day with that."

Okay, after we established that I wasn't offering money for sex, and insulting him for that matter because really? Fifty? After all that and my explanation of what I needed, we were left with him staring at me over the bed of his truck, appearing to weigh his options while I walked Ralph in a tiny strip of grass by the road.

"You haven't left yet," I said, coming back to stand on the other side.

"Don't take that as a yes," he said.

"So it's a no?" I asked. My stomach growled loudly and I clapped a hand over it.

He huffed out a breath and rubbed at his eyes, looking miserable. I felt bad for him. No one should lose their job.

"I'd have to stay overnight?"

"Well, I've already driven five hours, and there's another two ahead, so yeah, I'm not making the return back tonight," I said. "I'll stay at my aunt's house. There are three bedrooms there, you'd be safe."

He appeared to ignore my wit.

There was a long pause, and then he shook his head as if knocking loose the logical thinking. "I have to hit the pavement, sorry. I have bills—"

"A hundred?" I blurted. "Two hundred?"

He looked at me and then blew out a breath. "Lady—"

"Three—hang on," I muttered, turning on my heel and diving into the car for my wallet. Shit, shit, shit. I needed this. The guy couldn't have been more perfect for my jacked-up plan if I'd written it specifically for him. My win was right there; I could taste it, feel it. I could sell this crap to Carmen with him by my side, and as messed up as that was, I was about to sell my soul to find out. Or at least, a large portion of my wallet. I pulled out all the travel money I'd liberated from the ATM on my way out, clenching the bills like captive little flags. "Six hundred and change," I said, a little breathlessly. "It's all I have."

He looked at me dumbfounded. "You're crazy. You don't even know me."

"I'm desperate," I said, feeling a little choke pulling at my vocal chords. "And I have a gut feeling about you."

A gut feeling? Anything like intuition? No. More like delirium from hunger and onset panic.

"Shit," he muttered, turning in a circle, clasping both hands behind his head as if the action might keep it from exploding.

"Please," I said, holding out the money. "It's one day. Less than that, even."

His eyes dropped to the bills waving in the breeze, and he shut them for half a second.

"I'll—do it."

My lungs exploded, letting out my breath in one gush. "Thank—"

"Five hundred," he said, waving off my hand. "I'm not taking the last of your cash, you're on the road for Christ's sake. And come on, put that shit away, quit waving it in the parking lot like a loon."

"Deal," I said. *Really?* Like I had some kind of negotiation power. But hot damn and holy shit balls, I had me a Michael. "Oh, by the way, your name is Michael McKnight."

He pulled a face. "What, the other cheesy stage names were all taken?"

"Sorry, it's documented," I said, pointing behind me to the envelope on my front seat. "Can't change it now."

"Well, come on," he said. "Follow me to my place."

His place. Hang on. Visions of Lifetime movies played in my head. "Say what?"

Nick gave me a double take. "You asked me if I had a suit. I can promise you it wouldn't be in my truck."

"Good point. So—"

"So I'm not leaving my truck here," he said. "And unless you want me going reeking of old grease, I'm taking a shower."

I licked my lips and cursed my ridiculous options. "So I'm following you to your place."

"Yes ma'am," he said, slamming the door with a multitude of creaks.

* * *

The doubts that winged around my head like a flurry of butterflies as I followed Nick someone-or-other down a twisty road, didn't disperse when we pulled up to a double-wide trailer up on cinderblocks. What was I thinking? Asking a strange guy to come with me to Charmed for the reading of a will. What if Aunt Ruby was secretly hoarding money and leaving it all to me and they handed it to me in a giant laundry basket (because that's where she would keep it) and then he mugged me and stole my rental car and left me on the side of the road with nothing but Ralph and my empty laundry basket? What if he was a serial killer that preyed in unsuspecting diners, cooking and killing his way across the country?

Nick got out and gestured for me to follow him in. *Uh, no.* I rolled down my window.

"Give me fifteen minutes, and I'll be ready," he said.

I gave him a thumbs-up. "Cool."

He looked at me funny. "You don't have to wait in the car."

Have good manners. "I'm good."

He started to laugh and shake his head, and something in me—maybe it was the overwhelming hunger gnawing at my belly—but something stopped caring about manners.

"You think I'm coming into your house?" I asked. "I think I learned not to do that around age six."

One eyebrow went up. "Seriously?"

"As you pointed out, I don't know you."

He leaned against the bed of his truck and crossed his arms over his chest. They were good arms.

"Lady, I'm about to get in a car with you for an overnight trip to a town I've never heard of, to stay in some old house with someone so delusional she has to pretend to have a husband," he said. "If anyone should be afraid, it's me."

Heat—and not the good kind—flooded my face. "I'm not delusional."

"Look," he said, holding up his hands and pushing off his truck toward his house. "If you'd rather sit out here in the heat, be my guest."

He disappeared behind a screen door and another solid one, and I looked around. Nothing but land and trees and an old motorcycle that had seen better days. No other houses—or trailers—nearby. To his credit, the trailer was neat and he'd put a row of shrubs in front. And some sort of fern hung by the door on one of those plant stands. So he did care about where he lived, made an effort to keep it nice. Kept a fern alive. No spare toilet parts lying around the yard.

Maybe it was a little bit rude to ask him to trust me and then basically accuse him of being untrustworthy.

"Okay," I muttered, not really feeling okay as I stepped out of the car. I glanced back at Ralph. "If I die, good luck to you out here."

I rapped on the screen door, thinking I was probably too late. He was likely already—

The inside door opened and there he stood, still in his jeans but shirtless. A towel slung over one shoulder. Dear God.

"Um," I managed, pointing toward inside.

"Come on," he said, stepping aside as I pulled open the screen door. "No dog?"

"Well, I didn't think you'd want me to bring him in," I said.

"Won't he be thirsty?"

"Believe me, he's eaten and drank better than I have today," I said.

"Ah, that's right," he said. "The hamburger that never was."

"Yeah, let's not mention that," I said, my stomach growling loudly on demand.

"All right, I'll be out in a minute," he said, strolling down the hall, his jeans riding low as he started to unbutton them. He turned around with the top one undone. *Holy Jesus.* "There's a bag of chips on the counter. Help yourself."

That was the ticket to pull my eyes off his buttons.

As soon as the bathroom door closed and I heard water, I pounced on the bag that was waving to me from the kitchen. Sour Cream & Onion Ruffles. Oh, man. It's like he knew the mother ship was coming. I unclipped, unfolded, and stuffed as many as I could fit into my mouth. Just in case he was a quick showerer.

And then, as my blood sugar stabilized and I could see straight, I looked around.

It was nice.

Not fancy nice like expensive things, but clean, tidy, a little sparse like a man lived there alone, but a man who took care of his stuff and cared about appearance. The furniture, on closer inspection, was really nice. Leather. Wood. Almost out of place in a trailer, but maybe leftovers from a previous life. Like possibly divorce victims.

A table of framed photos was the only really personal touch. One of himself with another man, smiling and holding up fish. A brother? The others were mostly of a little girl with dark hair and the same chocolate eyes, at various ages. Some with him, some not. And one school photo of her, probably around sixteen or so. She was a jaw-dropping beauty, that was for sure, and looked just like him. Could be a niece, but that many photos of her screamed *daughter*. Which fit with the divorce theory. So a teenaged daughter—how the hell old *was* he?

Hottie cooking Nick as a dad—that did take down the serial killer angle a bit. Not that serial killers couldn't have families. In fact, most of them probably did, but I was choosing the route most likely to leave me in one piece.

I never heard the water shut off.

"Good chips?"

I whirled around with a yelp, hand to mouth to cover my chewing, and sidestepped to return the bag to the counter.

"Sorry," I mumbled around a mouthful as I clumsily clipped it back. And then I paid attention.

Nick was walking through the room in a towel. Dripping wet. Hair slicked back. Did I say dripping wet?

In a towel.

I almost forgot how to swallow. Apparently, having the delusional crazy lady in his house didn't scare him too badly.

He grabbed two bottles of water from the fridge, set one on the counter for me, and headed back to the bathroom.

"Not a problem," he called back. "I told you to eat."

A blow dryer came on and back off again.

"So I assume this is your daughter in the pictures?" I asked, resting on a bar stool. "Or a niece?"

There was the tiniest of pauses. I'd breached his personal space. Well, hell, he shouldn't have invited me into it.

"That's my daughter, Addison," he said, the sound of something spritzing—cologne, maybe—coming from the bathroom.

God, he was going to smell good, and I smelled like Ralph.

"She's beautiful," I said. "How old is she?"

"Just turned eighteen," he said. "About to graduate."

"Holy hell, eighteen," I said. "Then you're—"

"Old?" he finished, his voice farther away. Possibly in his bedroom, getting more naked. I needed to stop.

"You said it, not me," I called out.

"You have kids?" he called back. "Besides your dog?"

"No," I said. "And Ralph's not mine, either."

"You stole a dog?"

I rolled my eyes, not that he could see it. "I'm dog sitting for my neighbor while she's—somewhere."

I heard those words as they flew out into the room. I might as well have rented a billboard that read DESPERATE PATHETIC LOSER next to my photo. I could even add his "delusional" to it and draw an arrow.

"God, that sounded sad—" I muttered under my breath as I stood, turned, and nearly smacked right into him. *Sweet mama of all that is holy.*

My gaze took the trip while my jaw fell to the floor. Black on black with no tie. Looking like he'd just stepped out of a magazine. I licked my lips as my mouth went dry, and felt every blood cell in my body head south when his gaze dropped to watch me do that, and then take a little trip of its own.

Oh, hell no. *Breathe.*

"You look really nice," I said, backing up a step for safe space, and clearing my throat.

"Thank you," he said.

Don't think I didn't notice that he failed to return the compliment. But hey, drive five hours with a horse and see how fresh you look, Mr. Bond.

"I don't think I ever got your name," he said.

I held out a hand. "Lanie Barrett. And you're Nick?"

He took my hand with a slow grin that I knew instinctively would be my downfall.

"Michael, now," he said. "Michael McKnight."

* * *

It got weird in the car. I know, it was already weird in like five hundred different ways, but two strangers sitting in the car together with almost two hours left to go suddenly felt a little awkward.

"Should we do some homework?" he said, raking fingers through his hair.

Good, he was searching too.

"Great idea," I said, relieved. "So. We've been married about two years—"

"About?"

I blinked. "What?"

"You don't know when?"

"Um, well, I'm just going off when I told Aunt Ruby—"

"Have you ever been married?" he asked.

I blew out a breath. "No."

"Well we need more than an 'about' or no one will buy that," he said.

"When's our anniversary?"

I chuckled. "I don't think anyone is going to ask us that."

"You want to take that chance?"

I looked at him sideways. "Wow, you're really taking this job to heart, aren't you?"

He met my gaze. "If we're going to this much trouble, seems like we should do it right."

I nodded toward the envelope now resting on the dash. "There's a marriage certificate in there. I don't remember the date I picked."

"Already forgetting our anniversary," he said, shaking his head as he reached for the envelope. "Honeymoon must be over."

"So have *you* ever been married?" I asked.

"Didn't we already cover that?"

"No, you said you had a daughter, but last I checked, a ring wasn't required for that."

"Rings," he said, pointing at me.

I held up mine. "Check."

He glanced over at it. "Nice fake."

I frowned. "How can you tell?"

"And mine?" he asked, ignoring the question.

I gave him a look. "It's not required."

"It is for me."

"Excuse me?" Seriously? Out of all the strangers I could have picked up for this, I had to pick a diva?

"Come on," he said. "You started this game. Play it out. What's a twenty-dollar ring at Wal-Mart?"

"It's not a game," I said, popping my neck. This guy was making me tense.

"Okay."

"I started it to make my aunt happy," I said. "She did everything for me, and all she wanted was to see me *taken care of.*" I felt the tell-tale burn behind my eyes and I blinked back fast. "When she got sick, it seemed like the kind thing to do."

"Lie to her?"

"Make her happy," I huffed. "Give her peace of mind."

"I'd rather know the truth," he said.

"Well, I'll keep that in mind if you contract a terminal illness in the next twenty-four hours," I barked.

"Just sayin'," he said.

"So yell if you see a friggin' Wal-Mart," I continued. "We'll get you all official." I felt the need to stop and do some jumping jacks. Something to shake it off. Shake *him* off. He was getting under my skin. "You never answered me, by the way."

"About?"

"Marriage."

He sighed and reached into his coat pocket before pulling out a silver ring and holding it up with his finger and thumb.

"What's that?"

He cut me a look. "That's a yes." He slid it on his finger, and promptly slid it back off as if it burned, then put it back into his pocket. "Remind me when we get there."

"All that grief, and you had one all along?" I noted the change in his eyes, however. Glazed. One check mark in the getting-to-know-my-fake-husband category.

"Last minute-thought just in case," he said, looking out the passenger window.

"So how long were you married?" I asked.

"Seven years," he said, not looking my way.

I felt my eyebrows lift. "That's not chump change," I said. "That's—"

"Ancient history," he said. "So how long till we're in this Charming place?"

Okay, *check-check*. Ex-wife and daughter off-limits.

"Charmed," I corrected. I glanced at my GPS but I already knew by the exits we were passing. I could make this drive in my sleep. "And about an hour and a half." Ralph whined in the back seat and turned in a circle. "You can't possibly need to go again," I said. "And stay on that towel. Don't you mess up this car."

"*This* car?" Nick asked. "This isn't your car, either?"

"It's a rental," I said. "They think I'm coming from California, so I couldn't drive mine."

I felt the stare.

"Don't judge," I added.

"It can't be helped," he said. "You're certifiable."

"How nice," I muttered.

He started to laugh and rubbed at his face. "I don't know what's crazier about this day. That I got fired, or that I've ended up in a car pretending to be the spouse of a pathological liar."

"Hey!" I said, backhanding him in the chest. Which only made him laugh harder.

"Is there anything real about you?"

I frowned as those words sank into me. For one second, I could swear

I felt Aunt Ruby in the car with us, repeating those same words. Intuition.

* * *

We got to Carmen's office, a small building in the larger town of Goldworth, just outside of Charmed. My heart started to race as I pulled the keys and put them in my bag.

Deep breaths. You can do this.

"You all right?" Nick asked.

I met his eyes briefly. "Yeah. Just—I don't know. I never knew I'd have to compete for the house. And weirdly, it didn't matter until I found out about my cousins getting it. They couldn't possibly have good intentions for it. So now it's like—"

"You'd be letting her down," he said.

I nodded, feeling the tears brimming again. "No, no," I said, leaning my head back. "No crying allowed right now."

He pulled down my visor and slid the mirror open. "Here, fix yourself up."

I faced forward again and gave him a sideways look. There was a reason I didn't hook up with guys who were prettier than me.

"I look that bad?"

"No, you look beautiful, actually," he said. "But if we only drove from the airport, you might want to freshen up."

Damn, this guy was more on point with this charade than I was.

"True," I said, swiping under my eyes and digging for my makeup bag. "So, we good with all the details?"

We'd finally gone over the major points. Anniversary—May twelfth. Likes and dislikes—I love food and hate rap music. I'm afraid of fireworks. He loved reality TV and hated butterscotch. No major phobias. We both loved coffee and met in a coffee shop. Keepin' it real.

"I think so," he said.

I touched up my eyes and slapped on some powder and gloss. Refastened all the fallen hairs while Nick nicely took Ralph on a walk.

"Shouldn't be long," I said to Ralph as he jumped back in looking sad. I cracked the windows. "Then I'll bring you to a big yard you can run free in. Terrorize the squirrels."

"We gonna be able to stay there if—" Nick met my eyes. "Things go the wrong way?"

I hadn't thought of that, but of course we could. Shit.

"It's still my house in theory," I said. "I have a key. It'll happen." I took a deep breath and blew it out. "It'll be fine."

Nick gave me a long look and then blinked away as he pulled the ring out of his pocket. He slid it onto his finger, his jaw twitching as he did so. One hand landed at the small of my back as he turned me.

"Let's go do this," he said.

I stopped short. "Why are *you* doing this?"

He looked down at me, jaw twitching again. "Because I'm recently unemployed, and I need the five hundred bucks," he said. "You think *your* life is sad?"

Weren't we a pair.

I nodded. "Let's do this."

There was a one-story elevator ride, and then we were outside the door embossed with Carmen Frost, Attorney at Law. And then fingers were on my top button.

"What are you doing?" I whispered, batting his hands away.

"Relax," he said, returning to the scene of the crime. His fingers brushed the tops of my breasts as he unbuttoned the top button of my blouse. And arranged the flaps to lie there sexily. Heat rushed to my face as our eyes met. My fingers. Some other places. "You look too uptight. Remember, we're married. We're in love. We're comfortable with each other." He nodded toward the door. "And she's your old friend. She'll know if you're aren't."

Great. More to worry about. "True."

"It's a game," he said. "Think of it like that. Points we need to score. We're a couple."

"We're a couple," I echoed.

"You should walk in there totally at ease with the world. Like you're getting more sex than anyone in that room."

My jaw dropped open and a belly laugh sprang forth from pure shock.

"That's it," he said, opening the door in the middle of my laugh.

Oh, he was good. Walking into a room full of the enemy—not Carmen, but the five other people clustered together on all the comfortable furniture—with a laugh on my lips and a blush to my skin, that was genius. And instantly made me feel I had this.

"Lanie," Carmen said, warmly but not with the excited hug that she brought the last time. She couldn't, with a room full of legalities, I knew that. She couldn't take sides. She'd already told me too much.

"Hey, Carmen," I said, nearly tripping over my tongue when Nick interlaced his fingers with mine. I cleared my throat and smiled at the cousins. "Bryce, Treena, good to see you again." They smiled and fidgeted on the sofa with their clueless spouses. Bryce, the oldest, was balding and sweaty and looked to need a fresh shirt soon. Gross. The fifth woman, I didn't recognize. She was younger—wait—yes I did. She *was* at the funeral. The others weren't. She was the homely younger woman with the frizzy blond hair that I'd assumed might be the maid Aunt Ruby hired.

"Hi," I said, extending my unlaced hand to her. "I'm Lanie."

"I know," she said, chuckling as she took my hand in her limp fish one. Ugh. "I'm Alicia, the baby." She rolled her eyes as if that was cute. "Eight years younger than Treena. We probably never met as kids."

Well, since I'd barely met the other two, and they were a few years younger than me, probably not. Making her, what? Twenty-two? Yikes. She hadn't inherited good genes.

"Oh, okay," I said. "Well, nice to meet you." Nick squeezed my hand, and I remembered that whole *couple* thing. "This is my husband, N—Michael."

Balls. I almost blew it in the first sentence.

He shook hands all around, looking totally at ease in his own skin. In that suit. Good God, he could be a rich jet-setter just as easily as he flipped burgers.

"This will be a quick meeting," Carmen said, sitting on the front of her desk instead of behind it. She looked so together, with her blond hair pulled back loosely in a professional barrette, her simple form-fitting chocolate brown dress perfectly matching the strappy heels on her pedicured feet. My feet wanted to hide just looking at hers.

Nick pulled up the one remaining chair and gestured for me to sit while he stood behind me, hands on my shoulders. Damn good thing he knew how to play this game, because I was an epic fail.

"A lot of the outcome of this reading depends on you, Lanie," Carmen was saying.

"What?"

She smiled and blinked away, putting on some cheater glasses and opening a folder.

What did that look mean? Just what she'd told me, right?

"I'll begin," she said.

There was a lot of legalese. Small stuff. Personal stuff that went to me, which touched me even though I expected it. I was basically her daughter in every sense except blood, so anything sentimental was not a surprise. The cousins had to be wondering why they were there. Except if Bryce already had plans for the land, then he knew. Sneaky little shit.

"That brings us to the last two major things," Carmen said, addressing the room as a whole and not making eye contact with me. I felt chilled all of a sudden.

"Ruby Barrett had significant financial holdings, made up mostly of some smart investments and CD's. Her life insurance took care of her burial expenses, as you know." *I knew that because I made all the arrangements. What did these people know?* "So once her holdings were liquefied and the medical bills paid, the amount is substantial."

"What kind of substantial?" Bryce asked.

What a weasel. Maybe ten grand, dude. Take a breath.

"To the tune of eight hundred thousand dollars," Carmen said.

I sat forward, Nick's hands dropping free. "Excuse me?"

Carmen just nodded.

"That's—that's impossible," I said. "I would know if she had that kind of money."

"It wasn't in her bank account, Lanie," Carmen said. "It wasn't usable money, it was—"

"Hidden really damn well," I finished, patting my face. "Holy shit." Treena snickered, and I turned to face her. "What? Did you know about it?"

All three of them held up their hands and shook their heads.

"Okay then," I said. "Shock value justified. I mean, I was on her account and paid all her bills at the end. She had thirty-five dollars left after that."

Carmen nodded again. "Like I said, this was totally separate." She took a deep breath. "Okay, so next up. The house."

I sat back in the chair and blew out a breath, actually comforted by Nick's cool fingers returning to my shoulders and moving to the back of my neck, which had to feel like a million degrees.

"And actually, the money and the house go together as a package deal," Carmen said. "Bryce, Treena, Alicia, this is the part that involves you."

I laid my hand on my bag, it holding the fraudulent marriage certificate at the ready. My scalp started to sweat.

"Ruby wrote this part in her own words, and I'm to read them out loud," Carmen said, licking her lips and recrossing her legs. "The house and the money go to Lanie and her husband," she read from the folder. "Provided she can prove beyond a shadow of a doubt that she is indeed married."

I nodded, pulling the envelope from my bag.

"She told me she was," Carmen continued. "But I know my Lanie, and I know what she'd do to make her old Aunt Ruby happy."

My eyes filled with tears, and I didn't fight it this time. I blinked them free.

"I hope it's true, because I want love in her life. She did a lot of pretending in her youth, a lot of avoiding, and that's not something to play pretend with." Nick squeezed my shoulders and I shut my eyes tight. She was killing me. "Love is everything. Nothing is worth anything without that. Not even a few bucks and a rambling, creaky old house," Carmen read, a smile pulling at her lips in spite of the stark attempt at professionalism.

I laughed through my tears and swiped them away. The words hurt, but on the other side it felt good to hear Aunt Ruby talking to me again. Nick took my hand and held it there, and I thought *screw Bryce and Treena and Alicia-the-baby.* We were selling this. My childhood home was mine. The money was shocking and probably would be nice once I got my head wrapped around it, but honestly the house was more important.

"So I'm putting this condition on things, Lanie," Carmen read. "Prove it to me. Prove it to Carmen, to the powers that be. That you are happily married to your soul mate."

I held out the document with a prayer in my head.

"Live in the house together for three months," Carmen continued, not looking up.

My hand froze between us. *What?*

"I know that involves moving, and job issues, and all that," Carmen read, her voice going a little weak. "I know it's inconvenient, and maybe you'll have to figure some things out, and maybe you'll hate me. But life and love are not to be taken lightly, my girl."

I couldn't breathe as Carmen looked up at me finally, and I felt the cold again for a whole different reason as Nick's hands left my shoulders and let go of my hand.

"Three months," Carmen read. From memory. She fucking knew. "And if that can't be done or you fail, then at the end of three months, the house and the money go to my brother's children, Bryce, Treena, and Alicia Clark. To be divided equally."

Tears fell freely from my eyes as I saw everything slip away. Everything that mattered that I didn't even know mattered. There was no way. Not for me. Not for Nick. What was she doing? What was she thinking?

"What the fuck was she smoking?" I choked.

Chapter Four

"Don't ever give up. Fall down seven times, but get up eight."

"Carmen," I breathed. Begged. Pleaded with my eyes. "There—there has to be something—"

But Carmen was already shaking her head. "There isn't," she said. And then, almost low enough that it was just for me. "I've looked."

I blinked away, not wanting eye contact with anyone. Not her. Not the worthless cousins. Not the guy pretending to be my husband that I wasn't sure was even still in the room. If I were him, I'd be Googling the nearest bus station.

"Is there a problem?" Bryce asked, feigning concern. "I mean, if you two are really legit, what's there to worry about?"

"Really?" I asked. "You could up and move to another state for three months with no issues?"

He kind of jutted his head in a tilt. Was that a nod? "Sure. I work out of my car, so—"

"Well, I don't," I said. "And neither does Nick."

"I thought his name was Michael," Alicia said from her perch at the edge of the couch. She glanced over at Bryce as if to check if that was okay. *Balls.*

"My middle name is Nicholas," Nick said. "People close to me call me Nick."

Oh, thank God the dude was still back there. And that he could think on his feet better than me.

"The point is, who can uproot their lives like that?" I said, covering my face for a minute. I needed the solitude. "How could Aunt Ruby do this to me?" I whispered behind my fingers.

"Well," Bryce said, standing in all his sweaty glory. "Let me know what we need to do or sign or whatever to take care of the house."

"The house," I said, dropping my hands. "Is my home."

"And you just said you can't do what it takes to keep it," Bryce said, gesturing with a finger for his non-speaking wife to get up. "I assume you'll be turning over your keys to Carmen?"

On my feet in under a second.

"I will most certainly *not*," I said. "I'm—we're staying there tonight."

"I kind of have a problem with that," he said.

"I kind of don't care."

"Okay—" Carmen began, probably seeing a fight to the death about to play out on her carpet.

"She's already getting everything," Bryce said to Carmen. No, he whined it. Like a six-year-old girl. "Who's to say she won't—"

"Take what's already mine?" I asked. "What am I gonna do, Bryce, strap the house to the top of my car?"

"I'm just saying."

"You want her wooden spool collection, Bryce?" I asked. "Is that what's eating you? Do you even know why she collected them?"

He sighed dramatically and wiped a hand over his sweaty neck.

"I assume she sewed," he said, a bored tone to his voice.

"You assume," I said. "You don't know." The tears came then and I didn't try to stop them. "Yes, she sewed, but she didn't give a rat's ass about that. She kept the wooden spools so people would think she liked antiques, but in reality they would be kindling after the fucking Apocalypse while everyone else would be hunting for wood."

Bryce blinked, and I saw Carmen bite her lower lip.

"Do you know her birthday?" I continued, swiping at my face. "No, scratch that, you could get that off her grave. Do you know *Julius Caesar's* birthday?"

Bryce pulled a face. Yeah didn't think so.

"July thirteenth," Carmen and I said in unison. She met my gaze and gave a small smile. "If you actually knew Aunt Ruby, you'd know that," I continued. "But you don't know shit. And you think you deserve her house."

"Wooden spools are antiques?" he asked.

I dropped my head and focused on the swirly pattern in the carpet. He was an idiot. He wasn't worth murder. Orange was not the new black, and I looked awful in it.

"Hey, she wrote the damn will, not me," he said, corralling his people who filed behind him like ducks.

"Yeah, well, she was a lunatic," I threw over my shoulder, my voice shaking. "You would have known that too."

The door closed behind Bryce after some muttered comments about being in touch, and then it was quiet.

"But she was my lunatic," I whispered, sinking back into the chair.

"Lanie," Carmen said after a pause. "I'm really sorry."

I looked up from my misery. "You knew."

"I was bound by law not to tell you," she said, sounding for once like my old friend. "I already crossed like fifty lines of ethics telling you what I did."

I just nodded and leaned back in the chair, feeling all the anxiety of the day drain out the soles of my feet.

"And now that it's said and done and the Beverly Hillbillies are gone," she said, bringing a weary giggle up from my chest. "You two should know that if you're going to pull this off, you need more than a fake marriage license and a knock-off ring."

* * *

The ride to Aunt Ruby's house was eerily solemn, quiet except for Ralph's breathing. Nick had grabbed the leash and took Ralph for a brisk walk the second we got to the car—probably to give me lose-my-shit time, and probably out of remorse for the bail he was about to do. I didn't blame him.

So Ralph was panting heavily behind me, and *my-close-friends-call-me-Nick* was staring out the window again, a pensive look on his face and the ring safely back in his pocket.

It wasn't the post-meeting ambiance I'd expected. Well, maybe it was *before* I stopped at that diner, but honestly once Nick entered the scenario, I thought we had it in the bag. It never crossed my mind that I had more to prove. It never occurred to me that Aunt Ruby would be the one to double-cross me.

Unbidden tears pricked the backs of my eyes as we passed the big Texas-shaped **Welcome to Charmed** sign, glowing white and yellow in the sun with painted flowers and bees in the corners. *Home of the World Famous Honey Festival* was scrolled across the middle in honey-colored glittery lettering.

I always scoffed at the whole world famous thing, but at that moment

I was feeling so nostalgic and crushed that it nearly broke me. Aunt Ruby loved that stupid festival with its corny honey-themed everything.

The doomsday feeling must have caught because Nick pulled out his phone and pulled up a picture of the same girl he had a shrine to in his home.

What the hell were we doing? After what Carmen said, there was no point. I should have just left her office and drove straight back in the seven-hour direction I came, dropped him off with the five hundred dollars I'd just lost for nothing, and gone home to cry into a glass of Chianti and a tub of Blue Bell.

But I didn't have another seven hours in me. I didn't even have seven minutes. I needed out of that car and out of these clothes, slopping whatever cans of crap were still hanging around my aunt's pantry into the microwave.

Nick blew out a breath and clicked the photo closed, resuming his thousand-yard stare.

"What's up?" I asked, preferring anything to the running commentary in my head.

"Nothing," he said softly.

"Didn't look like nothing," I said.

"Well, you don't know what *nothing* looks like on me, so I guess you aren't an expert."

My jaw dropped and locked. Say *what?* I know he didn't just—

"I'm sorry, what are *you* put out about right now?" I asked.

He rubbed at his eyes as if he'd rather be anywhere else in the world. I was about to oblige him with the side of the road.

"Sorry, I know you just had your nuts handed to you." He cut a glance my way. "Rhetorically speaking. But now that acting school is over, I'm back to remembering I don't have a job. And I need one. Fast."

"I understand that," I said. "I'll get you home tomorrow." God forbid I hold too long to someone who uses *rhetorically* in conversation.

"We should have just taken turns driving back today," he said under his breath.

"What, the whole two hours to your place?" I said. "I have another five hours to mine. I'm cooked, Nick. I'm done." I slid him a look. "You were nice earlier. Can we find that guy again?"

"Fine," he said, wide-eyed, as if I was one of *those* females, having a moment. "I know you're grouchy too." Now I was grouchy. The day was getting better and better. "I'd be pissed if my friend sold me out like that."

"Carmen didn't sell me out," I said. "She's just doing her job."

I didn't harbor any bad feelings toward Carmen. She didn't have to tell me about Bryce's plans or point out that we were about as married as the dog she saw sitting in my rental car. She did that as a friend. To let me know we needed to step it up if stepping was in the plan. She was helping the only way she legally could. Unfortunately, it wasn't enough. I was about to lose a shit-ton of money I never knew existed and a house I didn't even know I wanted.

Unless I got married. For real.

What the living hell was Aunt Ruby thinking?

"And this aunt of yours was supposed to like you, right?" Nick added, just as I turned down Aunt Ruby's winding road.

The burn clogged my throat as I approached the clearing and rounded it to see the big old house sitting there like a grand old dame.

"That's the rumor," I whispered past tears that I was doing my best to shove down.

* * *

I couldn't get out. I just couldn't. Every moment I'd lived there, every young moment I'd lied to friends about why we couldn't hang out there, every time I was embarrassed by my goofy aunt and her eclectic house came rushing over in a flood of guilty waves.

"Lanie?" Nick said, his voice sounding like he was in a well. Or I was in a well. One of us had definitely left reality.

"This is my fault," I choked. "I lied to her. I lied to a dying woman and now she's calling me on it."

"Yes, I think we established that," Nick said. "But you did it to make her happy," he added quickly, as I geared up to let loose. "Beating yourself up about it won't change it."

Ralph whined from the back seat, either agreeing with him or wanting the hell out of the car. I swiped under my eyes. Either way, we needed to head in that direction and get off the pity train.

"Okay, Ralph," I said. "Let's go."

We got out, crunched across the gravel, and I let my gaze travel over the house I'd know if I were struck blind and had to identify it with my fingers. The big wrap-around porch with two giant oak rockers on either side of a stack of wooden egg crates. The roof that dipped down lower in front to protect from the afternoon sun. The upstairs windows, one of which used to feature me, looking out at nothing and wanting to be anywhere else but there.

I made it all the way to the porch banister—the wiggly one attached to the post with all my growth marks—before I lost it.

Ugly cry lost it.

Standing there, hugging a post, silently crying out the last vestiges of my sanity, while Ralph sniffed out the yard and Nick shouldered both our duffle bags, I officially hit bottom.

It was all going to be stripped bare, knocked down, ripped into splinters, and carted away. My life, my past, my touchstone. The leaky faucets and ornery plumbing and loose windows might be a pain in the ass, but they came with the hideaway closets, stained glass entryway, and memories soaked into every board.

The flood wouldn't stop once I opened that portal, and Nick turned and sat on one of the steps. Waiting me out. Looking like the weight of the world had wrapped around his neck. Petting Ralph and probably praying he wouldn't have to comfort me in some way.

That was okay. I didn't need a stranger to comfort me. I'd only shared air with the man for a little over three hours, so there was nothing he could say or do at this point to make things better.

"Lanie, let's get married."

Chapter Five

"Love makes the world go round. So does a really good juicy burger."

There are things a girl hopes to hear in her lifetime, and a marriage proposal definitely tops that list. A proposal offered as a business deal, probably thrown out in desperation to stop my meltdown and pending dehydration, however, was not what most women have in mind.

"Don't, Nick," I said, hiccupping through my sobs, trying to make it stop. "Don't play with that. Don't make fun."

"I'm not," he said, still facing forward, Ralph's face in his hands as if it were all addressed to him. "I'm dead serious."

I waited for more and it didn't come. Um, I needed more explanation than that.

Wiping at my face in vain, I leaned against the post and looked down at possibly the hottest man I'd ever met. Sitting on my porch in a black-on-black suit, asking me to marry him by proxy of Ralph.

"Why?"

Finally, he let go of the dog's large head and stood, turning to face me as though it was with his last dying breath.

"You need this house," he said, his words slow and precise. His dark eyes didn't blink, didn't look away uncomfortably, didn't falter. "You may or may not need the money, I don't know. I don't see you getting all emotional about that, but you're hugging the house, so I'm guessing the money's not an important factor."

"I didn't even know about that money."

"Which brings it to me," he said, closing his eyes briefly. "I need a job."

"Are you saying—"

"I'm saying I just got in a car with a stranger for five hundred dollars," he said. "That's how far I've fallen. Three months of my life—what would that be worth?"

My tongue felt as swollen and stuck as my eyelids.

That sentence, along with the glazed over look his eyes got and the hard set of his jaw, was possibly the saddest thing I'd ever witnessed. To be followed closely by the strong possibility of my saying yes.

The image of him staring at his daughter's photo in the car, and the haunted expression on his face floated across my waterlogged brain.

"This is for your daughter, isn't it?" I asked.

No blinks again. No twitches or tells.

Of course it was. He was too proud to have done any of this otherwise. I could tell that in the first ten minutes I'd known him. This man that I couldn't do any of this without.

I sighed, feeling everything sag as I expelled that breath. I was exhausted.

"Yes or no?" he asked.

I averted my eyes to a broken piece of step.

Is this what you really want for me, Aunt Ruby? A fake marriage?

"So what happens at the end of three months?" I asked, keeping my gaze down.

There was a pause that made me look back up. A look of defeat in his face that I knew had to mirror my own. He'd been married and it failed. He was volunteering to do that again on purpose.

"We make it look good for three months, get what we need, have a big public fight, and file for divorce."

"You make it all sound like a piece of cake," I said.

"It won't be," he said. "But we can manage. Can you, with your job?"

Oh shit, my job. I hadn't even thought about that again since I blustered about it in Carmen's office. I could take all my vacation and sick time, and then—then what? Quit? Who does that? "I—I'll figure something out."

He tilted his head. "So is that a yes?"

"How much money are you asking for?" I asked.

He looked away, an uncomfortable something passing over his expression. "You tell me what you're offering."

I put a hand over my forehead, which was suddenly boiling hot. "This is crazy," I whispered. Eight hundred thousand dollars. That was crazier. Where did she get that kind of money? More importantly, what was I going to do with it? And where would I be without Nick? Back to my last hundred bucks. "Two hundred thousand?"

He blinked hard and stared harder.

"Two hundred thousand?"

I stepped back. "That's what—sixty—almost seventy grand *a month*, Nick," I said. "What job is paying better than that?"

"No!" he said, holding his hands up. "I'm not—I'm saying that's too much. That's—I can't take that."

I blew out a breath. "I don't care about the money," I said, wiping my face for the fiftieth time. "If you're giving up three months of your time for this, you deserve it a hell of a lot more than the Clarks. Hell, you've already given Aunt Ruby more of your time than any of them ever did. So take a quarter of it."

He nodded slowly, seeming to process every word. "So it's a yes?"

"My singular goal in life at this moment is to make sure they don't get a penny or a splinter of this house," I said.

One eyebrow raised. "Which would equal—"

My heart squeezed. "Let's do it."

Nick took a deep breath and so did I. We looked at each other like cross-country runners probably do, anticipating a journey from hell.

He held out a hand and I shook it. Like I'd just purchased a car.

Or a husband.

* * *

Ralph was deposited in Aunt Ruby's backyard, with mumbled promises that he wasn't being punished. He sprawled out under a shade tree like Xanadu had arrived, so I figured my job was done. I looked around the sprawling living room with different eyes. Eyes that had been a visitor to my childhood home for many years, and hadn't thought about living here again, ever. Ever. The dusty books and shelves of odd knickknacks and random quirky things, like a basket of tiny clocks and a model of a pirate ship, crammed the shelves. A large handmade doily covered a side table, where a colorful mosaic lamp watched over a bowl of mismatched keys. A grandfather clock ticked ominously behind me. It was all familiar in that way that home is, when you see the items like stage props that are always there, but never actually *see* them. They were background noise. To Aunt Ruby, they were life. And that's what was missing. Her life. Her energy. Her buzz and the sounds of her moving around and the aromas of candles or homemade soaps or baking. There were no baked apple smells simmering in the air. Aunt Ruby always made baked apples and cinnamon when she was in a happy, carefree mood, or when it was time to celebrate something. My chest pricked with that sharp little pain of realizing I'd probably never smell that again. I could make them in my sleep, but it wasn't the same.

There were vague words about hunger and food, and explaining why there were fifteen cans of corn in the pantry and nothing else (one—no one lives there, and two—I'm the only one who visited. And I love corn), but it all kind of blended together in one swirly blur that ended with us sitting on stools at the lunch bar of the Blue Banana Grille.

You'd think two recently engaged people who just met at lunchtime— in another diner—would have a few things to talk about. A few things to learn about each other. Birthdays, favorite food, middle names.

Instead, after being accosted out on the sidewalk by honey pushers handing out samples, we were staring at blue laminated menus like normal people. As if any of this came close.

"So, why are they out there doing that?" Nick asked.

"The honey wars are coming up," I said. "It's part of the Honey Festival," I continued after his questioning look. "All the local honey farmers and amateur wannabes compete for the best honey. And spend weeks pimping it out. If you tell them theirs is the best yet, you'll get seconds."

He nodded. "Good to know. So, what's good here?" he asked.

I gave him a sideways glance, and did a double-take as I caught the stares of at least half a dozen other women in the diner. Not on me. On GQ over here. Not that I blamed them. He was delicious in that suit, like he'd worn them all his life. No one would ever suspect that he'd just been flipping burgers that morning.

"I have no idea," I said, peering back at my own menu. "It's been years since I ate here. Well, except for the pie."

"The pie?"

"And the honey," I said, pointing to a pyramid stack of jarred raw honey with the familiar local sticker sporting the Anderson Apiary logo and the scripted Made by Local Bees in Charmed, Texas. "Best honey in the world."

"So I've heard," he said.

"I used to come pick up a couple slices of pie for Aunt Ruby and me when I'd visit," I said. "After she lost her sight and couldn't bake anymore. It was the next best thing to perfect, and it's pretty out of this world."

"What kind?"

"All of them," said. "I do remember their chicken fried steak being amazing years ago too."

Nick slid me a look. "Chicken fried steak?"

"Yeah." I raised an eyebrow at the pause. "Why?"

"Do you *know* what cheap-ass cut of meat is used for that?"

"No, and I don't care."

"It's nasty," he said. "There's a reason it's beat to death and slathered in batter and fried."

I blinked and studied him. "Do you hear yourself sounding like a total food snob, Armani?"

There was a flash of fire in his eyes as he looked away, back at his menu.

"It's not Armani. It's the only nice thing I have left."

Hmm. There was a story there. No rush, though. Evidently I had three months to learn it.

"And I'm not a food snob," he continued. "I worked in a greasy spoon just like this."

"Then don't ruin chicken fried steak for me."

"Fine."

"Fine."

He cut a look my way. "Do you always have to get in the last word?"

"Frequently."

"Lanie Barrett," said a familiar voice as a petite brunette with impossibly dark eyes appeared from a hall behind the bar. She and Nick could have been siblings with those eyes. "Good lord, I don't remember the last time I saw you at my counter."

I was acutely aware of the state of my face, even though I'd done repair in the car, and of Nick listening. And of how many lies I'd told in the past year, spread so thin I couldn't remember to whom. That was easy when you were alone and could spin in any direction. A little weirder with a witness.

"Hey, Allie."

"Sorry to hear about your aunt," she said, grabbing a paper towel to wipe up some coffee.

Allie Greene was one of the few people I actually believed that from. She was always down to earth and sincere. A no-nonsense single mom since she was seventeen, growing up in the same trailer park Carmen did and running her dad's diner her whole life, she didn't have time for petty rumors or gossip. Even though she probably heard her share.

"I didn't know her well," Allie continued in her soft husky voice, a nostalgic smile on her face as she twisted her dark hair up into a clip she had on her jeans. "But she was always so sweet when she'd come in back in the day." Her smile broadened. "I remember she'd always slip me a quarter when I was out there bussing tables. Tell me to go buy a Coke."

I chuckled. "She still thought a quarter would get her a Coke up until last year."

She smiled. "This your husband?"

Here we go.

Nick looked at me, a touch of humor in his expression. *Well?*

God help me.

"Yes, this is Nick," I said. "Nick, this is Allie Greene, an old high school friend."

Which was stretching it slightly, and the small twitch in her cheek told me she recognized that. We were school friends in that way that the passing of years creates. When the fact that you traveled twelve years in the same building makes you comrades. In reality, we were aware of each other through Carmen, and through classes, but probably didn't have a real conversation till I started coming into the Blue Banana for pie.

"Nick McKane," he said, shaking her hand.

"McKane?" she asked, tilting her head. "I thought it was McKnight." She laughed. "Mc-something, I guess. I'm probably remembering the obituary wrong."

I didn't look at Nick or acknowledge the fact that I'd carried my lie into the newspaper obituary. Damn it, why did I ever give him a name? Thank God it was at least close.

"Y'all are dressed up today," she said, thankfully moving on.

"Had some will stuff to take care of," I said, setting my menu down. "Speaking of which, you know of anyone hiring?"

Allie's eyebrows raised a notch. "For what?"

"Anything," I said. "We just found out we have to live here in the house for three months in order to inherit it."

She pulled a face. "What the hell?"

"That was my reaction too," I said. "Plus a few stronger ones."

"What about your jobs? Your lives?"

I had no idea how I was going to pull off a three-month leave at work, get my rent-house sublet so I didn't lose it, and get everything I needed/wanted for three months packed up and to Texas, so we could start this debacle. Not to mention, I should probably call Carmen and see if she knew a judge that would do this quietly and quickly.

"Apparently, my sweet old Aunt Ruby had a wicked streak," I said, trying to keep the irritation out of my tone. "So if you hear of anything?"

"Well, nothing on your level, but off the bat I can say I heard that the bank is looking for tellers. I don't know how much they pay," she added. "Bash is always needing help with the hives—oh, and Dixon Lee said something about being shorthanded at the hardware store."

"Hives?" Nick asked.

"The honeybee hives," she said. "Bash—Sebastian Anderson—runs the largest of the Charmed apiaries."

"So that sign coming into town wasn't just being warm and fuzzy," Nick said.

"Nooooo," I said. "Charmed takes their honey seriously. Bash, even more so."

"Yes, he does," she said, a small smile on her face. "You haven't been here before?" Allie asked him.

Crap.

"Just once," he lied smoothly, chuckling with that knock-em-on-their-ass smile. "But it was a quick trip and I didn't pay attention."

He was good.

Allie nodded. "Well, like I said, there's not going to be anything here on the level that you're probably used to."

Just shoot me.

I smiled. "Can't afford to be picky."

She laughed. "If I thought that were really true, I'd hire you as a waitress or a fry cook. I'm down both. My head chef retires in a couple of weeks and Dave the fry cook is desperately trying to learn everything." She leaned over. "I wouldn't recommend anything too complicated right now," she whispered. "I'm about to go help him out."

"Sold," Nick said.

She blinked in surprise. "What?"

"Hire me," he said without hesitation. "But for the chef job, not the fry cook."

"You—you cook?" I watched Allie's eyes slide over his GQ appearance.

"I do," he said. "Very well." He pointed toward the kitchen. "I can go make you something right now."

She chuckled. "You know, there's being able to cook, and there's cooking on a line. In a diner kitchen."

"So I've heard," he said, a smile pulling at his mouth.

"And Chef would never let a patron in his kitchen," she added.

Nick laughed. "I understand that. So I guess you'll have to take me at my word."

Her lips curled up at the corners. "I don't have to do anything," she said. "I'm not the one who needs a job."

Nick paused a second, then nodded a concession. "True enough. But you do need a chef."

It was like watching a ping pong match, wondering who was going to catch the ball and put the paddle down.

Allie knocked her knuckles on the counter. "I'll be right back."

He winked at me as she disappeared.

"You still want a burger?"

God, was that today? It felt like a week ago.

"You heard her, he'll never let you back there."

"Yes or no?"

I hung my head. "That again."

"Come on, Mrs. McKane, burger or plate dish?"

That popped my head up, meeting those mischievous eyes of his. The game. *Mrs. McKane, indeed.*

"Burger," I said. "Well done."

"Spicy, or no?" he asked.

"Spicy."

He narrowed his eyes, a refreshed look about him, the challenge firing him up.

"Raw onions or grilled?"

"Neither."

Allie came back, tying on an apron as she grabbed a water glass to fill.

"You have fifteen minutes to convince Benny," she said.

"*Benny* decides?"

"In there, he does," she said. "He's been here my whole life, and runs a tight ship. Anyone replacing him, even short-term, needs to do the same." She turned back as Nick stood. "And if you get this, the deal is you train a replacement in that same standard before you leave."

"Deal."

He was almost vibrating.

"All right," she said, gesturing with a tilt of her head. "Get after it. But you—"

Nick was already sans jacket and rolling up his sleeves.

"Okay then," she said, chuckling in my direction. "A real go-getter you have here."

"Seems so," I said under my breath.

* * *

I snuck behind the counter to watch through the serving window, and did a double-take on the three women who piled up behind me.

"You're not supposed to be back here," I whispered, turning to look at them.

"Neither are you," one of them said.

"It's *my* husband," I said.

How frighteningly bizarre and normal that felt, rolling off my tongue. Having been engaged for all of thirty minutes, evidently that made me a pro at this *married* business.

"That hot guy? That was Lanie Barrett's husband," I heard someone say from somewhere else in the lobby.

Amazing how everyone still knew who I was, and I'd been gone forever. That was why. When you stay in a small town, you fade. You blend. But it's like there's some secret plaque somewhere with the names of those who leave, with a spotlight shining on it. The daring and the brave, who have seen outside the dome. And come home with James Bond.

Nick was walking the station while old Benny hovered, looking very unhappy.

"Do you mind if I peek in the fridge? See my choices?" he asked.

"I thought you were making a burger," the old man said, a frown creasing the skin over his nose. "How many choices you need?"

"I am," Nick said, thumbing behind him. "For her. I'd like something too." He turned to Allie. "Have you eaten?"

"Don't get cocky, Nick," I whispered to myself. Like I knew him well enough to say that.

She laughed. "You wanting to show off?"

"Not at all," he said. "But I do want to show that I know how to manage my time."

"Okay," she said. "Make me a chopped spinach leaf salad with sautéed chicken."

"That's all?"

"Caramelized with honey glaze," she added. "Cracked peppercorn dressing, crushed almonds, and shaved carrots."

"We don't have—" Benny began.

"Shhh," Allie said.

"Damn, Allie," I muttered. "Give him a chance."

He didn't look fazed, however, opening the big fridge door to scan over the contents whether Benny cared or not.

"When do I begin?"

"Knock yourself out," Allie said. "I'll be back in a bit."

Nick pulled out fresh ground meat, eggs, butter, three different kinds of greens, and a bag of something. Deposited those on a counter and headed to the pantry as feet scuttled behind me. I turned to see Allie standing with hands on her hips as my little posse of onlookers disbanded.

"Why are you behind my counter?" she asked, although her eyes held a glimmer of amusement.

I pointed. "I can't miss this," I said. *Play it, sister.*

Allie rolled her eyes and moved to take a new order. The women started to round the counter again and she made a clicking noise with her tongue.

"Lanie, only."

"Spousal privilege," I threw over my shoulder.

"Don't push it," Allie said.

He was already chopping leafy greens and spinach like he had a bionic arm. My God, he was fast. I'd never understand how they did that. He sprinkled something and tossed it all. Cracked fresh peppercorns into a bowl with olive oil and something else. Stirred honey into another bowl and seasoned it. Slathered butter on thick-sliced nutty bread and seared it, setting that on a plate. He chopped up peppers and onions and tossed half in a skillet and the other half into the bowl of ground meat, and then proceeded to season and press out the most beautiful meat patty I'd ever seen.

In three different pans, I watched him fry two eggs sunny side up, my burger, and the chicken, while cutting up fresh strawberries.

The magic happened when all at once, three plates filled up on a platter. My burger, gorgeously sizzling on an open bun with slices of avocado gleaming on top. Sliced strawberries were arranged in a little mound next to it. Allie's plate held her salad, all dressed in carrots and almonds and honey-glazed chicken that I could smell from the window. Two fried eggs on toast adorned another plate, next to a small pile of freshly shaved hash browns and strawberries.

"Allie, you want to see this," I said.

She walked back into the kitchen just as he finished plating, and gazed at his creations.

"Holy shit," she mumbled.

"Your salad, ma'am," he said, handing it to her.

She glanced up at him as she grabbed a fork and speared a bite of chicken and spinach.

"Mmm," she said, chewing slowly. "Damn."

"We don't have a cracked peppercorn dressing," Bennie said, clearly needing to make that point.

"We do now," she said, looking down at the other plates. "Okay, breakfast for you, nothing crazy there. Nice hash browns, though."

She picked up my burger and handed it to me through the window.

"Cut that and see if it's well done."

I did. It was. It was possibly more perfect than the last one I'd seen him do.

"Spot on."

But that wasn't all. I bit back a smile when I saw the corn. He'd made me Maque Choux. Cajun corn with sweet peppers.

Allie looked back at Nick, who was already nearly done cleaning up after himself.

"Go eat your food while it's hot," she said. "Let me talk to Benny."

"Yes, ma'am." He stopped to shake Benny's hand, and I saw the old man's expression change. "Thank you," Nick said. "It was an honor."

When he came out with his plate and sat by me with a heavy exhale, he met my eyes.

"Wow," I said.

And that wasn't just for the cooking show. It was a word that fell out of my mouth in response to all of it. The food, the confidence, and the very real roaring fire going on behind his eyes. If I were a betting person, I would have gambled on him having a hard-on from hell right then. He had loved every single second of that challenge, and it was so palpable I found myself holding my breath.

"Don't *wow* me yet," he said, nodding toward my plate. "Taste it first. Tell me what you think."

I picked up one of the halves, and shoved as much as I could into my mouth. I was past worrying about impressing him or looking feminine. I was ravenous.

"Om dnrr Gmd," I grunted around the heaven in my mouth. I closed my eyes and just savored every flavor.

"Good?"

"I'm in love," I said with a sigh, then cutting a quick look his way. "With the burger."

Nick grinned. "Of course."

"It's amazing."

"Worth waiting all day for?"

"No." He laughed out loud, and it made my skin tingle. "Seriously, I would have almost chewed on Ralph about now. But oh man, this is by far the best burger ever."

He sat back with a satisfied smile and dug into his own food. Just as the kitchen door swung open.

"Job's yours," Allie said, crossing her arms over her chest. "Can you be back in two weeks? Benny said he'd even stay a day or two over to help you get your bearings." She shook her head. "And Benny doesn't help anybody."

Nick looked at me, a question in his eyes. Two weeks. I had no idea. There was so much to do. Like get married. But there was something else in his eyes too. More than a need for a paycheck. A need for vindication. For appreciation. I remembered how they talked to him in that other diner. It would be different here; he would be in charge of the kitchen. And it glowed on him.

"If nothing else, you can come ahead of me," I said. "We'll figure it out."

"Thank you," he mouthed.

There were goose bumps again, but I told myself it was the food.

Only the food.

I bought a jar of the honey just to be sure.

That night, after a rousing game of Scrabble (I won) because the cable was turned off, and after we took turns using two different showers because the plumbing didn't allow for both at once, *and* after we spent an hour looking for shoes we'd just left in the foyer, we both passed out. Well, sort of. We retreated to separate rooms. I laid my head on Aunt Ruby's pillow and listened to Nick talk to Ralph down the hall.

Could we pull this off? Could I? Could I marry a man I'd just met today in order to keep this house? Not to mention live with him for three months. What if he was a serial killer? What if he was a chronic farter? What if he liked mustard?

The bed rocked as Ralph jumped up.

"Don't even think about it," I said. His big head sagged onto my knee as he laid down, looking at me all sad. Poor guy. He didn't know where he was or where his mom was. He was confused. I reached down and stroked an ear. "Me too, boy," I said. "Me too. But if you pee on me again tonight, you're riding as a hood ornament tomorrow."

Chapter Six

"Date the jock, but marry the nerd. He'll appreciate you more."

Two weeks goes fast when you're in a full panic. When every seed of logic feeds another seed and the what-the-fucks are taking you down.

I'd covered all the bases, even managed to somehow snow my boss into a sympathy rehire upon my return. Something about breaking into very real tears during a panic attack while quitting a perfectly good job.

Family emergency (not a total lie) and *I don't know what to do* broke her, and she told me not to worry, that she'd hire me back when I returned.

I'm pretty sure it was more about stemming my hyperventilation than it was about my superb work history, but I wasn't complaining. It was a blessing. Not hey-we'll-pay-you-while-you're-gone level of blessing, but still a significant burden off my shoulders.

I'd called the bank in Charmed and inquired about the teller job Allie had mentioned, so I had an interview in three days. Possibly a good thing.

A coworker had a niece in need of short-term living arrangements while she finalized a divorce, so my rent house was safe. Ralph was still with me for reasons I didn't yet know but Tilly had left me a message under a new number, promising to fill me in. Soon. Having a new number did nothing to make me really believe that.

And I'd had Aunt Ruby's cable and internet access turned back on so we'd have something to do other than stare at each other and play board games.

All the boxes were checked.

All except that *getting married* one.

I was in the car—*my* car—headed back to Charmed. Headed to

Carmen's office first, actually, where she would be waiting today with a JP friend of hers willing to break state law and issue a marriage license and marry us in the same day. As if we needed one more strike against us.

Nick would meet me there at one o'clock.

To marry me.

So I could keep Aunt Ruby's house.

And so he could help his daughter or fund the mob or make women's underwear or whatever the hell he needed the money for. We never covered that. We never covered anything. We never talked about anything, because we played fucking Scrabble and then went to bed and then drove home the next day with music blaring so we wouldn't have to. After a coffee debate first thing that morning, where he spent twenty minutes telling me the evils of caffeine after two cups. He'd told me he loved coffee. If I weren't so desperate, that could have been grounds for nixing the whole thing right there.

And now it was twelve-thirty and I was sweating through my sundress that I'd decided to wear, since it *was* my very first time to get married.

I swerved to the shoulder, opened my door, leaned out, and threw up.

"Oh my God," I choked, groping behind me into the center console for a fast food napkin. "What am I doing?"

Ralph barked from the back seat.

"I really don't need your commentary right now," I said, wiping at my eyes. "I'm kind of having a moment."

My cell rang in the next one.

"Shit," I muttered, hitting the button on my steering wheel. "Hello?"

"Hey!" Carmen's voice rang through the speakers. "How's the trip?"

"Great," I said, patting my face. "Just puking on my wedding day."

"God, I'm sorry, Lanie," she said. "This whole thing is crazy."

"You think?"

"Are you having second thoughts?" she asked.

"Second, third," I huffed. "Nineteenth." I sat back and tried to regulate my breathing. "But there's not really a choice unless I want to hand everything over to Bryce." My fingers closed on an empty CD case and I picked it up to fan my face. "It's just not how I pictured it all going down."

Not that I ever really pictured it. But driving to a JP alone with a dog and all I needed to sustain life for ninety days—to marry a man I barely knew—was never a fantasy.

"It'll fly by, though," Carmen said.

"You think?" I said, cranking up the air to just short of blowing snowflakes.

"Just stay busy, and remember the end goal," she said. "It will be worth it in the end. And hey, as husbands go, you could definitely do worse. Believe me, I know."

Husbands.

If I could have thrown my head between my legs at that moment, I would have.

"God, Carmen, you're gonna make me hurl again."

"No more hurling," she said. "You have to kiss him soon."

My face went hotter, if that was possible. "It's not that kind of wedding."

"Well, maybe not, but what are you gonna do, shake hands?" she asked. "Fist bump? Did you talk about sex?"

The image of Nick and—whew. Everything went hotter. Even with the snowflakes. It might have been a while.

"I don't think you want us doing that in your office," I said.

"Ha-ha," she said dryly. "So you think this guy is planning to live with a sexy woman for three months and not get a taste of it?"

Okay, I was missing professional tightly-wound Carmen. Where did she go?

"Whatever *taste test* happens on this little journey," I said. "It's like Pretty Woman. Sex is sex, kissing is personal. Personal leads to all kinds of intimate shit—"

"And heaven forbid that any intimate shit happens in a marriage," she said.

"It's not a marriage," I said, banging the steering wheel. "It's a business deal."

"True."

"Romance and love have no place in this," I said. "We are doing this for three months and then it's over."

"Okay, you were the one just puking on the side of the road, complaining that—"

"I know," I interrupted. "I'm trying to talk myself down, run with it," I said, pulling back onto the road. There was only one exit left before tying the knot, and I was running out of time to avoid it.

I blew out a slow calming breath. I'd already taken the exit. Carmen's office was literally like a minute away.

One minute. Till my life changed and then I was three months away from being a divorcee. Wasn't *that* a hell of a thought? I'd be one of those people who said things like *my first marriage...*

Carmen's office loomed ahead, and my mouth went dry. What if he didn't even show? What if he changed his mind? What if—

An old blue truck attached to a low-boy trailer holding an older motorcycle was parked off to the side. I remembered both.

"Okay, I'm here," I said, the words feeling like they were pushed through hot sand. "See you in a minute."

I had an overwhelming feeling of fight-or-flight. And if *he* didn't flee...

I took Ralph on a quick walk, halfway hoping Nick would come out and calm my nerves and halfway wishing I didn't have to face him at all. *You'll have to kiss him soon.* Surely not, huh? Damn, I wished I had some gum.

"Hey."

I spun around at the same time Ralph bolted past me, wiggling his way to Nick. And my skin prickled with goose bumps at the sight of him. He stood there in dark jeans and a long-sleeved white button-down shirt, hands shoved partially into his pockets. He looked positively edible.

If one was supposed to be thinking like that.

"Hey," I responded, watching him divert Ralph from jumping on him and then scratching his neck.

"You look nice," he said, his gaze dropping to take it all in. "Really nice."

"Thanks," I said, hoping he wouldn't have to touch me and see how clammy I was. Or how my hair I'd worn down in soft waves was now sticking to my neck. Or find out that my breath probably rivaled Ralph's.

"You do too," I said.

"So, you ready for this?"

Not even a little bit.

"Sure," I said. "You?"

God, if the next three months were going to be this painful, I needed medication.

"Ready as I'm gonna be," he said, patting a pocket. "Brought my ring."

"Oh!" I spun around and reached in my car before pulling a small box from my bag. "I got you another one," I said, holding it out to him.

His brows furrowed together as he closed the space between us, his gaze meeting mine. "You bought me a ring?"

"So you wouldn't have to wear your old one," I said. "I could tell it bothered you."

He opened the box to the silver ring inside. "You have no idea," he said under his breath. "Thank you."

"It's nothing fancy," I said. "You might want to try it on. I guessed at the size."

He slipped it on and I blew out a sigh of relief.

"It'll work," he said, handing it back to me. "Give me yours." I pulled mine off and handed it over. "Let's go get this done. My first shift at the diner starts in two hours."

* * *

"Do you take this man as your lawfully wedded husband, for better or for worse, and promise to make this journey together side by side?"

Carmen wrote custom vows and gave them to her judge friend, making the promises much more palatable. I was so grateful. I didn't know how I was going to lie gracefully about the *as long as you both shall live* part.

That, and she had an Altoid. Carmen was shaping up to be an excellent maid of honor.

It's a game. We're playing it out. Yet it seemed like the more I said that, the more ridiculous it became.

"I do," I said, slipping the ring on Nick's finger.

The judge repeated the question for Nick, who looked down at our joined hands.

"I do," he said softly as Carmen handed him mine. He put it on my finger and blinked away.

"By the power..." The judge rambled on, eventually getting to the *pronounce you husband and wife* part. "You may kiss your bride."

Our eyes met, and I wondered if mine looked as disturbed as his did as he leaned down and brushed a light kiss on my cheek. Yeah, that was every woman's fantasy.

It was done.

I was Lanie Barrett McKane.

Score one for Aunt Ruby.

* * *

We were just done signing the certificate when my phone buzzed from my bag on a chair. I didn't recognize the number and almost let it go, but answered it at the last minute.

"Is this Lanie Barrett?" a pleasant female voice asked.

Well, up until a few minutes ago it was.

"Who is asking?"

"This is Kristina with Cali Dynamics," she said. "I'm calling in response to a resume you turned in last year."

Oh. My. God.

"Cali Dynamics?" I echoed, searching for my voice. "As in the advertising firm? In San Francisco?"

"That's the one," Kristina said, chuckling melodically in my ear.

"You got my—" I stumbled. "I mean, that job can't still be open."

"No, it's not," she said. "But we are opening a new division and need a large headcount, so we're tapping into the interest from the last round."

"For—" My voice kept going hoarse, and Carmen and Nick were both looking at me funny. "For what kind of job?"

"Ad design," she said. "In a pool, actually. We'll have a pool of designers working on various projects, and the top performers will have a chance to move up."

I couldn't breathe.

"We see you're in Louisiana," she continued. "But your e-mail last year mentioned that you had no problem with moving? That nothing tied you to that area?"

"Right," I said, closing my eyes, feeling the ties circling my ankles as I spoke.

"Well, if you're still interested, we'd love to set up a phone interview," she said. "Skype or Facetime if you have it."

"Um," I managed. My tongue felt paralyzed. "I'm in my car right now," I lied, feeling the eyes and the sudden silence in the room. "Can I call you back with that?"

"Problem?" Nick asked when I hung up.

"No." I shook my head. "Come on, let's go."

* * *

My mind was spinning as we unloaded the vehicles and backed a dilapidated old motorcycle off the low-boy trailer. Was I interested? Of course! Five million times yes. But was I still available to move? Not exactly. Not right now. And not too many places waited three months for a position they could easily fill.

"So what's with the half-dead bike?" Carmen asked. She'd come with us to help.

"I've been working on it," he said. "Hoping to get it running one day. I'm a geek like that."

"You don't strike me as ever being a geek," I said.

"Most definitely," Nick said. "I wasn't into sports and big spotlight stuff like other guys. Give me an old motor that can't be fixed and I'd disappear for days."

"That's a nice one," said a voice behind us that hit me as familiar and *oh shit* at the same time.

Nick straightened from his bent over stance, probably reacting on instinct to the shift of testosterone in the air.

I turned as Alan Bowman, one of the cockiest, most arrogant people I'd ever met, strolled up wearing cargo shorts and a muscle shirt. He was also once my high school boyfriend.

"Alan," I said, surprised. "Where'd you come from?"

"Down the road," he said, thumbing behind him. "Bought the old Spivey place last year to set up hives."

He walked right up and hugged me. Tight. Finished it off with a wet kiss on the cheek.

"I heard you were coming back."

"Just—not really back," I said, wiping at my cheek. "We have to live here in my aunt's house for ninety days as part of her will."

"Heard about that too," he said, keeping one hand firmly planted on the small of my back as he reached out to shake Nick's hand. "Alan Bowman."

"Nick McKane."

"You've heard about a lot," I said.

Alan did a sort of self-deprecating shrug as he smiled down at me. "What can I say? My ear's to the ground." He pointed back to the motorcycle. "Nice bike. What year?"

I saw Nick's eyes fall to Alan's hand placement just above my ass, and I instinctively moved, picking up a random bag of clothes nearby. And instantly finding that weird in about forty different ways.

"Nineteen sixty-nine," Nick said.

"Sweet."

"Alan and I went to high school together," I said.

"Hell, we were a foursome once," Alan said, grinning at Nick. "Nothing quite like that. Me and Lanie, and Dean and Frosty here. We tore this town up at one time."

Oh, good grief, embellish much?

"Well, I don't recall much tearing," I said on a laugh. "But we did hang out a lot."

"So I guess you heard about Lucky Hart Carnival, huh?" Alan asked, looking at Carmen. "Did Dean tell you?"

I glanced at Carmen in time to see the color drain from her face and come back again.

"Dean and I don't really chat," she said, smiling politely. "So no, probably not."

I could see the anxiety in her eyes, though. Damn Alan for needing to push buttons.

Once upon a time, it was me and Alan, and Carmen and Dean Crestwell. Until the annual carnival came to town, sporting a new hot-shot carny. Sullivan Hart, the very hot and rebellious fireball son of the carnival line's owner, set his eyes on Carmen Frost, and nothing was ever the same. Carmen and Dean's on-again-off-again dance got more volatile every year at carnival time, becoming a famously rocky marriage and equally rocky divorce. Ending with poor what-could-he-ever-do-wrong pretty boy, Dean, being voted in as mayor, and Carmen avoiding Charmed social activity altogether.

She and I had kind of lost touch over the last several years, and I'd gotten most of this from my aunt, but the look I just saw on her face told me that Sully Hart still had an effect on her.

"The old man died," Alan said. "It was in the news I think too. Sully's in charge now."

Carmen nodded and licked her lips, looking away. "Hate to hear that," she said.

"So who knows what that means for the carnival coming here this summer after the Honey Festival," Alan said. "He was never as aggressive as his old man. If he decides to skip Charmed, it could seriously affect honey sales."

"Why would he skip Charmed?" I asked. "It's probably one of their more lucrative stops."

Alan chuckled. "Because his woman never shows up anymore."

"Screw you, Alan," Carmen said, pulling her keys from her pocket and walking to her car.

"Carmen, don't leave," I said.

"I'll catch up with you later, Lanie," she said, cutting an apologetic glance in my direction.

I let her go. In that look, my old friend peeked out. The one before controlling Dean and sexy Sully and a gossiping town took over. I remembered the push-pull she went through in the beginning. I'd never had a life-affirming, mind-blowing love like that, and watching her struggle back then was one of the reasons I hadn't. It always looked painful.

I turned to fix Alan with a what-the-fuck look as she drove away, but he wasn't even on the same field anymore. He was studying Nick's bike. As Nick sat on the tailgate of his truck, arms crossed over his chest, watching the whole show.

Eyes on me.

My stomach did a flutter.

Really?

Yes it did. Damn, the man definitely had sex appeal, I'd give him that.

"So, you do bee hives?" Nick finally said, turning his gaze to Alan.

"Do them?" Alan said, running a finger along the motor. "Yes. I guess you could say that. I'm not harvesting yet. I'm just working with Bash on increasing the local bee population."

"You work for Bash?" I asked.

"*With*," he reiterated. "Not for. I'm a freelancer."

"You're a bee pimp," I said.

Alan cut me a look. He was still okay-looking, or enough to get away with the tight muscle-shirt he had on. But too much sun over the years had weathered his face and bleached out his thin spiky hair to the point that his sun-reddened scalp glowed through.

"Whatever," he said." "So, my wife and I are having a get together in a few weeks." He tilted his head like it was no big deal. "We always have a few friends over for a little pool party right before the festival. Kind of kicks it off. Y'all should come, you'd enjoy it."

I couldn't imagine anything I would enjoy less, but I just smiled.

"Didn't know you got married," I said, moving to sit next to Nick on his tailgate. Strength in numbers and all.

"Well, you know I couldn't corner the market forever," he said, winking at me.

The reasons for dating him back in the day completely escaped me. I must have been hard up or starved for attention. Or the fact that a football player—the epitome of normal when that's what I craved—wanted me made me turn a blind eye to how obnoxious he could be.

"On that note," Nick said, standing. "I have to get to work."

He tipped my chin and leaned down to kiss the area *next* to my lips before I knew what was happening. A little gasp escaped my chest. It was more intimate than the wedding kiss on the cheek, more believable. The look he gave me with it said he was trying to sell it, and hell, he almost sold me.

And little lightbulbs flashed in my brain. He had the *Pretty Woman* thing, too. Well, he probably didn't call it that, but it was the same thing. He wouldn't kiss me, even if he wanted to. Because kissing was too personal, too dangerous, too real.

I totally got it.

"You gonna be okay, here?" he asked in a low voice.

"Yeah."

Whew.

Was I?

Chapter Seven

"Find something to laugh about every day. A day is wasted if you don't fall over laughing."

I was sitting out back watching Ralph sniff the fence—or sniff rocks crammed into holes under the fence—when my husband came home from work.

I'd been thinking things like that all day. Trying to wrap my head around the concept that I just got married. That morning. After puking my way there. Now that it was done, and I got over the lack of what I always pictured my wedding day to be—love and sex and googly eyes at each other instead of moving and talking shit with an ex-boyfriend—I was okay with it. I did sort of get kissed twice at least, even if it wasn't much more than brotherly, and kind of offered an interview if I ever called them back, so hey it wasn't *just* an ordinary day.

Nick walked through the back door looking exhausted but pleased. Well, why not? He'd just been handed his dream job, without having to quit anything. Plus, he had two-hundred grand coming. I'd be pleased too.

Not that I was feeling snippy at all. Or anxious.

"How was your day, dear?" I asked. "Need a beer? Foot rub?"

"A beer would be great, but you don't want anywhere near my feet," he said, collapsing in the chair across the patio table from me. The aroma of onions wafted over. "Do we actually have beer?"

"I don't think so."

He closed his eyes and leaned his head back. "Tease."

I chuckled. "Well? How was your first day as Chef Nick?"

"Like being a bug under a magnifying glass," he said. "With a beam of sunlight aimed at my head."

"I thought they liked you."

"They do, but Chef Benny hovers like a hawk. *We don't chop them that fine. We don't season that much. We don't use oil in the pasta. We don't mix honey into the butter.*"

"Oh, I think we need to," I responded, holding up a finger.

"Yeah, I pushed back on that one too," he said. "It's a town built on honey, why not make the best butter in the world?"

"Two points for the new guy."

"So how was your day?" he asked. "*Dear.* Did your redneck ex-lover stay long?"

I cringed. "He's not my ex-lover."

"You never did the deed?

"No," I said. "Not completely. I was actually still a virgin when I left for college."

"Wow," he said. "One of the few and the proud."

I saluted him.

"And that phone call today?" he asked. "When you lied about being in the car?"

I took a deep breath and went back to watching Ralph.

Nick held up a palm. "You don't have to tell me, it's none of my business."

I let my gaze fall back on him. That wasn't true anymore. He'd signed up for three months with me, and therefore anything I said or did or planned to do affected him.

"No, it is your business now," I said, raking my hair back. "That was a job I applied for another lifetime ago. A dream job that would have been perfect a year ago, even a month ago. And they want an interview."

"What makes it not perfect now?" he asked.

"It's in California."

His eyebrows lifted. "Ah."

"Yeah."

"So what are you gonna do?"

I shook my head. What could I do now? "I don't know yet. Stew about it some more, probably."

"Do you want to talk about it?" he asked.

"Not really."

He nodded. "Got it. So you do know that your—*our* new neighbor wants to make up for lost time, right?"

I chuckled, even though an involuntary shiver ran through me. "He's married."

"Just saying," Nick said with a shake of his head. "He was awfully grabby on another man's wife." I bit back a laugh. Was he actually jealous? He held up a hand. "He doesn't know if we've been married ten years or ten minutes. You just don't do that."

Okay, maybe not jealous, just disrespected. Not as sexy, but still kind of cute.

"Alan's the kind of person who needs to know that everyone wants him, married or not," I said. "It's part of his persona."

Nick evidently let that pass, blowing out a breath as he twisted the new presence on his finger randomly and then looked down at it as if surprised.

It made me look down at mine too. At the sparkly cubic zirconia that pretended to be something it wasn't. Very fitting.

"Odd, seeing that there, isn't it?" I said, spreading my fingers so it caught the light.

"More than you know," he said.

I looked up at him.

"So tell me, then," I said.

He rubbed at his eyes. "You don't want that whole sordid story."

"Kinda do."

He raised an eyebrow as he dropped his hand and slid lower in the chair. "You first."

"Me?" I laughed. "I have no story."

"Bullshit."

"Excuse me?"

"You're a gorgeous, sexy woman," he said. "There's no logical reason you aren't married already, or at least in a relationship. Yet you've chosen to create that illusion instead of living it. There's a story."

Of course I heard *gorgeous, sexy woman*, and stopped there. My own boyfriend hadn't even thought that about me, but this guy did. Or he at least was savvy enough to say it.

But there was more. Story, blah, blah.

"I was in a relationship, but it wasn't going anywhere," I said.

"So you made up the husband?"

"No—I—sort of did that before him," I said. "And it just took off. It was easier after a while to just go with that."

"Easier than falling in love for real," he said. It wasn't a question.

I fanned my hair out, feeling the heat start to lay thick on my skin.

"Let's talk about *your* love life now."

"You don't like to talk about that," he said calmly. Amusement pulled at his eyes.

"There's nothing to talk about," I said.

"You've never been there, have you?"

I pulled my hair completely up, piling it on top of my head. No, I'd never been there, and never planned to. It made people stupid.

"God, you're annoying."

Nick laughed. "Okay, I'll back off."

"And talk," I said. "I haven't forgotten it's your turn."

His laugh fizzled out on a tired sigh.

"You saw pictures of my daughter," he said. "She wants to go to this fancy art school up north. And she deserves to, she's amazing. She got a scholarship for part of it, but I could never afford to pay for the rest so she's pretending not to want it and settling."

"For what?"

"For a business degree," he said. "For a mediocre school, a mediocre life. A life where her dreams can't be realized." His jaw tightened and his eyes went hard. "Because of me."

I frowned. "What do you mean?" He shook his head. "Nick."

He fixed me with an impatient glare. Probably not unlike mine a few minutes ago.

"Let's just say that's why I took this gig," he said. "Because as much as she tries to be like me, I don't want that for her. I never want to see her settle for a lesser life."

The intensity in his tone gave me goose bumps, and I ran my hands up my bare arms.

"What about her mom?"

He looked away. "Addison's too stubborn to take money from her mom, and I'm too proud to ask for it."

"But if it's for your daughter?"

He shook his head. "Nothing is free with her mother. Everything has a string, a price, a fix I have to learn to let go of all over again." He shook his head. "Tara knows she can get under my skin. She always does." He looked at me. "So it's best to leave her out of things."

His eyes went to full shut down mode and he pushed his chair back to stand.

"Enough true confessions for one day," he said. "Let's save something for the next eighty-nine days."

* * *

Speaking of settling for mediocre. Every day was a new exercise in it. I got the bank teller job, if you could call it that. It was as an assistant teller. An *assistant* teller. I stress that twice because I kept saying it in my head and it still refused to make sense.

Not that I was dogging the teller positions. They worked hard. They dealt with the public all day, counted money, handled account issues. But assistant teller? It was like giving a secretary a secretary. I did nothing. Unless you call running bundles of cash back and forth, and doing a midday drawer count at each booth something. Evidently I had the opportunity to move up to a teller position after sixty days, but I might staple my wrists before then.

Oh for the boring days of ad copy.

And on that note—I still hadn't called Kristina back at Cali Dynamics. I wasn't sure why. I needed to call her and either one, tell her yes, let's Skype, and I'd figure it out later, or two, no, I'm stuck for three months. But something was holding me back. Something that told me leaving that dangling out there kept the dream alive, and facing it head on might kill it once and for all. In other words, I was being a big chicken shit baby.

Nick loved his new world, however. Chef Benny had finally left and Nick was running the kitchen his way, tutoring the fry cook to help him. He came home every night tired but happy, smelling of French fries and walking around the house in just a low-slung towel after a shower.

It wasn't fair.

For one, the towel thing was driving me mad. Yes, it had been awhile. Yes, Nick was incredibly hot. And yes, the constant towel-trolling was a tease. Also, his shower worked better than mine, and that kind of rubbed it in.

And did I mention he had a better job?

No, I wasn't feeling petty at all.

Carmen suggested we be seen together all over town, so we went to the grocery store every few days. Argued over the merits of fresh tomatoes versus canned tomato sauce until my brain started to melt, and I pelted him with grapes. He returned the favor by plucking a piece of ice from the meat market and dropping it down my shirt.

Basically, reasonable married adult activity.

We went out to eat a few times, being sure to reach for each other randomly, give a hand squeeze, a cheek kiss, laugh and smile at each other a lot. Nick became an expert at knowing just when to pull me to him affectionately when key people were around, and I learned not to react like it was something new.

Actually, that had become a weird kind of normal. Touching him, reaching for a hand, feeling his arms around me or his fingers on the back of my neck was beginning to feel natural. Even our evening TV schedule had become very domestic. My sitcoms merged with his reality shows. My need for popcorn slathered in movie butter sat happily next to his bowl of the sad natural un-buttered version. Because we both had a weakness for sour cream and onion chips, and that bonded the universe together. He even stopped rolling his eyes at my morning three-cups-of-coffee-and-veg-in-my-pajamas ritual, and I stopped rolling mine at his insanely vigorous morning run.

Saturdays were half days at the bank, so I decided to treat myself one Saturday to lunch at the Blue Banana. My first thought as I pulled into the parking lot was that it looked like a wait. My second, when I made it to the door, was that there was an oddly off base ratio of women to men. As in there were maybe five guys in the whole place, while females flocked every table and booth.

And then I saw why.

When *my husband* came out for a stroll through the diner, a smile on his face as he checked on each table as if it were a five-star restaurant. The black leather apron he wore over the black pullover shirt didn't hurt a thing, either. Holy hell.

All I could think of as I watched these ladies fall all over themselves as he spoke to them, was that they'd pass out cold if they saw the towel-trolling.

I stood there and watched a very buxom red-head with shorts too short for her age get up from her booth and hug him in thanks and appreciation for her delicious meal.

Seriously?

And then a hand to the chest as he patted her shoulder and she let go. And then a laugh and that same hand on his bicep.

Okay, for real? I mean, he did have a wedding band on. Usually that meant the man wasn't an all-you-can-eat buffet.

"He is bringing in the business," said Allie from behind me. "Daily sales have almost doubled since word got out about the new chef."

"Oh, I can see that," I said, crossing my arms over my chest as he caught my eye and smiled.

"Well, I won't lie, he's not hard on the eyes," Allie said with a poke to my arm and a chuckle. "But that wouldn't last him a day here without cooking good food. He's already added daily specials that aren't on the menu, and he's so damn fast."

"Hey, sweetheart," he said, walking up to me. I expected a hand squeeze or something, but instead I got his hand sliding to the back of my neck under my hair and a soft kiss pressed to my lips. *My lips.* My knees nearly caved; I was so unprepared for that.

And it must have shown, because he whispered, "Your cousin's at the bar," as he backed up.

Ah. *The game.* That's why.

Still. Holy mother of wiggly knees.

In every scenario, we had both avoided the meeting of the mouths. Every time. Now that, coupled with the intimacy of his fingers under my hair, had my toes awake and curling. And my stupid inner teenage girl memorizing how he'd kissed me.

"Working your fan base?" I asked, feeling every stroke of his thumb against my skin, and every envious eye on me.

"Jealous?" he asked, eyes dancing.

Oh no. No he didn't.

I tilted my head and slid a hand behind his neck, letting my fingers play with the hair at the nape as I laid my other hand against his chest and brought my face within inches from his. The quick inhale and darkening of his eyes sent a little rush to my belly.

Mm-hmm, take that.

"Only if you're cooking better for them than you do for me," I said softly.

His gaze got heavier as it fell to my lips.

Shiiitttttttt.

"Well played, Mrs. McKane," he said under his breath.

Jesus.

"Back atcha, Mr. McKane," I said just above a whisper as I watched him watch my mouth.

He wouldn't kiss me.

Dangerous.

Real.

And that made me want it a million times more.

"Gotta have the last word, don't you?"

I nodded, smiling. "Mm-hmm."

I backed up a step and let my hands slide down his chest as he blinked rapidly. As if pulling himself out of the moment too.

"Hi," said a squeaky female voice to my right.

I cleared my throat and looked to see fuzzy-haired Alicia smiling back at me.

"Hi," I responded.

"I have to get back to work," Nick said, his tone more polite now than playful. "Are you eating?"

"Yeah, but I still need to decide," I said.

"I recommend the chicken fried steak," Alicia said, to which Nick just shook his head and walked away.

At least six other pairs of eyes followed his ass, in addition to mine. It was a very nice ass.

"I wanted to apologize for my brother," Alicia said. "Bryce can be kind of overbearing."

Bryce could be a full-fledged prick.

"Bryce can do whatever he wants," I said. "As long as he stays out of my business."

"He's just very driven," she said. "He really wants that property."

"For what?" I said. "It's off the beaten path, next to nothing but an old ranch that Alan Bowman is using for hives. What good would it do him?"

She shrugged and grabbed her purse off a stool. "I don't know the details," she said, twisting a frizzled lock of hair.

I called bullshit.

"It doesn't matter," I said. "It's my home and I'm having to turn my life and my career upside down to hold on to it. I can promise you, it's staying right where it is."

There was a pause before she pasted on a smile.

"Well, have a good lunch," she said. "I have to get going. Oh—" She stopped and laid a finger on my arm. "Will we see you tomorrow?"

I went blank. "Tomorrow?"

"The Bowman's party," she said. "I thought Katrina said y'all were coming."

Okay, color me confused.

"Katrina?"

"Bowman?" Alicia said, as if that cleared it up. "She and Alan are having a party—"

"Oh, that's Alan's wife?" I asked.

"Yes," she said.

"And—you know them?"

"Bryce and Treena do," Alicia said in her goofy, self-deprecating way. "I met Katrina the other day. I think Bryce worked with Alan somewhere. They're always talking. Anyway, she mentioned that Alan invited you."

Oh, balls on a stick. I'd forgotten about that.

"Great," I said. "Well, we'll see. Depends on Nick's schedule."

She left, her cell phone out of her bag and to her ear before she was even all the way out the door.

Yeah. Don't-know-the-details, my ass.

* * *

"In a deer stand. She scared the deer away."

We were talking about "first times" after work, while I divulged my favorite secret place. An old rocky path that twisted into the woods on the edge of the property. You had to know it was there to find it, and as a kid I spent a lot of time exploring it. It went down to a trickling little creek by an old outdoor stone fireplace that was halfway gone now but still stood about six feet tall. Most of a stone bench was still attached to it.

I used to think it was where the magic came from. Aunt Ruby's magic. Before I got older and realized her skills were more intuition than *Abracadabra*.

"A deer stand?" I said, laughing. "How did that come about?"

Nick shrugged. "I was fourteen, I think. At our hunting cabin with my older brother."

"You were hunting?"

He laughed. "No. He brought a girl and she brought a friend." He grinned endearingly. "The friend didn't mind teaching me."

"Oh wow," I said. "So which question does this answer again?" I asked as we made it down to the fireplace. I sat down sideways on the bench and leaned against the cool stone. "First sex or first orgasm—with another person?"

"Same day." He grinned. "All day." He sat and pulled my feet onto his lap. "And you?"

"Oh, sex was nothing special," I said. "My first week of college, I think. I was away from home and drunk off my ass at a freshman party. I barely remember it."

"And the other?"

"That I remember," I said, chuckling. "At a movie theater."

His eyes sparked with interest. "Do tell."

"I was on a date with a cute nerdy guy named Wally," I said. "We'd been out a couple of times and kept passing dirty notes kind of as a joke to start, but then we got hold of some of his dad's liquor and got a little snockered before the movie."

"I see a trend," Nick said.

I laughed. "You could be right. So anyway, his hand was on my knee and when it started moving, I lost interest in the movie and my whole world became that hand."

Nick's fingers started making little circles on my ankles and the déjà vu of that was crazy.

"Pants or skirt?" he asked.

"Skirt."

"Nice," he said, one corner of his mouth twitching into a smile. "Proceed."

"So this took like an hour," I said. "I swear it was like a centimeter at a time, and he'd do—" I pointed at his fingers. "Like what you're doing right now. These slow little circles up my thigh. Until—" I stopped.

"Oh come on, you can't bail on me now," Nick said.

"I've never told anyone this," I said. "Not even Carmen."

He made a crossing sign over his heart. "Doesn't leave this spot."

I sighed. "Until he got to Ground Zero," I continued, feeling really warm all of a sudden. "Now by the time he got there we were both breathing like we'd run a marathon. I've never been so teased up and ready in my life, so when he finally made it under my panties, I literally lasted about three seconds before I came apart. And then so did he." I laughed. "Poor guy."

"Poor guy?" Nick asked. "I can promise you he still cherishes that memory. That's hot."

"I've brought towels to put down in the seats in theaters ever since," I said, making him laugh. "Seriously, think about how nasty those seats are!"

He was still laughing as he leaned his head back against the stone, his hands still resting on my ankles.

"It's nice down here," he said. "Peaceful."

"My favorite place in the whole world," I said.

"Okay next question," he said.

I groaned. "Is it as embarrassing as the last one?"

"Why do you hate fireworks?"

I blew out a breath. That was more complicated.

"That one's twofold," I said. "My mom and dad had a volatile relationship, according to my aunt," I said. "They were trying to get back together one July fourth, and we went to some picnic thing. Maybe it was the Honey Festival, I'm not sure. Anyway, they were fighting, and wanted to go home, and I wanted to see the fireworks because that's what my dad had been talking about all day. I'd never seen a big show. So I guess I whined too much, and he got mad and he grabbed me and brought me right up to where they were setting them off and yelled at me to *watch the fucking fireworks.*"

"Damn."

"Yeah," I said. "The people doing it yelled for us to get away but they went off and sparks went everywhere. He got a big one in his eye and I got them too." I pointed at little white scars on my arms. "He was screaming in pain and my mom was screaming at him, and I was crying about all of it."

"Did it blind him?"

"I don't know," I said. "He left that night and never came home."

"What?" Nick looked at me.

"Yep. My mom waited by the window for him for—I don't know. Months. She stopped being my mom. Stopped caring about anything." I took a slow breath and let it out. It had been a long time since I'd gone down that particular memory lane and it had my heart pumping. "My Aunt Ruby brought me to her house and I just never went home."

Nick was looking at me so intensely I could feel it on my skin. Like he was trying to see the story as I told it.

"And your mother?"

I swallowed hard. "She went into a depression I guess. Drank a lot. Took sleeping pills. The house burned to the ground one night while she was sleeping."

"Christ, Lanie."

I swiped under my eyes as they welled up unexpectedly. "I'll never know if that was accidental or not, but I do know that being psychotically obsessively in love with my father is what killed her. She never stopped waiting for that asshole to come home, even after what he did to me. She never had a life outside of him, and when he left, she died. Long before she actually did."

He squeezed my ankles. "I'm sorry that happened to you. And I'm sorry I brought up a bad memory." He looked around. "Especially down here."

I shook my head. "Best place to tell it," I said, chuckling, trying to shake off the funk. "The good magic down here overwrites the evil."

He smiled.

"I can see a little more about why this place is important to you," he said.

I just nodded. It was something I hadn't thought about in years, but he was right.

"Me too."

Chapter Eight

"Bee charmers aren't right in the head, Lanie. Anyone willing to risk death for a taste of sweet on their tongue needs mental help."

My phone dinged with an e-mail—a second one. From Cali Dynamics.

The first was to inquire if I was still interested since my weenie call, when I asked for more time due to a family emergency (not a lie, it qualified). The second had a form attached. For me to fill out on my preferred date to Skype, with all my info.

My insides quivered, and I tossed my phone onto the bed, where Ralph stared at it from his sprawl. He didn't look concerned, and I couldn't be, either. I couldn't deal with that, yet. I had swimwear to don.

"Why are we doing this again?" Nick called from down the hall.

I had been asking myself the same question at least fifty times in the last hour, as I dug for a swimsuit. I couldn't find my normal one, so I pulled out a second one from the bottom of a suitcase I hadn't unpacked yet. The way too skimpy one I bought on a lark, that I'd only worn once, and for some silly reason threw into the suitcase.

"Because the Clarks will be there. And we were invited," I called back.

"By your ex-boyfriend who still wants to do you," he responded.

"That again?" I said, more to myself, really. I tied my bikini top around my neck and held it to my chest as I rooted around for my long cover-up. "Seriously, his wife is there for one. And he's all hot air for—"

"Jesus."

I turned to realize I'd been bent over in just skimpy bikini bottoms, my back bare. I instantly jolted upright and pulled the strings around my back to tie them.

"If you're gonna be that naked, close your door," Nick said, suddenly behind me and taking the strings from my hands.

"Excuse me?" I said, trying to ignore the shiver that went down my back at the feel of his fingers sliding along my skin. "You walk around in only a towel. *Every night.*"

Dripping with water and giving me all kinds of increasingly un-game-like thoughts.

His hands moved upward. "Lift your hair."

"Why?"

He was already pulling the top string loose, and I hurried to grab my hair and clutch my top to my chest.

"Always have to retie," he said.

I felt the friction of fabric against fabric as he pulled it free, and heat rushed straight to my core. I suddenly felt entirely too naked to be this close to him. The swimsuit was too skimpy, and it wasn't even on yet. Every instinct was to back up against him, to feel him against me, and I had to shake my head to come back to reality. To shut down the mini-movie that had already begun in my head.

"Spoken like a man with experience," I managed.

A snort of disgust came entirely too close to my ear.

"My ex-wife practically lived in these things," he said then, even closer as he finished tying.

Don't back up. It's on if you do.

I turned around instead. And that wasn't much better. I focused on a long slow inhale to cover up the sharp one my heart slamming caused.

It was like the towel-troll but with swim shorts and all up close and I was definitely far too unclothed for this. When I made it to his face, I lost the feeling in my toes. His gaze was heavy-lidded and looked like he wanted to go swimming in my cleavage, which may or may not have been of my own fantasy, since I had a mad urge to lead him there.

But something—something knocking on my brain said that we were alone and that was playing with fire and we needed to save the sparks for the public eye.

"So the towel bothers you?" he said when our eyes met.

The game was all up in his tone, but we were home. There was no one watching.

"It's a bit distracting, yes," I said. "I am human."

"And you don't think *this* is distracting?" he said, his eyes panning south. "Or the tank tops with no bra at night?"

I felt the heat rush to my face at the knowledge that he'd noticed that.

Enough to make a point of it. "Sometimes I wear—"

"T-shirts," he finished for me. "Yeah, long ones with nothing underneath."

I put my hands on my hips. "I wear shorts."

"Well, it looks like you don't," he said, backing up. "You don't think that's maddening to see every night?" He raked both hands through his short hair, the muscles in his arms rippling, and God help me, that move was maybe right on up there with the trolling.

I licked my lips. I had to keep it together.

"We should probably go."

He nodded. "Please tell me you're wearing clothes over that," he said.

"Of course I am," I said, scoffing. "I'm not sixteen."

"I'm glad one of us isn't," he muttered, walking out.

"What does that mean?"

"Nothing," he said. "Did you do something with my black hat? The ball cap?"

"Do something?" I asked. "No."

He sighed and kept walking. "It was on my chair and it's gone. Along with the shirt I just put out to wear. Guess your aunt didn't like it."

* * *

The Clarks were already there when we came strolling up the road like natives. Our hands found each other as if on automatic pilot, our fingers interlacing so naturally you'd think we'd been together for years instead of three weeks.

They saw us coming, evidently, as Alicia was already waving and Bryce and his wife stood next to Alan, stoically staring at us as we approached. Nick transferred his hands to my shoulders as he stationed himself behind me and pulled me back against him.

Oh, dirty pool.

All the air left me for a second as the solid wall of Nick pressed against my back and warm hands traveled down my bare arms. He was getting too good at this.

Alan's grin went decidedly car-salesman-slash-politician as he winked at me and held out a hand for Nick.

"Glad y'all made it," he said.

I looked around at a yard full of people and a good dozen more in the pool. Which although it was off to one side, was technically in the front yard. Because that was logical.

It was like a who's who of Charmed. Anyone who had money, clout, or sway was there. Essentially, the whole upscale crowd from Bailey's Pond, where all the moneyed houses sat on the water on the north end of town with their cute little floating docks. Carmen's ex, Mayor Dean, was there. As was Bash, who owned Anderson's Apiary (But I liked Bash. And to his credit, he wasn't talking to Dean.). I recognized some city hall officials and business owners. So why the hell were we there? Why were the Clarks?

"Wouldn't miss it," Nick said, gripping Alan's hand, his words vibrating against my back.

"This is a few friends?" I asked.

Alan chuckled as if that made him super popular. I suspected it was either more about who he schmoozed to be there or about his wife. And I was willing to bet that the redhead strolling around in a tiny white swimsuit with tits the size of my head, laughing and handing out Jello shots, was said wife.

As she got closer, I saw more of her than I wanted to, as what little fabric she had was sheer and outlined pretty much all God gave her. I also remembered her. She was the gropey, short-shorted ginger from the Blue Banana that couldn't keep her hands off Nick.

Good times.

"Heyyyy!" she said, her eyes going as large as the areolas I could see way too well. "Nicky!"

Okay.

I turned in my Nicky space to give him the appropriate WTF look, but I never made it that far. I was halfway around when warm boobs pressed against my back. Or *boob* to be more accurate. The other one was on Nick. As she squished me into him and made me the filling in a Nicky/skank sandwich, floating in the scent of coconut oil.

"I'm so glad you came," she cooed, hugging him-slash-us.

I wrestled out a hand and raised it.

"Excuse me," I said, my face pressed into his collarbone. "Lanie Ba—McKane."

"Oh, I'm so sorry," she said, backing up and chuckling.

I turned to see those things moving like they were animated.

"Try not to accost the guests, honey," Alan said on a laugh, stepping forward to wrap an arm around her waist. "This is my wife, Katrina." He pasted on a grin for Nick. "Evidently you've already met."

"Nick's the talented new chef at the Blue Banana," Katrina said, with a wink at me like that made us soul sisters. "You know I love that place. And what he can do with an alfredo sauce is just—"

She closed her eyes and parted her lips, and I swear everyone in a five-foot radius stopped breathing while she looked to have a sexual experience. Bryce sweated more. Alicia snatched a Jello shot and walked away. Even Alan's eyebrows went up as he watched Katrina.

"Guess I need to try this magical sauce of his," I said, gazing lovingly up at my husband. I laid a hand against his abs, letting it slide to settle just an inch or two lower. Just for the satisfaction of feeling his muscles twitch. "*Nicky's* never made it for me."

"I'll make it for you any time you want," he said, running a finger from my cheek all the way down my neck. "A special private tasting."

I had no idea if the five-foot radius thing applied that time, but all the blood left my head for other journeys.

Yeah. Game was definitely on.

"Nice to meet you," Katrina said with a head tilt. She did look genuinely sexy-ditzy, to the untrained eye, but I caught the spark of intelligence hiding back there. The one that said she totally knew what she was doing and just how to play it.

"You too," I said.

"I hear you and Alan were an item back in the day?" she asked, winking at me again. I wanted to give her a pirate patch for that eye.

"Oh," I said, chuckling. "A very small item." And then I heard what that sounded like. "I mean, we just hung out in high school," I tried to amend as Alan's scalp glowed a little brighter. "Us and Carmen and Dean. Is Carmen here?" I asked, trying to divert.

I knew she wasn't. She wouldn't be caught dead at the same event with our esteemed Mayor Dean Crestwell, who—dammit—was walking toward me. Or even anything with Alan, for that matter, after that little word swap on the day we arrived.

The day we got married.

Good Lord, that felt like three months ago instead of three weeks.

"No," Alan said. "I never saw her again to invite her."

Yeah, tried real hard, too, I was sure.

"Lanie!" Dean said, hugging me right out of Nick's grip.

"Dean," I said, giving the polite pat. "How are you?"

"Good," he said. "Mayor. Have to behave and all that, can you believe it?"

I laughed. "Like that would stop you."

"Well," he said, giving the endearing smile that had initially won Carmen over many moons ago. Before Sully Hart smiled better. "I just have to work harder at not getting caught."

Everyone laughed. That Mayor Dean—what a charmer.

Not.

I knew too much.

"Hey, I'm sorry about your aunt. Let's grab a coffee or something and catch up later, okay?" he said, a hand on my shoulder as his eyes already panned to his next networking opportunity.

I nodded with a placating smile as he already moved on. "Sure thing."

No way in hell.

"Nicky, could you come help me with the hors d'oerves?" Katrina asked, looking totally innocent. "I think they need a little something. I know you'll know just what they need."

Really? I bet I knew what they needed too. A little caress and rub down from the hunky chef?

I felt Nick's hesitation, but we needed to look comfortable with that sort of thing. Like we weren't attached at the hip. Alan and Katrina were certainly way past comfortable. Bryce and his wife were—I don't know what they were. They were like mannequins with sweat glands.

"It's okay, babe," I said, reaching up to touch his cheek. The soft stubble sent zings through my fingers.

It wasn't just zings, however, when he squeezed that hand and kissed my fingertips. Holy shit balls. That was a clear point, set, and match in his favor.

"Okay," he said. "Be back in a bit."

"Bring me something delish!" I called after him as Katrina curled her arm in his and dragged him off to God knows where, slapping Mayor Dean on the ass as she passed. "Should I send in the cavalry if he doesn't make it back?" I asked Alan.

He laughed and threw an arm around me. "Kat's harmless. Let me show you around out here." He walked straight away from the Clarks, who didn't look the least bit put out by it, and little bells sounded in my head. The kind that come with stupid-sticks to poke at me.

It was a setup. To separate us and either get the truth, or individually cop a feel to prove a point and start shit. Or both.

"So have you ever had the Cajun infused honey that Mrs. Boudreaux sells at the feed store?" Alan said, his fingers lazily tracing my shoulder before they pointed ahead. "I buy it like crazy to glaze these stuffed jalapeno wraps."

My mouth watered on command, as he probably remembered it would. I was nothing if not shamelessly in love with food, and that hadn't been any different then.

"Oh wow," I said as we approached a card table that was nicer than my rent house.

Alan picked one up and fed it into my mouth before I could stop him. And the visceral reaction to it couldn't be stopped either, as the sweet and salty and spicy combined to give me a euphoria I hadn't known in a long time. I closed my eyes to savor it. I probably needed to get laid.

My eyes sprang open on that thought, and I looked around in case I might have said that out loud. I might need sex, but not for another two months and some change. Not till I wasn't married anymore, or at least till Nick and I were coming up on the end of it.

God, did I just think that?

Not that I planned to have sex with him. I actually had most definitely decided to *not* have sex with him in the beginning. But that was three weeks ago. Things were getting a little—warm—at times now.

Three weeks ago. Good grief, I was saying that in my head like that was such ancient history.

"Man this is really good," I mumbled, trying to be ladylike or mannered or any of the things I'd never been.

"Isn't it?" Alan said. "They're like my crack cocaine," he said on a laugh. "I have to make them once a week, I can't quit. Hopefully, one day I can try to match it. Enter the honey wars."

I rolled my eyes. "The honey wars."

"You know how competitive that gets," he said. "And believe it or not, it affects sales. I'll bet you ten dollars if Mrs. Boudreaux enters this stuff, she'll take first place and be sold out at her store for six months."

"Cajun honey?" I asked. Wanting another one so badly it gave me a twitch, but I was really aiming for that ladylike thing.

"Yeah, she won't give up her secret, either," he said, his hand back on the center of my back, steering me around and away from the food porn.

To the pool. Where there were all manners of fake boobs, made more prominent as five women suddenly decided to all float on their backs at the same time. It looked like a bunch of life buoys decided to dress up.

"So, what makes you want to come back here, Lanie?" he said, that hand sinking lower. "I mean, I remember you practically attaching a rocket to your ass when you left for college."

It had been true. And up until the reading of the will, I thought it still was. So having to defend that train of thought was a little shaky. Funny how that part didn't feel like ancient history.

"Yeah," I said. "And I can't honestly say that I know—" I cleared my throat. "We—that *we* know what we want to do. It all kind of happened quickly."

"Well, if you ask me—"

"I'm not," I said, smiling as sweetly as I could in the sweltering sun. Or maybe it was the conversation that was melting me on the spot. Or his hand now riding just above my ass crack. "It has nothing to do with you, Alan. It barely involves me. It's my aunt being a pain in the butt to make a point, turning everyone's lives upside down."

"So then walk away from it," Alan said, his greasy smile starting to nauseate me. "There are other players on the field, what's keeping you here?"

"My home."

"Excuse me?"

I raked my hair back, suddenly feeling like I could jump in that pool with all my clothes on. I lifted it off my neck and cursed not bringing a hair tie. Or a pair of scissors. It was like it was suddenly weighing me down.

"It was my home, Alan," I said, taking a step away from him and his need to touch me. "My only family. Whether I live there forever or not, it's my roots."

My phone buzzed with a text, and I looked down to see the California number, ironically.

Sent you an e-mail, please advise that you have received.

Shit.

And why *shit*? I had no idea. It was the job I'd always wanted. But to have to tell them I was stuck here for a while, and hear them give their regrets and move on… I didn't think I could bear it. Plus there was Nick.

Wait, what? No. There wasn't Nick.

"You okay?" he asked, panning from my tapping foot to where I held my hair up.

"I'm—just feeling twitchy," I said. "My hair's heavy. Must be the heat."

"Well, hop in the pool," he said. "I'm sure Kat has a swimsuit you could borrow."

Right. If we had two volleyballs to stuff the top with. And then some sanitizer for me to bathe in to rid myself of the full body slide trip his eyes took at the mention of me in his wife's swimsuit.

"I have my suit on under this," I said. "Just waiting on Nick. Do you think your wife hid him in a closet or something?"

Alan laughed. "I don't know, if she jumped him, we may have to retaliate."

I laughed too, but it was more the uncomfortable I-might-puke version. "I'm gonna go find—where can I get some water?"

"Right up there on the porch." He pointed. "There's a big wooden cooler with a variety of drinks."

"I'll show you," said a tall, dark, and gorgeous guy, swooping in to loop an arm through mine and never losing a step.

"Bashhhhhh!" I squealed quietly as we walked away so Alan wouldn't know my great giddiness at being escaped.

"I heard you were back," he said.

Sebastian Anderson had always been either in the row next to me in class or two lockers over in the hallway. He was drool-worthy and usually dating a cheerleader or something, but we always said hi. Senior year, when we ended up science project partners, we hit it off big. As buddies. Then he left for the Marines and got even hotter before coming back to Charmed and kicking off his own bee business. It kind of wasn't fair.

"Sort of," I said.

"Also heard you were married," he said.

"Like recently?" I asked. "Or from my aunt?"

"Your aunt," he said. "She told me every time I saw her."

I laughed with relief. "So are you here because you want to be?"

"God, no," Bash said. "Strictly business."

"With Alan?"

Bash shook his head. "I throw him a bone now and then to shut him up, but I'm here simply to put a face with the label." He nodded toward a group of way too shiny looking men clustered together. "Money." He sighed. "I have to give up watching baseball in my recliner to come talk to people with money."

I laughed and patted him on the arm as we approached the porch and he hugged me as he headed to the money people. Just in time to hear a full hearty female giggle that got louder as the French door opened. Nick came out adjusting his shirt, looking uncomfortable as he quickly shut the door behind him.

No. Way.

Chapter Nine

"Keep your lies simple with an element of truth, so you can look people in the eyes."

"Seriously?" I said.

He just shook his head. "These people are some kind of messed up."

"Yeah, I don't think that's a shocker to anyone around here," I said, looking back at the door. "Did she tackle you?"

Nick blew out a breath, taking my hand and walking us both away from the house. "Let's just say the appetizers she wanted me to taste weren't food related."

My mouth fell open and my feet stopped cold. "Are you fucking kidding me?"

I knew we weren't a real couple. *He* knew we weren't a real couple. But these people didn't know shit. For all they knew, we were madly in love and fucked like rabbits every night.

"I took care of it," he said.

"Oh, she'll see *taking care of it*," I said, turning on my heel. "That bitch has some nerve—"

"Lanie," he said, pulling back on my hand. "You don't have to. I seriously told her that she was completely out of line. Let's just walk away."

"Excuse me? Do you remember the *ten years or ten minutes* conversation a few weeks ago when you first met Alan?"

He gave a look of concession like a boy caught telling a lie. "Okay, touché."

I felt like a hot mess. "Oh my God, what is with all these people, hell bent on calling us out."

"You think it was a setup?"

"Oh I know it was," I said. "Divide and conquer. Katrina snags you for a little taste test, and Alan whisks me off for a touchy-feely trip down memory lane."

"He touched you again?"

All his muscles bowed up at attention, and it was adorable.

"Now who's going off the rails?" I said, turning back to walk with him. "He fed me peppers slathered in honey. Want to get in the pool?"

Nick reached back and pulled his shirt over his head without another word, bringing appreciative gazes from every woman there and maybe a few men too.

"Need to cool your jets?"

I didn't know if I could pull off the move that smoothly while we were walking, but I gave it a hell of a shot. I nearly tripped over a decorative rock while my tank top was still over my head, but thankfully Nick guided me around it.

"And take down the silicone ratio in there," I said.

He chuckled. "You saying you're all what God gave you?"

"One hundred percent."

After tossing his shirt on an empty chair and kicking off his shoes, Nick walked down into the pool. I hesitated to watch him. He was truly spectacular.

I mean, yes, I saw the towel-version of this every night, but I always felt like I shouldn't be looking and made myself look away. This was fair game, and I feasted on it. He wasn't hairy; just the right amount of hair peppered his chest and led a dark line down to—and the abs on this guy were absolutely lickable.

I blinked that thought away as I dropped my shirt onto his and tried to remember how to unzip my shorts.

It felt like too many eyes were on me as I walked into the pool. Not that I was all that, but I'd walked up with Superman here, so naturally the envy comes out and where he is silently celebrated, I knew every inch of my body would be picked apart and studied for flaws. My lack of visible lickable abs for one thing. Of a hard body. My waist was small, but my love of food made me soft and curvy.

I felt every one of those curves as I paraded in front of so many nosy eyes, but a burn started in my belly at the look in one pair.

Nick was all the way across the pool, against the far wall, watching me in a way that heated my blood. So I did what any logical-minded woman would do. I went under. Pushing off in the silence, I passed legs of all kinds, some intertwined in ways you wouldn't guess from the surface. And then there was the bottom half of Nick in all his glory. Until I was about ten feet away, and he went under to wait for me.

Something slammed inside my chest as his eyes met mine. Something hard and soft and cold and hot and about to be squeezed as a move so random and playful and harmless was so damn intimate. My feet stopped kicking but my momentum kept me moving forward, slowly inching toward him.

It said *I've got you*. Like out of all the legs I swam by, he was there for me. I pulled my feet under me and pushed to the surface. He popped up too.

"Most women refuse to get their head wet at a party like this," he said, slicking his wet hair back.

I leaned back to rewet mine and let it slick itself. And give myself something to do besides think. "I'm not most women."

Nick laughed. A low, deep sound that did nothing to settle my inner shakes.

"No doubt about that." He stretched both arms out along the pool wall. "So what did Mr. Loverboy have to say?"

"That I should let Bryce have the house so that I can get on with my life," I said. "He reminded me that I couldn't wait to leave here."

"So what do you think his stake is in this?"

I shrugged. "His property butts up to mine. I'm willing to bet he and Bryce have struck up some kind of deal if he wins.

Wins.

Like it was some sort of game.

There was familiar loud laughing and splashing behind me, and Nick's expression told me what I needed to know.

"Crap," he muttered.

"There y'all are," Katrina said, cozying up against Nick's outstretched arm.

All I could see through the resurging anger that filled my head was naked Katrina trying to seduce him.

"You were looking for us?" I asked through my teeth. Heat flooded my head so hot I had to be glowing.

"Of course," she said, laying a hand on Nick's chest. His bare chest. Something *I* hadn't even done yet. *Did I just say yet?* "Nicky left before he could finish sampling my snacks."

Oh no.

I could not be expected to tolerate this. Fuck no.

"Aw, did he?" I said. "Damn that's a shame, because I sampled some of your husband's *snacks* over there, and oh my God. Melted in my mouth."

Katrina's eyes narrowed in that way of hers that showed a brain, and I knew she was questioning what Alan might have done. I didn't care. My heart was pounding so hard in my ears it hurt.

"And for the record," I continued, my words flowing on a fog of red haze that took me past logic and good sense. "My husband doesn't need any of your snacks, Katrina." My hands went to the strings around my neck and pulled them free, before palming my boobs and pushing them up for her. There was a collective gasp heard around the world. "He has these to *snack on* whenever he pleases."

"Okay, enough," Nick said, pulling me to him protectively, wrapping his arms around me as he pressed me against his chest. My naked boobs against his chest, that I bared for the town. Oh my God. What had I done? "The show's over, you can all go back to talking about people. Katrina, can you maybe go chat with someone else?"

I felt her storm off. Felt, because I was facing Nick's neck with my eyes shut.

"I've got you," he said against my ear.

The irony of his words almost broke me.

"I just did that," I whispered. "Fuck balls, I really just did that."

He chuckled. I felt that too. Naked chest to naked chest. God help me.

"Yes, you did," he said.

"I can't face these—oh my God, my cousins are here. And Dean," I said, pressing my forehead into his shoulder. "And Bash."

"And they are?"

"People I went to school with, who should have never seen that," I whispered. "I'm so sorry. That's not me. She just made me so crazy."

"Are you kidding me?" he said, chuckling again. "That was the hottest thing ever." I chanced looking up, and instantly knew I was too close, and too undressed, and just too everything. "You fought for me with your one-hundred-percent boobs. I can honestly say no one has ever done that."

"Oh God. Please try to forget that."

His face came down lower, a teasing look in his eyes. "Oh, I will *never* forget that." He grinned. "It's okay."

"Can we leave?" I asked.

"No," he said, looking down into my eyes.

"Why?"

One hand slid from its hold on my back, down to right above my ass, and pulled me tightly against the biggest rock-hard hard-on I'd ever felt. And where he settled? Was spot on. I sucked in a breath.

"That's why," he said against my ear, his voice sounding strained.

I went dizzy. All the blood in my body rushing to one spot in two-point-two seconds will do that. His hand sliding lower to curl fingers into the soft skin of my ass cheek didn't help. My hands went to his sides automatically, my nipples grew hard against the coarse hair on his chest, and my legs wanted to wrap around him in response. But I wouldn't let them. If I did that—

"And I'm thinking that a raging boner in response to my wife's tits probably doesn't say we've been married for a while," he said, his breathing a little rougher against my ear.

"True," I said. Or someone said, using my mouth. I needed to get dressed. To get my shit together and my head back on this planet. I slid my hands up between us, bringing my bikini top back over my breasts. "Can you hold me while I tie this back? I can't reach the bottom here."

Both hands went to my ass, pulling me tightly against him, and my control wiggled as my mouth went dry.

"Not quite what I meant," I said hoarsely.

"Sorry, I'm a little drunk on no blood right now," he said. "All roads are leading there."

I tied it back as well as I could with shaky hands, and then pushed back gently, my hands on his chest. *There, now I'd touched his chest.*

Yeah, a little distance might be good," Nick said, sliding under and coming back up. "And some cold water on my head."

"Good id—"

And I was under, the sound of my own bubbles closing over my head. I came up spitting water at him.

"Now, that's sexy," he said, laughing.

"Cute," I said, splashing water in his face.

And just like that, he set everything back on its axis.

He had that talent.

I moved to the wall next to him and tried to will my body back into compliance.

"Thank you."

"For?"

"Coming to my rescue," I said. "Even though it was awkward and uncomfortable."

A smile pulled at one corner of his lips.

"Anytime," he said. "But before you go making me all noble, let me assure you that nothing in the last five minutes was a sacrifice."

I laughed. "For me, either. In fact—" Should I go for the admission?

What the hell. I had already shown him my boobs. "Probably a good thing we're in public."

"It's a very good thing we're in public," he said. "Although honestly, a few more moves and I might not have cared."

The heat rushed back with a vengeance.

"Oh?"

I was playing with fire. And he knew it. The mischievous spark flashing in those dark eyes told me so.

"Do you need a do-over?" he asked, his tone all shades of delicious.

I smiled and gripped the concrete like a lifeline.

"I'll take a rain check on that."

What. Did. I. Just. Say.

The pool had to be drugged. With aphrodisiac water. Maybe Alan threw oysters in it before the party. I clapped a hand over my eyes that really should have been over my mouth.

"Okay, we really need to leave this place before I say or do one more thing."

Nick laughed heartily and removed my hand. "Lanie, relax." He glanced around and lowered his voice, leaning in. "I think we both know that this game we're playing with—it's fire and matches. We live together. We're always in each other's space." His gaze dropped to my body and water splashed as he ran a wet hand over his face. "And you drive me mad. It's probably gonna happen eventually."

You drive me mad. Jesus, that didn't help. At all.

"I'm just shooting for the later side of that," he continued.

"Me too," I whispered. Thank God we were on the same page. Sort of.

"Because—"

"We have a long way to go," I said.

He nodded. "And if we went there now," he began.

"It could—It would get—" The words froze in my throat.

"Complicated."

Boom.

Exactly. I saw my every thought looking right back at me.

Translation: It wouldn't just be once. And more than once equaled need. Need turned to feelings.

Neither of us could afford that.

"Yeah," I said. "So—"

He glanced down at himself. "So I need to quit talking about this or we're never getting out of this pool."

Was it bad that him being turned on by me was a hot rush? That I really wanted to reach over and feel it for myself? *Yes. Yes it was, Lanie.* I smiled.

"So tell me about your daughter, then," I said.

He frowned. "That'll do it."

"Her name is Addison and she's brilliant and beautiful and wants to go to art school," I said. "That's all I really know about my stepdaughter."

"Oh man, that sounds weird," he said. "Shit, I need to tell her."

"You haven't told her?" I said. "You talk to her every other day."

"I talk to her once a week, thank you very much," he said. "She just texts a lot. Teenagers do that."

"And?"

He blew out a breath. "Tell her over the phone that her old man got married for the money to send her to college?" he said quietly, lifting his eyebrows. "No. That hasn't come up."

All the hot steamies and the warm and cozy moments of the last half hour felt decidedly cooler.

"I'll tell her tonight," he said on a weary exhale.

"That's still over the phone."

He shook his head. "I'm headed home tonight."

"You're—what?"

I had no claim and he owed me absolutely nothing, but something in that sentence stabbed me in the gut. He looked at me funny.

"It's Addison's graduation on Monday. I put it on the calendar on the fridge."

That sounded so married and domestic. Except that truly married and domestic would have probably involved a conversation. And possibly travel for two.

And that's where my brain shut down my heart. Right there on that thought path. With a roadblock from hell. Where in this journey had I *ever* thought he'd bring me home to meet his family, his daughter, his life? That was never in the plan, and I was breaking my own internal rules.

I shook my head and laughed. "Of course. I'm sorry. I just—never think to look at that."

"So you're okay with it?" he asked, looking a little confused. Probably wondering why he was asking.

I scoffed. "Please. It's your daughter's graduation. Go! Enjoy!" I pushed at his shoulder like a friend would. Like a buddy. "Video like all the other nerd parents."

He chuckled. "That'll be her mom." He shook his head. "For someone who never wanted to grow up and be a mother, she loves these big moments. Goes all out."

The woman who always got under his skin was going to be there. Fuck, of course she was going to be there. Where else would she be on her daughter's high school graduation?

"Tell me about her," I said, sensing he was actually open for once.

"About Tara?" I nodded so he'd continue, but his eyes took on that slightly pissed off look they always did when the subject of his ex-wife came up. "She's usually the person I try to avoid if at all possible, but this time is out of my hands." He exhaled slowly and stared off into something I didn't see. "She was the spoiled rich girl I had no business having. Then she was the love of my life. Until that wasn't enough."

Chapter Ten

"You're always so anxious to grow up, my girl. Slow down. One day you'll be begging to build a blanket fort in the living room to hide from life."

"Y'all need to step it up."

That was Carmen's grand advice. Nick's departure that afternoon led to a little girl's night therapy at Rojo's. A Mexican restaurant that had been there since before our time and possibly before Aunt Ruby's. Not that I needed therapy. Or was upset or uptight in any way. But venting was definitely in order, and Ralph wasn't cutting it as a sounding board. He wouldn't even come inside much anymore he was so into his kingdom in the backyard.

"Step it up how?" I asked. "I flashed my boobs to the entire town, defending his honor, and then we practically rounded third base as he defended mine."

Carmen clapped a hand over her mouth before she could spit out a mouthful of chip and salsa, and laughed silently in her chair.

"God, I wish I'd been there," she said finally. "That has to be the story of the year. It'll definitely be the story of the festival this year. You know that, right?"

"Whose side are you on?" I said, throwing a chip at her.

"I didn't know we were picking sides," she said. "I'm just saying. Telling Katrina Bowman off like *that*—it's epic."

"Well, you *don't* wish you would have been there, because Lean Mean Dean was working the next election like a pro," I said, using the nickname he used to call himself.

Carmen shook her head and dipped another chip. "Sad that he's become that—that thing. That stereotypical politician. He used to be a good guy."

I gave her a look. "A good guy that worked you like a puppet and then threw you under the bus when his ego took a hit."

She chewed in silence, ever the protector of the innocent. Carmen was always the pretty one. The one that turned guys' heads. The striking looks with the perfect boobs and bouncy blond hair that could have any man she ever wanted, except for the one she truly did. She never cheated on Dean, not even when they were kids. Not even when Sully entered the picture. They were broken up when it started, and after he left—well, after that, maybe her heart strayed but her body never did.

At least to my knowledge.

"So, back to you and your apparent exhibitionist streak," Carmen said, ducking when I aimed a chip at her head. "You're right, that'll be hard to follow."

"And why do we need to?" I asked. "We're doing just fine—or sort of. Except for that leaving without telling me thing. But the town is buying it. We're playing it."

"The town isn't who you need to convince," she said. "It's those rotten cousins of yours."

Wow, how far we'd come from the polite and respectable presence of Attorney Carmen just a few weeks ago.

"I think Alicia is up to something," I said.

"They're all up to something," Carmen said. "Bryce has been schmoozing at City Hall, I've seen him there twice. And I just got the heads up that he's paying Alicia to play private eye."

I sat back in my chair. "Say what?"

"Yes, ma'am."

There weren't enough what-the-fucks for that.

"She needed the money, and he probably figured she was a hell of a lot cheaper than the real deal. So all these times you see Alicia?"

"Oh man, I'm totally upping the freaky scale," I said. "Maybe I'll start wearing wigs and pick my nose in public."

"Just start showing a little more intimacy," Carmen said. "Don't give them a reason to go digging and find out you just got married." A big bowl of queso came and we both moaned.

"Again—flashed my boobs and stayed that way in his arms for what felt like half the day," I said. I wasn't thinking about the massive hard-on and his hands gripping my ass and how close his mouth had been. Nope, not at all. "Stepping that up in public would probably get us arrested."

"Not step *that* up, dorkus," she said. "*Kiss* him."

My entire body broke out in goose bumps. She said that like it was so simple. The one time we'd bumped lips was at the diner for Alicia's benefit, and it had nearly given me a coronary. If I would have gone there today along with the—I couldn't even think about it without going hot in all kinds of places.

"We don't do that," I said.

"So start," she said, her eyes wide like she was talking to a child.

I licked my lips at the mere thought of it, and she pointed at me.

"Uh-huh, that's what I thought," she said.

I frowned. "What?"

"You might not *do that*," she said, doing finger quotes. Really. Finger quotes. "But you want to." She narrowed her eyes at me with her lawyer stare and a grin pulled at her lips. "You want to, bad. You're falling for your husband."

I scoffed. "I totally am not."

"You are, and you're buying the next round for lying," she said. "The next two, if you're really that clueless and don't see it."

"I'll throw in a dessert just to bring an end to this topic," I said with a wild grin.

"So let's look at all the points, shall we?" she said, ignoring me.

"Oh hell no, you aren't lawyering me."

"First, you're all out of sorts because he left town," she said.

"I have no problem with Nick leaving town," I countered.

"To see the love of his life," she added.

My jaw locked a little on that one. And my left thumb twitched. That wasn't a problem, right?

"He's going to see his daughter graduate," I said. "Have dinner with her tonight. Perfectly normal. The *love of his life* chick just happens to be there."

"And if you only saw your face just now," she said. "That bothers you."

"No it doesn't, lawyer lady, move on." I stopped to point at her. "And I was not out of sorts. I just had a problem—not even a problem, actually. Just an *issue* with him springing it on me like that. I mean, married people tell their spouse when—"

"And so you see the two of you as a real married couple," she said. "Check."

I picked up my drink and shook my head. "Uncheck."

"Point two," she continued. "The thought of Katrina Bowman hitting on him drove you to rip off your clothes—"

"Excuse me?" I said. "There was no ripping. I calmly untied

the string and—"

"Held your baubles up for the world to see," she finished. "To show her just whose man he was and to keep her grimy hands off."

My mouth opened and closed twice like a friggin guppy. Had I done it like that?

Yes. I had.

"Next," I said. Rather weakly.

"Third, you just went ten shades of panicked when I mentioned kissing him," she said. "And finally—I know this droopy preoccupied look of yours. It hasn't changed in all these years."

"What?"

"When you have it bad, Lanie," she said, taking a long swig from her fruity drink. "You wear it all over you. You get all flushed and blinky when you talk about him, or when his name comes up unexpectedly."

I just glared.

"You're full of shit," I said. "Nick, Nick, Nick, Nick. No blinking. No pinking. No problem."

"So if I said he just walked in?" she said, glancing past me.

My heart felt like it went up my throat and hurtled itself against my skull, as I whirled around in my chair, knocking my beer over in the process.

"Fuck!" I exclaimed, grabbing at it, my napkin, my wallet, my phone— all while craning my neck to find him. "Seriously?"

"No."

I turned back around, my ears still pounding with my heartbeat. "What?"

She started laughing. "No, he's not here. And you just made my case for me. Thank you, Your Honor, no more questions."

I sat there blinking, catching my breath, one arm and thigh drenched in beer.

"I hate you right now."

Carmen tilted her head sympathetically, handing me some more napkins. "Sorry?"

"No you're not," I said, sopping up the mess. "You love that lawyer shit."

"Not really," she said. "I'm good at it, but it's just going through the motions."

I glanced up. "So why do it? Do something else."

Carmen scoffed. "Right, just *do something else*? Blow off the fact that that's the only thing I'm trained to do?"

"I mean, if you're not happy," I said.

God, I was a hypocrite. *California, much?*

"Happy would be travelling the world, drinking coffee in dive cafes and never having a mailing address, remember?" she said. "It's not about happy, it's about reality. And that's here. Chasing court dates instead of dreams."

I remembered. Carmen's mom was a big dreamer, raising her on her own but working odd jobs because she was always looking for some magic fit she never found. Carmen inherited that itchy nature in the form of wanderlust. Not that she ever got to act on it.

"Anyway, we were talking about you," she said. "And your love life."

"No," I said. "No we weren't. You were making a court case all by yourself and I was listening."

"The point is, y'all do need to make more appearances," she said. "Intimately. Holding hands. Kissing. You know Alicia will be everywhere. What about the dance?"

I laughed. "I don't see us going to the Honeycomb Dance, Carmen."

"Perfect opportunity," she said. "Will he be back?"

"Supposed to be back on Wednesday, and the dance is that night, so yes, but—"

"No buts," she said. "I'll even—ugh," she began, rubbing her face as if the words she had yet to say were going to hurt. "I'll even meet you there."

My eyebrows shot up. "You? At a Charmed public event? With people?"

"I know," she said. "Take that as proof that I have your best interests at heart. I want to see you get what you want."

There was a double meaning all up in her eyes and tone, but I refused to let her steer me there.

"What if Mayor Dean is there?" I asked.

"I'll say, *hey Dean*, and keep walking," she said. "Alan's a different story. Him I might have to maim." She held up a finger. "I have one other question."

"Crap."

"Why haven't you called that California job back?"

I huffed out a breath as I sat back in my chair. "How do you know I haven't?"

"Have you?" she asked, one eyebrow lifting.

"Sort of."

Her eyes narrowed. "Meaning?"

"I still have to schedule an interview."

Carmen nodded and signaled our waitress for another beer for me. "So what's stopping you?"

"I'm kind of stuck here, Carmen," I said. "Thanks to Aunt Ruby, I still have another two months left on my sentence."

She chuckled. "You can still do the interview, and tell them it's something else. Make it sound important. You're on a special project at work and can't leave them in the lurch till it's done in two months. You're willing to take three weeks' vacation instead of four in gratitude for their patience."

My jaw dropped. "They aren't going to give me four weeks, anyway."

"Play it like they are," she said. "Build your worth up. Lanie, this is the chance of a lifetime. A chance to get the hell out of here."

Sounded more like the chance of *her* lifetime. She'd settled on life in Charmed with Dean after Sully Hart left her behind. It hurt my heart a little that maybe that's why we drifted apart after I left. Because I got to leave.

"I was already *the hell out of here*," I said. "Not all it's cracked up to be."

"This one's different," she said. "It's your dream job. It's starting over. You can tell them whatever you want them to believe."

I shook my head and grabbed my new beer. "Maybe I need you to do my interview for me."

My phone dinged, and my belly tightened as I saw the name on the text message.

Nick.

Only because we kept talking about him. Shake it off.

Then I pressed it, and there was a different belly burn.

A selfie of Nick and his daughter, head to head, at a restaurant. It was an adorable photo. She looked so much like him it was incredible. He looked so friggin proud I could feel it through the pixels.

If only it wasn't photo bombed.

By his ex-wife grinning over their heads.

Looking like a family. The real kind. I inhaled slowly and took a long drink from my bottle. Tried not to think about the earlier activities of the day. Tried not to let anything cross my face where Carmen could pounce on it.

Evidently, I failed, because she plucked the phone from my hand and looked at the screen.

"Why did he send you this?" she asked.

My stomach felt nauseated, all the chips I'd just ingested turning into concrete.

"It's—it's a good picture of him and his daughter," I managed.

"*That's* what you see there?" she said. I took my phone back and started pressing and scrolling. "What are you doing?"

"I'm filling out a Skype form," I said.

Chapter Eleven

"Life's too short for melodrama and uncomfortable shoes."

I ran through the door at precisely 11:28, having ditched out of work fifteen minutes before my lunch hour officially began. One of the tellers quit unexpectedly, so I'd been pre-promoted from the cursed assistant position to a real girl with my own station. At eleven o'clock, however, while listening to yet another female customer in my line wax on about the Greek god that was my husband and how he made her want to eat at the Blue Banana every day of the week and how lucky I was… I'd looked down to see that my phone had 2 percent battery left because I couldn't find my charger that morning and my Skype interview was at eleven-thirty. I was going to have to go home, and pray that my laptop (still in its case) was working.

"Please, please, please," I chanted as I jogged up the stairs with Ralph on my heels, sweating through my silk blouse that hopefully they wouldn't be able to see.

I gave a quick look around my bedroom just in case the phone charger *that was always plugged into the outlet by my bed* had made a reappearance. It hadn't. Really?

"Aunt Ruby, you are seriously pissing me off!" I yelled. "Quit hiding things!"

I yanked open my closet door and grabbed the laptop case leaning against the wall, thankful to feel weight inside. The way things went missing in this house, even though I'd never taken it out, it was a fifty-fifty shot.

"Cord, cord, where's the—" My fingers closed on it, and I hurriedly hooked it up, plugged it in, set it up on the side of my bed and knelt on the floor. I drummed my fingers ever faster as it cranked to life, mentally willing it along. I had just clicked on the Skype app and brought up my webcam, when the call came in.

I stared at myself wide-eyed.

I looked like a clammy, deranged freak. Eyeliner was bleeding south, my hair was sticking up on top and looked sweaty at the hairline, and there was a pile of dirty laundry behind me.

"Shit!"

I swiped under my eyes, shuffled on my knees to the left so that the background was a bookshelf, and attempted to smooth my hair. And clicked *Accept.*

Three people filled the screen. Three people who looked much more put together than I did, sitting at a table instead of a bed and not covered in a sheen of perspiration. I put on my best professional smile.

"Hello," I said.

"Good morning," said the middle one, a blond lady with a perfect twist on her hair. Morning? Oh yeah, it would be nine-thirty there. "We're so glad we could make this interview finally happen," she said. "We're anxious to get our team put together and really hope that you're a perfect fit, Lanie."

"Thank you," I said, tilting my head, remembering Carmen's words of advice to sell myself. "I feel that I am. I—"

I saw Ralph's head in the small screen with me at the bottom right before I registered him next to me. Before his extraordinarily large tongue came across my face.

* * *

On my way back. Should be there around 3ish.

It was a text from Nick after I got back to work. Like I needed more stress after the interview from hell. I didn't text back. I was feeling grumpy and irritable and noticing stupid things like he didn't add the word *home* after *back.*

My hormones had to be ape-shit out of control or something. Of course this wasn't home for him. It was a job. He was being paid for this. It wasn't really my home either, and when it was all said and done and we won this ridiculous game, I was going to have to figure out what to do with Aunt Ruby's house.

On the crazy chance I actually pulled off the ghetto interview with

Ralph making his cameo appearance, and I made the cut on the California job...*and* they went for my proposal of starting in two months because of the important project I was currently on (thank you, Carmen), I would be leaving not only Louisiana but Texas too. Should I close the house up and leave it vacant for a place to come home to? That didn't feel right. Leaving Aunt Ruby's home vacant and unloved just didn't feel right. I could rent it, but finding renters in Charmed that I could trust not to screw me would be tricky from across the country.

Even if I just went back to my old life in Louisiana, the decisions remained the same. And it all gave me a sick, sad feeling in my stomach that I couldn't explain. The only thing becoming increasingly obvious was that it was no longer just about the house.

Thank you, Carmen, *again*.

I pulled up to the house and felt my belly tighten at the sight of his truck in front. Yeah, that *complicated* thing we were trying so hard to avoid? It was knocking on the door and peeking in every window.

Ralph met me at the door, all wiggles and tongue, moving me a good two feet in his gusto. I had to admit I'd learned to enjoy his presence. He was part of our merry little dysfunctional family—for sure he fit in as well as we did. I'd miss him once he was gone. Assuming he ever was. Tilly had kind of gone radio silent.

"Hey," came a voice from the stairs, and I looked up to see Nick descending, wearing jeans and pulling down a white T-shirt as he went, giving me a flash of perfect abs. The knock against my chest wasn't just about that, though. "I just got here, was changing clothes."

So I saw.

"Hey," I said, deflecting Ralph. "How was the drive?"

"Same," he said. "How was work?"

"Work." I swallowed hard and sank onto the couch. "I had my interview today."

He stopped in his progress to the couch to join me, his feet faltering just for a second before he continued on.

"The Skype one?"

"Yep."

Nick sank onto the opposite end, sitting sideways to face me as had become our way at the end of each day. The move tugged at me. I didn't realize that I'd missed him.

"So?"

I looked at my hands. "I don't know. I wasn't very impressive."

"I don't believe that," he said, kicking my foot.

"No, seriously," I said, chuckling. "I had to come here and use my laptop and Ralph joined me." Ralph thumped his tail from across the room at the mention of his name. "So it was kind of a comedy of errors. We'll see."

Nick gave me a long look I couldn't really read. "Guess so," he said finally. "What if you did impress them, though? What then?"

I looked away. At the TV, the wooden bowl on the coffee table, my fingernails. "I told them I'm on a special project at work so I wasn't available for two months, so if I still somehow miraculously make the cut—"

"That's brilliant," he said, a grin pulling at his mouth. "Makes you look important and needed."

I smiled. "That was the plan. And Addison's graduation?"

And her mother?

Stop.

"Awesome," he said, his eyes going warm with memory. "And hard to believe. Damn, it seems like that girl was just starting kindergarten." He sat up and pulled out his phone. "Come see."

He scrolled through pictures as we sat shoulder to shoulder and I looked at a beautiful, young, smiling female version of him. Some just her, some with her mom, and some of just him.

"Who took these?" I asked, bumping against him.

"Addison stole my phone at one point, so lord only knows what she—

That thought was addressed pretty quickly.

A moment caught of Tara and Nick, her arms wrapped around his waist as she gazed up at him and he looked down at her. He didn't have his arms around her, just his hands on her arms, but it still—I just—if I had nuts to be kicked, that would be the feeling that stabbed straight through me.

He hit delete, and another one came up right behind it, this one with her hands on his face like she was about to kiss him. To his credit, he was frowning. But I had to get up or stop breathing, so I rose to my feet.

"Lanie, that—"

"Is none of my business," I said. "It's your family."

"Family?" he said, laughing shortly. "No. Addison's my family. Tara acts like that when it suits her. When the mood strikes her or it makes a good appearance. *Family* doesn't stay in Lake Tahoe partying when their ten-year-old daughter is in the hospital with appendicitis."

"So—how old *were* you when Addison came along?" I asked, forcing the nut kick down.

"You've been dying to ask that, haven't you?"

"Kind of, yeah," I said.

Nick smiled and rubbed at his eyes. He looked exhausted. I felt bad about springing the dance on him, but after seeing that picture I was a little less remorseful. Okay, so some of the nut kick still lingered.

"Seventeen," he said.

"Wow," I said, grinning. "You were a naughty boy."

"I guess," he said. "It was a crazy time, and Tara and I were so—" He made a circled crazy motion with his finger. "Off the charts. Couldn't get enough of each other. Couldn't think straight if we wanted to."

Oh, good. That was such a fun fact to get back to.

"It wasn't a great moment at first, for anyone, as you can imagine," he said. "But by the time Addison got there, Tara's parents had softened on me. They—they knew their daughter. She was as flighty then as she is now, and I think they looked at me and saw stability. A hard worker. Someone who wasn't going to wake up and book a flight to Bali on a whim. Or buy two thousand dollars' worth of new clothes because I had a bad day."

I frowned. "Excuse me?"

"They had money," he said. "They *have* money. And Tara was spoiled with it, to the point that she became reckless and didn't care. By the time her parents began to care, she was who she was. No amount of scolding or cutting her off mattered. She—has a way. She has a charm. People love her no matter what she does. No matter how she treats them."

"And this was the love of your life?"

It fell out of my mouth before I could vet it, and the sharp gaze that met mine told me it hit a mark.

"You know that person that you can't forget, that taught you everything you know about love now and can still knock you on your ass even though they are toxic for you?"

My breath caught in my chest. The way he spoke those words, so passionate, so full of hate and love and anger and sadness and irritation, it hurt me. It physically hurt me. No one had done that to me with words before, and he wasn't even talking about me.

"No," I said, the word not being much more than a whisper.

He blinked and swallowed hard. "Sorry, I forgot you said you'd never been there." He raked a hand through his hair, making it stick up. "Well one day you will. And it makes you do and think things you never thought you'd be so stupid to do."

"That's why," I said, finding my voice. It came out a little rougher than I intended, but that was okay. I was ticked. The pictures. The gut-stabs. *I forgot you'd never been there. One day you will.* A burn built behind my eyes, and that made me even madder. "Love makes people stupid. I prefer to keep my wits about me."

Nick's expression changed and he closed his eyes. "Your mother."

"For one."

"Lanie, I'm sorry," he said. "I—okay. Point taken."

All the ire was sucked right out of me, like air released from a balloon. The look in his eyes pierced my insides more than the other things had.

"So," I pushed out, my voice croaky. "Addison?"

"Addison came along and we gave it a good shot," he said. "Tara tried, I'll give her that. She still tries. But her demons and her habits run deep. She still runs when she gets stressed and maxes out credit cards when she's sad. Thankfully, Addison never picked up any of that." He blew out a breath and his jaw tightened. "She's so far the other way, so rebellious against the wealth that is her birthright, that she'd marry a street singer and live in her car just to prove a point."

I sat back on the arm of the couch. "What? Did she?"

Nick shook his head. "No, but she's sporting this new boyfriend and that's exactly what he does. And she eats that shit up like candy."

"It looks like she's okay with her mom from the pictures," I said.

"She is, to a point," he said. "For show. In small doses."

"Did you tell her what you're doing?" I asked.

He chuckled. "Oh yeah. That was fun."

I slid back down next to him. "And?"

"Got accused of—let's see, selling out, being no better than Mom, prostituting myself."

"Oh my God."

"Yeah, that was my personal favorite," he said.

"Does she not get that you're doing this for her?" I asked, biting my tongue to keep from adding *the ungrateful little shit.*

"She does, and she apologized," he said. "After a while. I think it was Tara who actually told her to quit acting like a brat and show some respect."

"You told Tara?"

I don't know why that bothered me but it did. Especially after the touchy-feely picture. I wanted to go right into those pictures and pull her off of him. Carmen's words rang in my head about Katrina.

To show her just whose man he was and to keep her grimy hands off.

Good grief.

"There wasn't much alone time with Addison," he said. "It was either tell them both or not at all." He gave a face shrug. "Surprisingly, Tara was supportive about it. Acted like a model mom after that."

Imagine that.

"I'm beat," he said, patting my leg and getting up. "And hungry for something bad for me."

I could teach him how to make baked apples. It was happy food. Aunt Ruby had taught me that, although the way I made them quickly in the microwave would probably not pass muster. For either of them. Man, those two would have liked each other.

"But I'm gonna go pass out instead," he said.

"Um…"

He stopped and turned around. "We have something to do, don't we?"

"We do."

He grimaced. "How much of a something?"

* * *

"Okay, did Lanie fill you in on everything?" Carmen asked.

We were at a picnic table next to a display of pies, eating ridiculously small slices given as samples. Townspeople milled, the air was thick with the aroma of raw honey everywhere, and music thumped inside the town hall building next to us. It was the annual Honeycomb Dance that kicked off that "famous" Honey Festival the highway sign bragged about.

I had changed into a cute sun dress that flattered my figure and made my boobs look amazing. It had stopped him in his tracks halfway down the stairs. It was dirty pool. I knew that. But those photos of his ex-*love of his life* in his arms, mixed with remembering *being* the one in his arms just the other day, had me all over the damn place, zapping from one live wire to the next.

He hadn't exactly gone grungy Farmer Bob, himself. Nick looked drool-worthy in dark jeans and a black, untucked long-sleeved shirt rolled up to show the perfect amount of forearm. He might have been wiped out, but he sure faked it well.

And that's what we were all about, after all.

"Alicia's a spy, the Bowmans are in on it, and we need to molest each other in public," Nick said, ticking the items off as if it were a grocery store list.

"Pretty much," Carmen said, separating her tiny pie from the tinier drizzle of honey. "I mean, make it look married, not first date horny, but yeah."

Not first date horny. She had no idea.

"God, is there nothing in this town that isn't dripping in this crap?" Carmen said, wiping the honey essence from her plastic fork.

"You don't like honey?" Nick asked. "Is that legal here?"

"Not really," she said. "Another reason I don't fit in." She winked at me. "I won't even grow flowers in my yard because I don't want bees around."

"Wow," Nick said. "You *are* the black sheep."

"Well, tonight I'm faking it, kind of like you," she said with a small smile. "So go make it look good."

Faking it. Right.

"All right, sweetheart," I said, smiling up at him and squeezing his bicep, which almost made me do it again. "Are we ready to go be sexy?"

It was like a first date. With some kind of weird permission to push the boundaries. Everywhere we stood, every conversation we had with others, involved Nick's hands on my body in some way. He'd play with the ends of my hair, his fingers brushing against the sensitive skin of my neck and shoulders. His hands would run up and down my bare arms, or he'd have a hand at the small of my back, one finger making maddening little circles that more than likely a married woman would not notice. I, however, could zone in on every touch like a drone, and didn't remember half of what anyone said.

I loved it. It was a bad idea to love it, and I knew that, but it was like being Cinderella at a ball. I knew I had limited hours left of such physical intimacy before we went back home and to our separate rooms, and I was loving every second of his hands on me.

And my hands on him.

Because that was just as much fun.

I pointed out the Clarks, and made sure we were always in Alicia's line of vision. Katrina Bowman was the center of attention as usual, in a low-cut pixie dress that almost didn't have a purpose, but so far she had kept her distance. Carmen talked with us some, but made sure she was never in one place too long. I didn't blame her. I knew she was an out of place butterfly in this situation, and just who she was avoiding.

Three different people made comments about the boob flashing, thankfully by hearsay and not by personal witness. All of which I was able to laugh off and tone down.

I was feeding Nick a piece of Key lime pie for Alicia's benefit, and enjoying running my thumb along his bottom lip and watching his eyes go dark, when Mayor Dean walked up with Alan. And by walking up with Alan, I mean that Dean walked up and shook Nick's hand. It was Nick's expression that alerted me something was about to happen when Alan came up behind me and slid his arms around my waist.

"Hey, sexy," he said, pulling me back against him.

Recoil and repulsion put my whole body in motion. That, and the murderous look on Nick's face. I had about two seconds to wonder if it was jealousy or just plain dislike that fueled his step forward, but Dean put a hand on his shoulder at the same time I gently pulled Alan's hands off me.

"Easy, big guy," Dean said. "He's just messing around. No harm done."

I instantly wrapped my arms around Nick's waist and pressed my chest against him to get his attention back. We didn't need a cock fight tonight. I'd already done enough of that with the battle of the boobs.

"Hey," Alan said, laughing, holding both hands up. "Don't shoot. I was just getting a hug from the party girl."

"Party girl?" I said, chuckling. "Hardly. I tend to find the corners like this one and hope no one finds me."

Hint.

"Oh, I'm not talking about this party," Alan said, winking. "I'm referring to you showing off that beautiful rack of yours at mine." He shook his head as his eyes landed unabashedly on my chest. Like now he had that right, because they were community property or something.

"Alan," Dean admonished, looking at me apologetically. "Dude, come on, let's move on."

"Why?" Alan asked, grinning at us all. His eyes were a little overly red.

"Because maybe you've had a little too much of something," Dean said, his eyes scanning the room and then coming back to me. "Sorry, Lanie."

"We can go talk to Frosty for you," Alan said.

The look in Dean's eyes kind of broke my heart. As much as an asshole that he was during their divorce, and even some of their marriage, he still held a torch for her. An unhealthy and twisted torch maybe, but still.

"Why don't we just go find your wife," Dean said with a smile, turning Alan with ease and guiding him along. "See y'all later."

I looked up at Nick and he gave me a downward glance as I was still wrapped around him.

"Thank you for not sucker punching him," I said.

He ran a finger along my cheek that felt decidedly real. Breathtakingly so. Then he pulled my arms free and turned me around so that I was in front of him. He draped an arm over my chest in a hug from behind, his other arm around my waist, pulling me against him with my ass up against—oh my.

Chapter Twelve

"Love is messy. It's up and down and everywhere. Don't try to make sense of it or understand it, it makes no sense. I've never understood anything in my whole life and I'm the happiest person in the world."

"As you can tell," he said against my ear. "You have this way of taking all the blood from my head so that I can't think straight."

Shitballs. Holy crap. If I felt all his touches before, I was positively zinging with them now. I knew where his arm was warm against my breasts. Where his fingers rested along my neck. Where his other hand was splayed on my belly. And where his dick was settled nicely against my ass and sending all my nerve endings into a frenzied dance.

"And you think this position helps?"

"Not even a little bit," he said on a chuckle. "In fact, it probably makes it worse. But I'm most definitely not thinking about punching Alan Bowman for copping a feel on my wife."

I started to laugh, because that made the goose bumps dissipate that had sprung up when he said *my wife* against my ear. I was hopeless. I was screwed.

"Well, success, then."

"We should get T-shirts made," he said. "*I saw Lanie McKane's boobs and I liked it.*"

"We could have sold them at the festival! We could definitely get a booth at the carnival next month," I said, angling my head up to look at him and feeling my belly twitch right where his hand was. His face was so close. And that was okay, because—because we were supposed to do that, and it was the perfect time, but it didn't feel like the plan or the game or the anything as he looked into my eyes.

"That's my girl," he said finally, a small grin pulling at his lips, and I faced back forward, counting the seconds of my breaths.

We stayed that way, rocking a little to the music. His arms around me and his face against my hair, my hands hugging his arms. I closed my eyes and mentally took a picture of this moment. This was what real must feel like. With feelings.

My eyes opened. Slowly, I disentangled myself and turned around, patting his chest.

"I'm gonna get some punch," I said. "You want some?"

He shook his head. "I'm good."

I glanced downward. "Are you?"

The grin came back, sending a shimmy through me. "It's why I untucked my shirt."

My brows furrowed. "You did that at the house."

"I know," he said.

Damn he was good. "Okay, I'll be—right back," I said.

I needed something cold and some space between us before my head made me do something crazy. Something like scale him like a tree. I poured myself a cup of punch and knocked it back, blinking and coughing at the unexpected burn.

"Seriously? Is this junior high?" I choked. "You can buy beer here."

I caught Carmen's eye across the room, where she was talking to a good-looking guy I didn't know. Good for her. She needed some attention here besides the moony-eyed mayor that was eyeing her over his beer. She nodded back toward the corner, though, and I turned to see what the deal was.

"Are you shitting me?"

I filled my cup one more time and knocked that one back too. What the hell. Maybe a little liquid confidence was what I needed. One step in that direction, however, and guess who? Yep.

"Dance?" Alan said, stepping in front of me and very nearly sticking his outstretched hand into my cleavage.

"Not right now," I said, moving to walk around him.

"Hey, I'm—" he began, angling to stop me again. "I'm really sorry about a few minutes ago. Dean's right, I probably need some food. Or some coffee."

I turned and picked up a cracker slathered in raw honey, the crystallization sparkling under the lights.

"Here you go," I said, shoving it into his mouth before he could protest.

I walked around him without hesitation, only to be stopped with a hug from Alicia.

"Hey, cousin!" she said, like we hadn't seen each other in years and didn't have a pending case of crap between us.

"You people need to stop," I said, backing out of her hug. "See that guy?" I pointed at Nick, who was fending off Katrina Bowman's hands. I saw red. Again. I had about had it with other people getting to touch him more than I did. A slow song came on, an old one that spoke to me somehow. Or spoke to the moment. The lights dimmed, and the time had come. "The hot one over there getting molested by Alan's wife? That's my husband. And I'm going over there to rescue him and pull him out on the dance floor. So whatever stupid plan y'all have to divide and conquer is going to work out about as well as the last time did."

"I—"Alicia began, her fuzzy hair trembling, but I was already on my way.

"Hi, Katrina," I said, removing her hand from his abdomen and taking his. "You don't mind, right? I need to dance with my husband."

I didn't look back, and I didn't care. Nick's hand was warm in mine, and when we reached the dance floor they'd cleared a space for, he tugged back gently to make me turn around. The look in those dark eyes nearly took out my knees. He pulled me into his arms, leaving no room for imagination, and I let my hands slide up his chest to his neck, and around back as his eyelids grew heavy.

Roberta Flack crooned softly, *the first time...ever I saw your face...* And something in me went warm from head to toe. Something besides whatever was in that punch. Something more real than that.

"Nice save."

"I tried."

"How was the punch?" he asked.

I wound my fingers into his hair and pulled his head down.

"See for yourself," I said, the last word finished against his lips.

Sparks ignited throughout my body as our lips met. Soft. Slow. Wet. Needing. Our bodies moved as one with the music, so close, so tightly pressed together I could feel his heart beating. My hands traveled slowly back down his chest and around his middle as his came up into my hair. When his tongue ran over my top lip, I knew he could feel my gasp. And when I pulled him in deeper to taste him, I felt the low growl in his chest rumbling against mine.

His fingers twisted in my hair as he dove deep and then pulled back, deep again and back, teasing me, pulling back to kiss my lips one at a time, as I kept clinging tighter. I was drunk on it. Breathing shallow. My fingers curling into his shirt with the need for *more*.

The first time...ever I kissed...your lips...

It was erotic, the way he kissed me. The way I kissed him. Slow, matching our movements. Intimate. Electric and emotional at the same time. And so full of desire and barely restrained need, that my body was trembling with it when he held my face and leaned his forehead against mine.

I wanted to keep my eyes closed. Absorb the feel of him, the song, the words, the taste. Just hold on to it a little longer. But I felt the heat of his gaze and my eyes fluttered open. And everything inside me turned to liquid fire. No one—ever—had looked at me like that. Had *wanted* me like that. The mirror image of what was churning inside me was all over him. In the desire mixed with the trouble haunting his eyes. This wasn't the game. That thought hit me like a sucker punch to the gut. This was—

His mouth covered mine again, hungrier, hotter, and I melted into it. The burn in my chest at the realization of just how fucking real this was, stole at my breath, and I didn't care. It was more than we were supposed to be doing but—God, it was so good. It was so good my heart felt like it was swelling to the size of the room. Wrapping around us as his hands cradled my face and he broke from the kiss, moving his lips along my face, my cheeks, back to my lips, both of us breathing fast. It was *more*. Nick was giving me the more. It wasn't just physical; it was bursting inside me.

When he pulled me to him, I buried my face in his neck and held him as tightly as I could as the words slowed to an end. I didn't want it to be over. I didn't want to let go.

I could hear my heart in my ears, pounding with every breath. He smelled like soap and something woodsy and Nick, and I always knew that but being up close enough to lick him made the smell intoxicating.

The music stopped.

The lighting was changing. I had to let go of him, and the second I moved he backed up too. Just a little. Just enough for me to see the mouth I'd just gotten to know intimately. His gaze fell to my lips as well, before dragging up to my eyes. Things had changed. In the course of time it took for that song to make its evolution, our reality had shifted. And the real kicker was that I think we both knew it already had.

"So, the punch is decent?" he said.

The humor pulled at my lips. "It's spiked."

"Perfect," he said. "Need some more?"

"No, I'm gonna—" I pointed in the general direction of where I thought the bathrooms were, and he moved my hand to correct it, making me chuckle. Always the one to put me at ease. "Thanks."

Except that nothing was at ease. As I made a beeline for the ladies' room, dodging fifteen people's attempts to draw me in with boob anecdotes, I felt the weight sitting on my chest. I pushed open the door, sent up a prayer of thanks for an empty room, and leaned over on the old Formica countertop.

"Oh my God," I whispered. "Oh my God oh my God oh my God."

Sweat popped out on my forehead, I could feel it. I ran the cold water on full blast and stuck my wrists under the stream like I'd heard you should do. The door opened behind me, and I grimaced.

"Yeah, I'd be looking for anything short of ice cubes after that too," said Carmen's voice, flooding me with both relief and the knowledge that I might have a meltdown.

"You wanted us to kiss," I said, not looking up.

"I wanted you to kiss, not procreate," she said, laughing. When I looked up and she saw my face, however, she stopped. "Hey, I'm kidding. What's wrong?"

The elephant on my chest shifted all the way to my throat and eyes, and the burn was too much to hold back. Hot tears spilled over before I could blink them away.

"That—that was—" I began, pointing at the door as the tears tracked down my face. I shook my head. I couldn't say it. "Fuck balls."

"That was hot," Carmen said. "Looked as real as it gets. I can't imagine faking—" I was nodding and crying harder and she stopped and tilted her head. "Oh my God."

"Yeah," I hiccupped.

"Come here," she said, pulling me into a momma bear hug. "I'm sorry. You did say you were falling for him."

"*You* said I was falling for him," I squeaked.

"And I was right," she said, rubbing my back. "Good God almighty. But you know, it's not the end of the world to have feelings for someone."

"In this case, it is," I sniffled. "In two months, it is literally the end of this particular world we've created. He goes home. I—go home or move across the country. We—have taken steps to avoid this."

"And then he fell in your mouth," she said.

"Actually, I pulled him in," I said. "Katrina Bowman pushed me over the edge and I pulled him with me. Damn it, it's always her fault! Every time she's around, I give up a part of my body and my sanity."

My phone buzzed, and I glanced at it, halfway hoping it was Nick. From outside the door? God, I really had fallen.

It was a text from Tilly.

It was an unknown number, but it was Tilly.

The *How's my sweet boy?* line gave it away. Then *Bad news. I won't be coming home for a while. Like a long while. Have some issues to take care of. Hope you're not mad. Hug Ralph for me and tell him I love him.*

I sputtered out a cry. "And now I have a dog. What else?" I waved my hands in the air. "No, not what else. I didn't mean that, universe, don't jinx me!"

Carmen let go of me, and directed me back to the sink.

"Splash some water on your face and get yourself together," Carmen said. "I'll go run interference. Need a drink?"

"No, I think that helped me get here," I said. "I'm good."

I wasn't good, but it was as good as it was going to get. We'd crossed the very line we'd been toeing for a month. *Only a month?* It felt like six. Funny how in the beginning the thought of crossing that threshold with him just sounded like sex. Now—no, don't go traipsing down that *now* path.

* * *

It took longer to walk to the car than it did to drive home, namely because the fireworks started and I jumped like I'd been shot.

"I've got you," Nick said, stopping to put his arms around me. "Here, turn around." He turned me with my back against him. Both arms went around me tightly. "Focus on the beauty of them," he said against my ear. "How majestic they are."

Each explosion made me shake but he was right. I'd never let myself actually watch the blossom and bloom and three-dimensional effect of them, but they were beautiful.

"Nothing's gonna hurt you now," he said. "I won't let it."

My eyes were leaking by the time it was over, but it wasn't out of fear. It was just emotional. No one had ever done that for me before, and when he let me go, I missed it.

"You okay?" he asked.

I nodded, and he took my hand and walked slowly with me to the car, where once we were inside, it changed. It felt like forever, in that tiny space all closed in and trapped, with suddenly nothing to talk about and both of us locked in a memory of everything, namely a hot embrace to stop time.

Or I was, at least. I couldn't speak for Nick. For all I knew, he was thinking about his motorcycle or what was on the menu for the week or hell maybe he was thinking of Tara—the last woman he had in his arms.

That was so not fair, and I wanted to slap myself upside the head for going there, but the little green jealousy troll invaded me in my moment of weakness. The thought of that woman in his arms, in his life, in his mouth—it made my chest hurt. It made my damn chest hurt! This was why I didn't do these crazy things.

We pulled up to the house and I opened the door almost before the car stopped. Before we could start talking. Luckily, Nick didn't try to change the course and he made for the front door as quickly as I did.

"So, you have to work tomorrow?" he asked as we both deflected Ralph's enthusiasm.

"Half day," I said. "Then I'll head out to the festival. I signed up for a couple of events for work and one to help out Bash's apiary."

Nick nodded, and that was it for the small talk. It made my insides hurt in a different way. We talked all the time. We basically never stopped talking. And now we were dancing—no, not dancing. We were skirting around the giant purple rhinoceros in the room, making small talk like strangers. Because we'd just made out like lovers.

Annnnnddddd that thought pulled the air right out of my lungs.

"I'm gonna go crash a little early," Nick said, standing maybe a foot away. Not that I was measuring, but I could just about feel the inches. "Been a long day, driving and all."

And other things.

"Okay, sleep good," I said, turning to find something—anything—to busy myself with. "See you in the morning."

There was a pause. "Lanie."

Oh, fuck.

When I turned back his way, he was staring at me with an intensity that covered my body in goose bumps. *Jesus.*

"What?" I asked, the word coming out breathy.

"You looked beautiful tonight."

Heart in the ears again. Pulse racing. Chest felt like a pinball game. Damn, this guy was going to kill me.

I tilted my head to try to be cute, and a strand of my hair brushed across my cheek.

"Kinda had it going on, yourself, Mr. McKane," I said.

The grin that tugged at one side of his mouth disarmed me, rendering me unprepared for the hand that came up and tucked my hair behind my ear. Rendered him unprepared too, by the look of want that crossed his face when he touched me. My breath caught in my chest as what felt like magnets sucked me into his space.

He breathed in deep and shook his head slowly, letting his hand fall.

"And that," he said softly, leaning forward with a wink. "Is why I'm going to bed."

I felt the air move as he passed me.

When did that happen?

Chapter Thirteen

"Do the crazy stuff. Be bizarre. If you don't do anything stupid when you're young, you won't have anything funny to remember when you're my age."

I woke up feeling like Ralph was lying on top of me, and I lifted my head to make sure he wasn't. I was exhausted. Lying awake all night pondering the designs in the ceiling texture will do that.

Hitting the snooze button three times didn't really add to the quality of my sleep—or my peace of mind getting ready—but it did allow me another twenty-seven minutes to dwell on every kiss and every touch and every skin-tingling moment in Nick's arms the night before.

Seriously, what was I expecting? For him to devise some plan for our future and surprise me with it over breakfast? A declaration of undying love from a man who had already made it clear that he didn't do that anymore? A complete turnaround in my own code of life that said love wasn't worth my time? Not that this was that. I wasn't saying anything like that. I just—had never experienced anything like last night. I had never experienced anything like Nick McKane. Ever. He was head-to-toe, everything I should run away from. Far and fast.

So then why was my first thought after turning off my alarm about the need to go see if he was up and what he was doing?

I sat up in bed. When had I become one of *those* women? The ones who go ass wipe stupid over a man?

No, I thought as I swung my legs down. It was a new day, and that was not going to be my path. Not in this lifetime. I got up, showered, thought a little bit about the kiss in the shower because—I'm human. Geared up to go downstairs and was admittedly a little disappointed that Nick was nowhere. Not over his absence (of course), but over my silly worry of it. That was thirty good coffee minutes I wasted.

I was just headed for the coffee maker, when the back door opened and in huffed Nick and Ralph. Fresh in from a run, breathing hard— Ralph, not Nick.

Hair sticking up. Shirt sticking to him. Nick, not Ralph. Muscles all outlined and wet. I'd never been one to understand what was sexy about sweat, but Nick pulled it off.

"Morning," he said, opening the fridge for a bottle of orange juice.

"Morning," I said. "Coffee'll be ready in a few."

"Don't need any today." He opened the bottle and knocked back three-quarters of it before pouring the remainder into Ralph's bowl.

"You don't need coffee?"

He hit his chest with his fist. "Good hard run today, that's a natural stimulant."

"Naturally crazy," I said, filling the machine with water. "Oh, by the way, I forgot to tell you we have a dog now."

I had a dog now. Me. When this was over, Ralph would come with me.

Nick looked down to where Ralph was sprawled on the cool tile, tongue lolling. "Another one?"

"No, this one," I said. "I just don't think he's on loan anymore."

Nick nodded. "Cool. So you done with the shower? Don't want to piss off any plumbing ghosts today."

"I'm good."

He gave me a thumbs-up. "I'm on it, then."

"Good deal," I said as he disappeared.

His head reappeared around the frame. "Really?"

I nodded, and he left again.

"Yep."

I heard a sigh, and bit my lip.

Well. That was interesting. Like nothing ever happened.

Okay then. That's how he wanted to deal with it? Go back to the way it was a month ago, before things got—complicated? Hey, that was okay, right? That totally fit in with today's new cause. There would be no reason for obsessing from either one of us.

Cool.

Got it.

Awesome.

* * *

Did you see her and her husband out there last night?
Damn, I wish my husband still kissed me like that.
You think they're really married?
If not, I want to be the first in line for a piece of that.
Y'all, that man makes me sweat a hundred different ways.

The thing about being a bank teller, is that when you stand behind that little partitioned window, people think you can't hear them if they aren't talking directly to you. You're invisible to a point. And at least a third of the town had gone through my line today, talking with their line buddies about the steamy scene that had gone down at the Honeycomb Dance. It was like being back in high school, but with a paycheck.

I smiled and played their pretend game of *I can't hear you*, letting them think they pulled something over on me. It worked to my benefit. Not only did they talk trash on me, but I also ended up getting the scoop on the Bowmans and even my crazy cousins.

Not only did Bryce play a dirty little scam of Pin the Tail on the Rich Guy quite frequently, but he also had a habit of losing his ass in any bet within a five-mile radius. And he and his wife had just lost their house in Denning to foreclosure and were living in a double-wide just outside of town. Telling me he was probably desperate to get his hands on Aunt Ruby's house and money, and get those condos going.

Little Miss Katrina evidently wasn't the only one with wandering fingers. Her grabby husband (yes, I'd rather refer to him as that than as my ex-boyfriend) had become quite well known for dipping his *toe* into other people's ponds. Also, while he was freelancing in a little beekeeping and trying to build up some business with Bash Anderson's apiary, his name was thrown around a lot as a short-term high-interest pocketbook for the temporarily desperate.

Bryce Clark, for example.

Amazing, the things you can learn when you just blend in.

By the time I got off at noon, I had a plan. It was simple, really. Stay under the radar. No more big scenes, mouth-to-mouth, boobs-to-the-world, or otherwise. Nick and I weren't strong on subtle, so we just needed to stay quiet and not draw attention to ourselves for the duration. Normal married couples did that. We could do that.

It was a pretty day, low humidity, so we decided to walk the half-mile to the festival. Or Nick did. His no-coffee-good-strong-run day had him taking it in stride, while I was puffing at the end, keeping a good foot or two between us for good measure.

"You all right?" he asked.

"Perfect," I responded.

"Sounds like it," he said as we rounded the corner to the main avenue into town and all the action came into view. His fingers laced into mine, and that both poked at my heart and annoyed me. It was just the game again.

That's what you wanted!

We kept it low key. Acted like everyone else. Tasted honey samples at the various booths and filled out voter ballots. Checked out the craft booths and bought him a set of cooking utensils and me a painted T-shirt that said *I Like It Raw*.

Cracked me up. Okay, maybe *that* wasn't totally low key, but I thought it a minor infraction.

Then it was time for the games. All the local businesses competed in a series of crazy games, all in good fun. Or all in good play-to-the-death competition. There was a water balloon fight, a rope climb, a cake-eating contest, and a three-legged race, all culminating at the end with a marathon of all four events with the top four. Those four were paired off into two teams, and the winning team shared the glory.

Once upon a time, there was only one winner, but someone decided that sharing with another business promoted community teamwork and goodwill, so it was changed. Honestly, I think it was more about having to live with one person's bragging for an entire year.

The cake-eating contest was first, and I was playing for the bank. It was my favorite one of course.

"I'm a cook," Nick teased, sitting next to me. "I've got this."

"Just because you can make a cake doesn't mean you can eat it," I said, rolling my head on my shoulders and popping my knuckles. The four-layer cake in front of me was daunting. I formed a strategy, one slice at a time.

"Big words, Mrs. McKane," he said.

Calling me that sent goose bumps trickling down my spine.

Why?

It wasn't the first time. But something about sitting next to my husband in a goofy town festival cake-eating contest suddenly felt so domestic. So normal and real.

Focus, Lanie.

The bell rang, and we were off. We each had knives, but those of us with experience skipped that time consuming task. Hands worked just fine, and going for big bites with minimum chewing was optimal. The winner was Berty Carson from the barber shop, an elderly man who obviously had been practicing judging by the girth around his waist.

Still, I had three-fourths of my cake gone compared to Nick's little over half.

"What was that, Mr. McKane?" I said, putting my cake-covered hand to my ear. "Was that the sound of losing?"

Nick grabbed my hand and stuck one of my fingers in his mouth, sucking the cake off with his tongue. Everything stopped for me for a moment, the world going on tilt, and he winked as he licked his lips.

"What was *that*, Mrs. McKane?" he said. "The sound of shock?"

Oh, what a dirty, dirty boy. He didn't play fair. I would so remember that.

Next up, was the rope climb. Some thick fire station rope with knots tied in hung from two ladder trucks. Now—seriously, come on. This one was tailor made for the guys. Well, the guys and the hard core females with a chip on their shoulders. Nick hit his rope like a pro, steadily climbing hand over hand, while every woman watching—yours truly included— had a near sexual experience.

My turn was next, and Nick grinned at me. "You can do this."

"I know," I said sarcastically. "Although it might work better if you put an angry bear at the bottom and an ice cream cone at the top. Something for motivation."

The bell rang, and Missy Yancy, a Zumba instructor with zero body fat and thigh muscles that could snap a man in half, scaled that rope before I could get to the third knot. Which was a good thing, considering I might have still been there at the same time tomorrow.

"Don't feel bad," Nick said, close to my ear. "They throw out the two very bottom scores."

I shrugged. "I guess my thighs are just used to wrapping around bigger things."

The desire that darkened his gaze and took his power of speech away was so worth it. *Take that, pretty boy.*

"What do we think?" said Allie Greene, walking up between us. "Time for the water balloons?"

Nick double-blinked away from me like he hadn't heard a word. Like he was still back there with my thighs. I had to admit, the image was sticking with me too.

Not that I was obsessing. Or acting a fool over a man. Just after last night's extracurricular activity, I was having some difficulty separating the somewhat impure thoughts from all the other thoughts. Yeah. That was it.

"What?" he asked.

Splat.

Allie smashed a large green water balloon into Nick's torso, soaking his pullover shirt and outlining his ab muscles in fabric.

"Sorry," she said. "It was on a dare." Allie shrugged devilishly. "And being your boss, I was the safest person to deliver the job."

Nick held out his arms as everything dripped, looking down at himself and then at Allie as all the females cheered.

Wow.

"Oh, it's on," he said.

Allie shrieked and ran, and someone brought four coolers full of already filled water balloons into the center of the ring.

It was like a bunch of five-year-olds arrived in adult bodies. Everyone scrambled to get handfuls, armfuls, even shirt-fulls of balloons and retreat behind lines, but Allie's jumpstart on Nick changed the atmosphere. The ice cream store ladies threw early at the cell phone store guys, and all the employees at the flower nursery decided to wage war with each other. What was designed to be two lines taking aim at each other, turned into a free-for-all frenzy mixed with a wet T-shirt contest.

Mayor Dean got several shots to the head, someone's carefully aimed balloon popped Katrina Bowman on the side of the neck, and then a warm water explosion down my cleavage got my attention. Not as much as the hand that remained resting against there did.

"Alan," I gasped, as he then playfully picked me up around the middle and swung me around, using me as a human shield. "What are you doing?"

What the fuck *was* he doing? Treating me like we were a couple, and familiar, and intimate. His moronic wife standing no more than ten feet away.

And my husband—was stopped in his tracks, staring at us as I shrieked, water balloons still slamming into his back as every muscle looked poised to strike.

"Put me down," I said, kicking one foot backward into his knee.

"Ow, okay," Alan said, laughing and obliging.

I turned on my heel when I landed, intending on giving him a piece of my mind, but the bloodshot whites of his eyes stopped me. He was feeling no pain. No inhibitions. No logic. His life wasn't the grinning perfection that it appeared to be, and working with extortion had to be exhausting. I walked away, away from Alan, away from Nick. Just off to the sidelines a bit to escape the craziness. It wasn't worth making a scene.

"Lanie." I turned at the serious tone in Nick's voice. "Are you okay?"

"I'm fine," I said, automatically reaching for him and wondering when that became automatic. He detached a blade of grass or something from my cheek and the imprint from his fingers that was left behind was warm.

And then I wanted to slap myself. "Really. He's just drunk."

"Already?" Nick said, looking back at where Alan was blearily grinning in the crowd. "This early?"

"Evidently. Just let it go."

"He basically just felt you up," Nick said, one eyebrow coming down in irritation as his gaze lowered to my chest. My dripping wet chest that was now covered in wet white fabric. Great. I had to wear white today. And Nick saw the water balloon score to first base. Awesome.

I pulled my wet T-shirt away from my chest and fanned it to hopefully lose the cling factor. Not that it was anything Nick hadn't already seen, courtesy of me.

"Please."

I had another epiphany as déjà vu hit. When Katrina was mauling him, and then put her hands on his bare chest in the pool, something *I hadn't even touched yet*. That's what was eating him. Alan got something Nick hadn't had yet.

Yet.

We moved on. Watched the other competitors. Were treated with honey-drizzled pecan pralines until the sugar high was at a peak. Till it was time for the four winners to be announced. I was not expecting anything, as my performances (except for the cake-eating) weren't all that. I didn't even know how they were judging the water balloon debacle.

"The winners to perform in the grand finale are," Mayor Dean announced over a microphone someone handed him. "Alan and Katrina Bowman," he said.

"Of course," I muttered. "Although Katrina did no better on that rope than I did. Missy Yancy should win over her."

"And Nick and Lanie McKane," Mayor Dean finished.

"Say *what*?" I exclaimed.

It had to be rigged and planned and part of the bigger picture. That's all there was to it. No way in hell that—

"And to make it fair and interesting," Mayor Dean was saying. "Couples can't be teamed together, so Nick will be with Katrina, and Alan will be with Lanie."

All the fucks in the world couldn't cover this.

"This is—" Nick began.

"Supremely jacked," I finished.

"Rules are this," Dean continued. "The rope is done as a team. Figure out how to work together to reach the top. Then a three-legged race from there to the finish line, where you'll have another cake to finish off by feeding each other."

I felt ill. For both of us.

Mostly for him, which by default was for me, because the thought of Katrina's hands all over him, her body all over him, Nick sucking the cake from her fingers like he'd done mine—oh my God, my blood ran hot and angry and I needed to quit.

Alan and Katrina walked up to us, her smiling in her innocent I'm-not-trying-to-be-seductive scam.

"Hey, partner," she said, sidling up to Nick, while Alan just gave me the drunk eyeball. Up and down.

I might puke before we ever got to the cake.

We set up on the two ropes, Alan and I both peering upward. I didn't see his first attempt, so I had no idea if he was any good at it. And honestly, I didn't care. I signed up to do this at work, thinking it would be fun, and now that I was the only one left in the running, were any of them around to cheer me on? Hell no. I was on my own. Go me.

I only had one thought. *Dear Lord, please don't let me fail in an embarrassing way in front of Nick.*

Well, it was good to have a goal.

"Here's how this is going to work," I heard Nick tell Katrina. "Take your shoes off. I'm starting and going to that first knot, then you're going to climb me, and I'll shove you up. Then you'll stop and lock on, and I'll climb you to the top."

Katrina's eyes went foggy and I think she probably orgasmed right there. I would have. As it was, my insides were going to molten lava with anger that she was going to be all over him like that.

"That sounds like a good plan," Alan said, pulling my attention back. *Balls.*

Thunder rumbled in the distance, and I looked around for the non-existent rain. What were the odds that the sky would open up and drown out this little event? Like—before I had to climb Alan.

The bell dinged, and a crowd of people gathered around, whooping, hollering, laughing and cheering us on as four people climbed each other like uncoordinated drunk monkeys.

"Would you have ever thought when we were dating in high school that you would be climbing my body like this all these years later?" Alan teased loudly as I attempted in the most ungraceful manner possible to scale him.

Huffing and groaning, I advanced a full foot.

"Please stop talking," I said.

"Just bringing up old times," he said.

"You lost the right to chat about *old times* when you joined forces with my cousin," I said. "Against me."

Something alarming flashed across his eyes as I reached that level, and I glanced passed him to see Katrina wrap her legs around Nick's waist.

With a grunt of disgust, I pushed on.

"I don't know what you're talking about," Alan said.

"Sure you do," I said, using his hips as leverage and toe holds for my feet. "You're funding his little pet project, aren't you? With a 100 percent interest, I'm sure."

It was that point when my hoo-hah was in Alan's face and he growled playfully against it, probably trying to distract me, that I lost it and made an executive decision. First by kneeing him in the eye and making him drop a foot in pain while I stepped on his head. Then after I looked over to see Katrina rubbing her boobs in Nick's face, taking her sweet time climbing on my husband, I found a sudden surge of energy. Screw this taking turns thing. I had to get it over with. I couldn't be body-to-body with Alan again, and I needed to help get Nick out of Katrina's chest and before she was hoo-hah level with *his* face in her tiny short-shorts.

Grunting and making noises I didn't know I could make, I climbed. I didn't stop for Alan; I kept going. Foot by foot, I squirmed my way up, not stopping till I reached the little yellow flag at the top. It wasn't ice cream, but some crazy intense motivation, just the same.

The crowd cheered, and I looked over to see Nick grinning proudly at me. Completely oblivious to the hoo-hah waving at him. A surge of warmth came over me. Even more so when he removed her legs and climbed down.

All that remained was the three-legged race to the cake. Alan tied our legs together, his knuckles brushing almost illegally close to third. He glanced up and I glared at him, not caring that his eye was bruising. He was lucky I missed his teeth.

At the start line, we lined up. Alan and I with our arms around each other, and Nick and Katrina the same. Almost done. *We're almost done.*

"You have a spirited one here, Nick," Alan said. "Lucky you."

"I think so," Nick said.

Aw.

"How long have you been married?" Alan asked.

Shit. Did we ever say? Had we ever decided? *Shit!*

"Long enough to know not to grope another man's wife, Alan," Nick countered. "How long have *you* been married?"

Wow. See, this was why my Nick was the bomb.

My Nick?

"Nice deflection," Alan said. "Funny how I was under the impression that you two were married for at least five," he said. "But a little bird told me that an internet search brought up—"

"Go!" Dean yelled.

Katrina and Nick instantly pulled ahead. They'd evidently talked strategy. Whereas Alan and I fought each other, our legs out of sync, probably due to my impending heart attack at the mention of an internet search. What was he playing at?

We finally got our timing right, yelling what leg to use, but Nick and Katrina made it to their cake table before we did. They were halfway through one, shoving cake into each other's mouths, when a particularly overzealous cake shove on our part knocked us off balance. I groped the air but got a handful of cake instead. Alan crammed a large piece into my mouth on our way down and we hit grass. It was funny. I had to admit it was funny, and I started laughing but it was short lived.

Before I knew what was happening, Alan's cake-covered face was on mine, and he was kissing me. Cake, and all. Laying on the grass.

Stunned wasn't a strong enough word. Shocked and appalled was a better description. I heard the amused gasps of the crowd, and I pushed at him but the angle and positioning was so odd I had no leverage.

"Alan, stop!"

Then weight was lifted. In the span of five seconds, Nick was looming over us, free of his leg ties with Katrina, a murderous look on his face and Alan in his hands as if he were nothing more than a heavy pillow.

There was a snap and I was free of my ties as well, and I rolled to the other side as Nick hauled Alan up against an electrical post.

"That's the last straw, man," Nick hissed through his teeth. "You and your psycho wife stay the fuck away from us. And if I *ever* see you put your hands on my wife again, I will break every one of your fingers. Do you understand me?"

"Your *wife*," Alan drawled. "Please. You didn't even know Lanie a month ago. Don't act all noble."

I was on my feet as I heard the words, and a sick dread went down my spine. *You didn't even know Lanie a month ago.* Nick didn't seem to be affected by it however, as he pulled him off the post and pushed him into it again.

"Don't speak her name," Nick seethed. "Don't *breathe* her name. Treating her like this and what you're trying to do to her, you're lucky I don't beat the shit out of you right here."

The goose bumps. They took over. The protectiveness coming off him like sonar was unreal.

"Nick, he's drunk," I said, touching his arm. He was as hard as steel.

"I know," Nick growled. He dropped him and backed away. "He's not worth it." He turned to me then, his hand on my shoulder. "Are you okay?"

"I'm fine," I whispered as thunder rumbled again, closer, and the sun disappeared behind a dark cloud. "Let's go."

But we only made it four steps when we heard the yell. The sound of a stupid, inebriated man, charging his prey and announcing it like a screaming banshee. The whole thing lasted seconds but I saw it in slow motion. Nick shoved me sideways, spun in place, and met Alan's open roaring mouth with his fist.

Chapter Fourteen

"There's no such thing as almost. If you get to almost, it's done in your head."

Alan's head popped back, his feet went out from under him, and down he went on the grass, blood gushing from his upper lip and Katrina shrieking at his side.

I clapped a hand over my mouth as the crowd did a collective chorus of gasps and cries, and Mayor Dean leaped in out of nowhere to work crowd control and hold a hand up in front of Nick.

"Go home, man," Dean said.

"That's what I was doing," Nick said, his lip curling.

"I know," Dean said, nodding. "Just go."

"He hit me!" Alan yelled, blood dripping from his mouth as he sat up, Katrina kneeling beside him. "He's a fraud and he threatened me! You all heard it!"

Several of the people watching waved a hand at him and walked away, disgusted with his behavior. And even Dean picked him up and muttered for him to shut up.

"Lanie, you okay?" Dean asked me.

I nodded and went through the motions of cleaning myself up from the cake fiasco, shaking from Nick's words, from his coming to my rescue. No one had ever done that before.

Nick stood like a statue on fire, anger radiating off him. When the crowd was gone, and it was just him and me, he finally met my eyes.

We both heard the things Alan had said, and that wasn't good. Even if Alan was a blowhard and no one believed him, the digging would start.

Something needed to happen.

Something already was.

My gaze fell to his hand, and I reached for it. "You're bleeding."

"I'm fine," he said, pulling it back.

"Nick—"

"I'm done with this today," Nick said. "With this place and this town and—I'm going back to the house."

"Wait for me," I said, my mind reeling. "Let me—"

"Take your time," he said, holding up a hand half-heartedly. "A few minutes by myself walking home will do me good."

I watched him walk off, slinging cake from his hands as he did and flexing the fingers he'd hit Alan with. He was pissed, or upset, or—just tired. I could understand that. I was too. I was exhausted from this game. From always having to be on and pretending.

I cleaned myself up and started walking home, just as the first drops fell from the sky. Oh, the drama that could have been saved if that would have just come around ten minutes earlier.

By the time I reached Aunt Ruby's front porch, it was a full white-out, and I was clean of all things cake-related. I didn't care how soaked I was. All I could think about and see over and over, was Nick hauling Alan off me. Defending me with his words, defending his wife, churning inside me so deeply I had to wrap my arms around myself to contain it. All because of this place. This house. Because of me.

I looked up at the sky, at the raindrops coming from what looked like infinity, and felt the heat behind my eyes join the trouble in my chest.

"Why?" I asked softly, blinking against the rain. "Why are you making all of this so hard?" A sob shook me as the warm rain mixed with my hot tears. "What did I ever do but try to make you happy?"

No epiphanies came. No intuition. Aunt Ruby left me high and dry. *Here's your house, child, but only if you jump through fifty different hoops and cartwheel down the street every day. But hey, the wooden spools and the carnival glass is my treat.*

I left my shoes on the porch, and walked in, noting that Nick had left the front door unlocked for me. I peeled off my shorts in the living room, not even caring that he was there somewhere. I was too tired to care. Too exhausted to play the charade right now. And too annoyed to be modest. I yanked my wet T-shirt over my head as I topped the stairs and buried my face in it, dropping it when I heard the bathroom door.

Nick in a towel.

Of course he was.

His expression looked as beat up as I felt, but his eyes took me in in my tiny but plain white undies and bra, soaked to probably see-through. One look at my face, however, and Nick's demeanor changed.

He reached for me immediately, pulling me into his arms, and the warmth of his skin against mine took my breath.

"I'm sorry," he said, his mouth against my hair. "I shouldn't have left you there."

I shook my head, unable—or unwilling—to form words while my face was against his chest. One hand came up under my wet hair and the other trailed patterns down my back.

"You did nothing wrong," I said, my voice a whisper against his wet skin. "I'm just—"

I had no idea what I was. The feel of his hands moving on my body again made my head all foggy, and the ratio of underwear to towel was calling to me. My fingernails dragged themselves up his back of their own accord. I couldn't help myself. He was—he was—oh God, he felt amazing.

His response was even better, splaying both hands down my back to my ass, squeezing me against him and then moving up to my head and cradling it as he pressed his lips to my hair, my forehead, down over my eyes.

"Lanie," he whispered against my cheek. "Tell me what you need, baby."

Everything inside and out turned hot and liquid at that sentence.

"You," I breathed, dragging my lips along his jaw.

Nick pulled my face back to meet my gaze, his eyes heavy with need, with desire, with places we didn't go.

"I'm yours."

His mouth landed on mine with a hunger we hadn't tapped into yet as he backed me into the wall. Last night was about tasting, exploring. Now it was—it was just on. Like a fucking freight train with no brakes, kind of on. It was everything we said we shouldn't do, diving into each other, pushing every boundary. I didn't care. I wanted him. I wanted this man like I'd never wanted anyone in my life. I wanted more. I wanted all of him.

One flick of his fingers and my bra was gone, replaced by his hands, caressing my breasts and rolling my nipples between his fingers. I groaned as his kisses traveled down to meet them, sucking, licking, his mouth making love to my breasts.

"God, you taste so fucking sweet."

"Come here," I gasped, pulling him back up. I tugged at his towel and it dropped at our feet and in less than a second he was in my hands, huge and hard.

A guttural roar shook his body at my touch, sending every ounce of blood in my body to one hot burning place. He slammed a hand against the wall as if to hold himself up. "Fuck, Lanie, what you do to me."

"I need you," I begged, stroking him against me.

"You have no idea," he said against my neck, his hands traveling me again as if they might not get another chance.

Then I left the ground. I wrapped my legs around him as he lifted me effortlessly, not caring where we were going. He could have taken me to the roof for all I cared. I just wanted this. All of it. When he sat down on his bed, pulling my legs tighter around him, I moaned into his mouth, moving against him.

His fingers dug into the soft flesh of my hips as I moved, guiding me; one thin little strip of panties was all that kept him from pushing inside me.

I was about to go off the fucking rails. Shaking with need, every nerve ending in my body reaching for this man who was driving me to the brink of insanity. My fingers twisted in his wet hair, pulling him impossibly tighter, kissing him with all I had as we moved against each other in the tease from hell.

I pulled back and held his face in my hands.

"Please."

It barely held sound.

It didn't need to.

In the time it took to blink, Nick wrapped an arm around me and had me on my back, his eyes boring into mine with something—something that made my skin tingle. Something beyond the dance our bodies were doing. Something I couldn't look away from if I tried, until he did. And that was only because he curled two fingers into my panties and was sliding them down, then standing at the edge of the bed with the world's most glorious hard-on.

"God, you're beautiful, lying there," he said, almost to himself, as if it wasn't meant to be out loud. Which hit my heart and brought prickles to my skin.

His fingers ran up my calf as he crawled up my body. "Goose bumps."

The trail of flames his fingers left behind made my toes curl under.

"You do that to me," I whispered, my breaths shallow and fast as he dropped light kisses on his way up and I reached for him. I needed to feel him on me, in me, over me—like now.

His eyes met mine as if no one had ever told him that before, and that was inconceivable. He was breathtaking. He was maddening.

He was mine.

Tears pricked the backs of my eyes as that thought landed hard. As his mouth covered mine and a hand cupped my face as the other one lifted my leg. He was mine. Nick was *mine* as he touched me, making me arch into him, *mine* as he poised himself to join me. His ass was in my hands, and I was ready to pull him inside.

When the doorbell rang.

* * *

Really?

Ralph howled.

Let them go away.

That's what his eyes were saying as the same thought played in my head. Potentially the hottest sex I'd ever had was about to unfold, and a visitor was the last thing I needed. Maybe it was the doorbell going out. Or Aunt Ruby trying to be funny.

It rang again. Ralph set up a barking frenzy like it was the second coming. Damn it, it was a person.

"Expecting someone?" he asked.

"Not ever, for the rest of my life," I said, pulling his face back down to mine.

Our lips had just touched when it went off again. This time in a cute chopsticks pattern. Which froze his progression. The deepening of the line above his nose told me volumes. Namely that we weren't letting whoever it was go away.

"Hold on," Nick said, rolling off of me, and then rolling back. "Don't move. Don't change a thing. Please." He kissed me. "I'll be right back."

He got up and grabbed a pair of jeans from a chair and pulled them on commando. Somehow that was even hotter than the sight of him naked. Maybe because I could see myself sliding my hands down those jeans to take them off in a few minutes.

I heard his quick footsteps on the stairs and smiled as I thought of him turning someone away so he could come back up there and ravage his wife.

His wife.

That kept wrapping around me like a warm—

Female laughter broke my thoughts, and I sat up. I heard the rumble of Nick's voice and then the female voice again. No more barking. I scrambled off the bed in a panic. Who the hell? Carmen? No, it didn't sound like her. The only other woman I could imagine just dropping by would be—ugh, Katrina. But she wouldn't be laughing with him right now. Not after he just socked the shit out of her husband for mauling me.

Still, he wasn't coming *right back*, so he knew her.

I ran down the short hall to my room and snatched my white robe off the back of my door. The one I stole last year from a fancy hotel and then had to pay $80 for, but hardly ever wore. It seemed like an appropriate time.

Wrapping it around myself, feeling kind of pleased with the thought that Nick would know I was naked underneath all the fluff, I finger-combed out my wet hair and sauntered down the stairs.

And stopped midway.

A stunning brunette woman was hugging Nick around his shirtless torso, her head thrown back in that effortless hair-tossing way that some women have, looking up at him adoringly.

My breath froze in my throat, and my fingertips went numb. I didn't know her, but he did. I didn't know her, but I'd seen her before. In the pictures on his phone.

Tara.

Random thoughts pinged through my brain, with no logical progression or connection.

Tara was here. In our house. In my house. Funny how it just became my house again. He told her where we live. She has sex hair. The bitch has sex hair. And better boobs than me. Did she tell anyone? She's the one that always got under his skin. Under his skin.

And fuck if that wasn't the thing that lodged in my throat and threatened to take me down in a chokehold. This was the woman he couldn't forget, the love of his life, the mother of his child, the one that he could never quite shake, that he kept coming back to. She looked like a million bucks in tailored capris and a blingy fitted T-shirt that most definitely was not purchased at Target. With skin that most definitely had a more expensive care regimen than Noxzema pads and Oil of Olay.

She was flawless. And wrapped around him like a tumor. A hot, sexy tumor.

Dark, perfectly lined eyes drifted my way, and I suddenly wished for a large pair of tweezers to pluck me right out of the picture.

"Hi!" Tara said, letting go of Nick and walking toward me with one hand trailing behind along his abs. Her face was smiling, but that move was on purpose. *He's mine*, it said. Interesting that I was thinking that very thing just moments earlier. She held a hand out at the bottom of the stairs, which propelled my feet to keep moving that direction. "I'm Tara McKane."

McKane.

Another good zinger on her part. Throwing out those possessive vibes. Staking her territory.

"Lanie—McKane," I said, tempted half a second in to go with Barrett and then spun it back, adding a chuckle for bonding.

"Wow, that sounds weird," she said, laughing, turning back to Nick. I looked at him for the first time since I entered the room, and the pure what-the-fuckery in his expression kicked me in the gut. I saw the *under the skin* thing. Right there. Because if he were really over his ex-wife, he would have stopped her at the door and said he was busy. Servicing his *new* wife. Or hey, how about he would have never told her where to find him in the first place.

"Not really," Nick said, his tone flat as he locked eyes with me in a look I couldn't read. "I've gotten used to it."

What was he talking about? Oh yeah. McKane. Were we still there? Hadn't it been like a week?

Ralph licked her fingers and pushed at her hand, and she looked down, scratching at his head and cooing. "Hey, big boy, what's your name?"

Ralph melted. As probably most men did.

"That's Ralph," I said.

"Hi, Ralphy," she said. *No. Ralph.* "Well, it's nice to meet you." Tara looked up and shook my hand genuinely. "Nick had great things to say about you last weekend. He's very fond of you."

Number three…ding ding ding!

Fond.

Generic like, as in I'm fond of chicken fried steak. The girl was good. She was charmingly putting me in my place and making me feel smaller and more insignificant by the second, and in my own house.

"Well," I said with the only smile I could find in my now numb face. "The fondness is mutual. He's a great roommate."

Probably not the most slamming cut I could have come up with, but the oxygen was still trapped in my head from five minutes ago when he was sucking on my tits and about to fuck me into oblivion. So wittiness was a bit foggy.

"So, did I miss something about your coming here?" I asked. "I've been crazy busy lately so I might have."

Hint.

Aunt Ruby would have said something snarky about unexpected guests and diarrhea, but I was slightly more tactful.

"No," Nick said, shaking his head free of the kicked-in-the-nuts look. "I had no idea. Tara, why are you here?"

Tara smiled back at Nick as if they shared a secret. "I had a couple of days free and thought it would be nice to come chat a little." She tilted her head in a way that said they had intimate private talks. "Maybe finish our last conversation?" She gave a quick inhale and pasted on a smile for me. "And come meet the woman that's helping out my baby girl."

I just smiled back. *Our last conversation.*

Was it anything like ours?

I couldn't think through the slamming my heart was doing. I had to get out of their line of vision.

"Who wants coffee?" I managed to push out as I walked past both of them into the kitchen, taking my first deep breath since Nick pulled me into his arms—literally minutes ago.

Minutes.

Tell me what you need, baby.

The coffee pot landed a little hard on the countertop.

Don't cry. Don't you dare fucking cry.

"In the middle of the day?" Tara asked, chuckling as she walked in behind me.

"I wasn't suggesting spiking it," I said. *Okay, dial back the snippy.* I grinned to soften it. "I can drink coffee any time."

"She can," Nick said, following her in, pulling a T-shirt over his head that he must have had tucked in a secret hiding place reserved for when crazy ex-wives come to call. "Never seen anyone as—fond—of coffee as Lanie."

My eyes shot up to meet his on the word. He was giving me something. A new definition for fond to match my coffee addiction. Okay, that was sweet, but still, grow some damn balls, dude. Problem with the kid? Of course the ex comes into play. You are always parents. You are always connected. But this?

No.

"Great house," Tara said, perching on a stool.

I'll bet. "Thanks," I said. "I grew up here."

"That's what Nick said." She rested her elbows on the bar and looked around. "So much life and character here."

"That it has," I said. "Along with broken plumbing and finicky air conditioning."

"And Ralph!" Tara said, rubbing his head when he laid it against her leg.

Traitor, I sent to him telepathically. Just in case. Aunt Ruby's house and all.

"Ralph came with me," I said, letting my gaze drift back to Nick. "And he'll go with me when this is over."

It was my own zinger, and I'm the one who felt the stab as I watched his eyes. I had to give it to him. This woman was by far possibly the most beautiful person I'd ever seen, and Nick wasn't looking at her at all. He was leaning against the far counter, arms folded over his chest, staring deep burning holes through me. Well, hell, why not? Wet hair and rained/cried/kissed off makeup, bulky robe—what on earth was there not to feast your eyes upon?

"And when is it over again?" she asked.

Her expression was open and innocent, but I didn't just fall off the turnip truck.

"We have a little less than two months to go," I said. "Then everybody gets what they want."

I didn't look at him that time. I couldn't bear to look at him and see that confirmed.

Tara just nodded.

"So I saw a sign for a festival on the highway," she said. "Along with probably twenty more in town." She laughed. "Small town charm."

I wanted to guffaw.

"Something like that," I said quietly.

"Can we go?" she asked. "It sounds fun."

I did look at Nick then, hoping like hell he'd catch my subliminal message, but he was already shaking his head. Thank God.

"We just got back from there, actually," he said. "I'm beat."

"So tomorrow, then?" she asked. "Do y'all work tomorrow?"

My jaw dropped. Or in my head it did. Did she just—?

"Are you staying?" Nick asked, the lines above his nose deepening.

"Well, I'd love to," she said with a brilliant smile. "I brought a little bag just in case, but if you don't have room, I can grab a hotel."

There were no words.

My mouth opened and closed like a guppy, and the only thing that saved me was the ringing of my phone. I didn't even look to see who it was because it didn't matter. I would have answered a call from the devil himself to remove myself from this conversation.

Chapter Fifteen

"Don't waste time being jealous, my girl. You got the same pants to be glad in as anyone else."

Call me a chicken shit, but I didn't go back. Carmen's call allowed me to make my escape to my room, and I just stayed. Put on one of my tank tops with no bra and some shorts just because, and curled up in my bed with a book. He was a big boy, and she sure wasn't here to see me. He could entertain his own damn guest.

Forty-five minutes later (I'd wagered myself an hour, so he did at least surpass that expectation) my door opened. No knock. Just a walk-in.

"And if I'd been getting myself off?" I said, not looking up from the book that I hadn't turned a single page of.

"I would have stood here and watched," he replied, sitting at the foot.

"Well, I'm not sure what you're expecting," I said. "But if you came in here to take up where we left off you're gonna be disappointed."

"Don't insult me," he said, his voice edgy. "I came in here to check on you."

"I'm not breakable," I said, pulling my eyes up to meet his.

"You didn't come back."

"I don't think she's here for me, Nick," I said. "I figured since you have a conversation you need to finish—"

"Don't," he said. His voice was low and irritable, like he'd been arguing already. "Don't play games, Lanie, you're better than that."

"Okay then I'll shoot straight," I said. "Why is your ex-wife in my house?"

"I didn't invite her here."

"You didn't tell her to leave, either," I said. "You stood there like a broken puppet, while the woman *that always gets under your skin* batted her eyes and pulled your strings."

"Jesus," he said, getting up and pacing. "Of course you'd latch on to that. Do you want to know what happened last weekend?"

I laughed bitterly. "No thanks."

"Nothing," he said. "For the first time *ever*."

I raised an eyebrow. "You—want a gold star for not hitting the sheets with your ex-wife? That's kind of not normal."

Nick ran a hand over his face. "I'm not saying that, I'm saying things usually get weird with her. That's why I avoid her. But this time—" He shook his head. "This time, you want to know who I couldn't get out of my head? You."

I blinked, my thoughts pinging all over the place.

"And not just because of the boob flash, either," he said. "Before you go there. I found myself missing you. Wanting to get back here—to you. You want to know why she's really here?" He laughed. "To check you out. Because I didn't want to fuck her."

"That's twisted," I said, while mentally filing away the missing me comment. I couldn't enjoy it right now, but I could pull it up and pet it later.

"Well, that's Tara." He stopped pacing and sank into the chair across from the bed. "She's got a different way of thinking about things. And it usually has very little to do with Addison and very much to do with her ego."

I met his troubled gaze. "You told her where we live. Where *I* live. Where I may or may not still be when this is over—"

"You are all about pointing out the end of this, aren't you?" he said.

I let a couple of beats pass. "That's when you get your money," I said softly. "When you're free."

Arms crossed over his chest again. "And you?" he asked. "What does the end look like to you?"

I looked away. I couldn't answer that. Not anymore.

"So is the first Mrs. McKane spending the night?" I asked, trying to ask that without an attitude or reaction.

"I'm not making that call," he said. "This is your house. You tell me."

"Oh my God, Nick, make an executive decision," I said, swinging my legs down and getting up. "If you want her here—"

"I *don't* want her here," he said, suddenly standing in front of me. "I didn't tell her to leave because—she may look sweet, but she's not. She would march right down the street to whoever would listen and sell us down the river."

I nodded, my arms crossing over my body. I needed space and he was blocking me. I needed to not need him. To not need to walk into his arms and bury my nose in his neck and inhale the very Nick-ness of him. To not need to feel his hands in my hair and mine going up the back of his -shirt, but all of that was all over me and I didn't trust myself to get close enough. I couldn't do that now. We'd already crossed that line but I didn't need to jump over it fully. Not when his feelings for the supermodel downstairs were questionable.

"Then I guess she stays," I said.

That topic being settled, I saw the change in his expression.

"Lanie—"

"Good night, Nick," I said, sliding past him.

"*Lanie.*"

It was loud and forceful and full of *look at me* vibes. I shook my head, looking at the chair he'd just vacated instead.

"No," I said. "I'm not—*this* is why I don't do this."

"Don't do what?"

"This," I said, thumbing between us. "Getting—involved. Giving a shit. It's never a good idea."

"You give a shit?"

I closed my eyes and counted backward while I cursed my inability to—

His lips were on mine in less than two seconds, followed by hands holding my head. My first reaction was to balk and be indignant, but that one was quickly squashed by the coup my body threw. My hands moved up his chest and around to his back before my brain kicked in and poked me.

I pulled back and he leaned his forehead against mine, not letting go.

"I'm not—"

"I'm not asking you to," he said softly. "I'm just kissing you."

Just kissing.

With Nick, that was like saying the Grand Canyon was just a ditch.

"Why?"

He gave me a look. "You say the damnedest things." I raised an eyebrow and he sighed. "Okay so maybe I give a shit too."

It was possibly the sexiest thing any man had ever said to me.

* * *

I was up early for coffee. Partially because I didn't sleep well, and partially to see if Tara was a coffee person. And what she looked like with morning hair.

I sat outside at the patio table and fiddled with the little peg game Nick had left out there one day when he challenged me to a competition (that he always won). Ralph had come downstairs meekly and was now lying on one of my feet.

"I know what you did," I said under my breath. "You never came to bed last night." Ralph's little Groucho eyebrows took turns going up and down. "I know where you were."

Ralph settled his head a little higher up on my foot.

"Yeah," I said, sipping my coffee. "Men. Snuggle up a little more and all is forgiven, right?" Ralph's tail thumped. "What I thought."

The door opened to my right, and out came Mr. Hot Stuff, in a gray muscle shirt and shorts, ready for his run. The butterflies that hit my stomach I chalked up to being hungry and not caffeinated enough yet. *Not* the result of yesterday's antics and last night's kiss that kept me up all effing night replaying it all on long loop. God, when did I become such a girl?

Be normal.

"Morning," I said. "Looks like the rain is go—"

My words were interrupted by the door swinging open again and producing a female version of Morning Nick. The perfect hair was slicked back into a shiny ponytail, a bright blue sweatband that looked like it had never been sweated on held back the tiny hairs. Matching blue tank top that possibly grew from her skin, black running shorts, and a face that still looked perfect while free of makeup. She could have tried out for high school cheerleader right now, and probably make it.

Of course she'd be a runner too. Why wouldn't she be? They were like brunette Barbie and Ken.

"How far do you go?" she said, bending over to stretch and literally touch her nose to her knees. "Distance or time? Morning Lanie," she said, glancing my way as if just realizing the lump in the chair was breathing.

"Cheers," I said, halfheartedly holding up my cup.

"Since when did you start running?" he asked. "You used to be all about sleeping late."

"That was the old me," she said with a smile, propping a leg on a chair to stretch it. "I've gotten into healthy living lately."

"Really," he said, his tone insinuating he didn't believe her.

"Actually, why don't you just see if you can keep up," she said to Nick, tossing that ponytail with a wicked grin as she took off from the patio and disappeared around the side of the house.

He blew out a breath and landed his gaze back on me, where I just held up my cup again.

"Have a good time."

"Her idea of healthy living usually involves carrot cake as a vegetable," he said.

"Well, if she can live on carrot cake and still look like that, more power to her," I said. "Now, if you don't mind, I've already shared too many words for this time of the morning. Go be energetic somewhere else please."

There. That sounded a little disconnected and not bothered at all by the circumstances, didn't it? Like I wasn't jealous of her or affected by him or any of the monumentally stupid things people start doing when they—give a shit.

My phone dinged with a text as he disappeared around the corner. Carmen.

Are you up?

Unfortunately.

Does she drink coffee?

Sigh. *She just took off running with Nick.*

Ugh. That's just wrong.

If she comes back looking better than she left, I give up.

* * *

She did. She even pulled off sweaty and messy as more of a healthy flush and shine. I would be red-faced, splotchy, wet hair sticking to my face, and probably dry heaving in the corner.

Nick walked past her, pulling off his sweaty shirt as he did. Both of us watched. Hell, I couldn't blame her for that. Not that many people had exes who looked like him.

"I'm taking a shower," he said, as he always did. Every morning.

"Me too," she said.

"You have to wait till he's done," I said. "The plumbing goes on strike when two showers are going at once. Or my dead aunt likes to play with the pipes."

"She haunts your pipes?"

"I wouldn't put it past her," I said.

"I'll be fast," he said. "I have to get to work."

Tara plopped down in a chair opposite me, taking a long drag from her water bottle. Great. Girl time. Awesome.

"So, what are you doing today?" she asked.

"I'm off," I said. "I work tomorrow." Bad plan. Come up with something. Something she won't want to do. Like cleaning out the attic. No, with my luck she'd enjoy cleaning out the attic and I'd be stuck actually cleaning out the attic.

"We should go to brunch," she said.

It was still early, so my head lean was justified. "I'm sorry, what?"

"Brunch?" she said. "Don't y'all do that here?"

"Um, maybe," I said slowly. "I usually just call it eating early."

She chuckled. "Then we should have an early lunch. At the diner."

Bingo.

"I don't know if Nick would be happy about that," I said. "He's kinda weird about being distracted at work."

He loved being visited at work, but I didn't think this would qualify. Plus—trapped in a car babysitting her? No. No. No. No thank you.

"Let him be distracted," she said. "I want to get to know you." Uh-huh. "We should go to the festival."

There were maybe a hundred places I could think of off the top of my head that beat out that festival on places I'd like to go today. Like the chiropractor. And getting my oil changed.

"It's really not that exciting," I said. "Basic small town snoozefest. With honey."

"I love honey." Of course she did. "Do they make it locally?"

"Yep," I said. "It's a bee charming, honey farming town."

She grinned and took another drink. "They should put *that* on their welcome sign."

I chuckled. "I'll hit up the mayor for it. Then again," I added, twisting my lips. "He's not real fond of me right now so maybe not."

"Uh-oh, town drama?"

I bit my top lip. You could say that. "Nah, just—personal disagreement. We grew up together and probably know too much."

"Ohhh, juicy?"

"No, he dated my best friend, and—" How and why was I talking so much? How was she drawing this shit out of me? "Anyway, small towns are bad about that. You can't get dressed without everyone knowing the color of your underwear by noon."

"Oh, I love that stuff," she said. "I'm so drawn to books and shows about it. I grew up in downtown Dallas, so the only small town life I ever had was when Nick and I moved in together when Addison was a toddler."

And it had begun.

"It's not like the movies," I said. "Pretty boring." Now to take a play from her book. "So where did you and Nick live?"

"A little town north of Dallas," she said. "It's not little anymore, everything has exploded around there, but when we were there it was adorable."

"You didn't get married right away?" I asked. Yeah, I was digging. Sue me. "I mean, Nick told me y'all were young, but he never really got into the details."

"No," she said with a laugh. "We were still in high school, and my parents were a little less than thrilled, understandably." She shook her head. "I would have died if Addison had come up pregnant at that age. I don't know how my mom kept her cool."

Money buys good therapists.

"So what about you?" she asked. "Ever been married? Before now, I mean?" she added with a grin.

"No," I said. "Never been a big believer in it."

"Really?"

"My dad skipped out when I was little," I said, wondering if there was any duct tape in the house. I needed it over my mouth. "And I watched my mother just bleed grief for a year. She was so hopelessly in love with someone who was never coming back, she—" I couldn't go into that detail again. "She died before I was eight."

Tara's eyes got huge. "Oh my God, I'm so sorry."

I shook my head. "No need to be. I had a great life with my aunt. That's why it's so important to me to save her house."

"Wow, that's so much like Nick's story."

Ding ding! That got my attention.

"What do you mean?" I asked, trying to be vague, not wanting her to know that we hadn't actually delved into personal pasts that much. Outside of her, anyway.

"His brother Leo raising him after their parents died," she said. "And then just taking off and disappearing one day. He had major trust issues for years. Still does," she added, looking away.

Nick walked through the patio door, not in a towel, thank God, or I might have yanked it off him and strangled him with it. He had on his work white T-shirt and jeans, his hair finger combed and spiky. His expression a little leery on what we might have been chatting about all this time. I would have given my right boob to go be all up in him right at that moment.

"So you grew up here," Tara said, switching tones and giving me a wink. "Did you ever have sex in this house?"

Yesterday, nearly, till you got here.

"Not quite," I said, glancing at Nick.

And then I realized what she'd done. She got me all comfortable and buddy-buddy and then popped the question to find out if Nick and I had done the deed. And I fell for it. Dear God, she really could get under your skin.

"Shower's free," he said. "Watch the hot, it gets finicky."

"Lanie said it's haunted," she said, getting up and patting his chest as she passed him.

"Well, there's that," he said. "Good luck."

The door closed behind her.

"She's good," I said. "Scary good."

"Told you."

Chapter Sixteen

"Keep your friends close and your enemies closer, Lanie girl. Sometimes it's hard to tell the difference."

Brunch was a bad idea. I felt it in my bones. But Tara was determined to go to the diner with or without me and I figured with would be easier to explain. A stranger in town always drew attention. A stranger that looked like her would have tongues wagging. A stranger that looked like her and was attached to Nick and I in some way—especially after yesterday's fiasco—would send up the bat signal.

She flounced through the door of the Blue Banana all large and in charge, her hair twisted up in a messy bun that looked divine on her and would just look like bedhead on me.

"This place is adorable," Tara cooed, sinking onto a stool at the bar.

I was surprised at how many people were actually there that early. Some eating breakfast, some hitting up lunch already. It wasn't even quite ten. I didn't get it.

"Maybe let's get a booth," I said, glancing around at the curious eyes.

"Nah, this is where the action is," she said, looking like a kid in a candy store.

I laughed, taking the next stool. "I seriously don't know what kind of action you're expecting, but—"

"Look who dares to show up here after that spectacle yesterday," came a voice I'd learned to cringe over in a very short time.

I turned to see Katrina Bowman standing behind me, one neon-pink nailed hand propped on her overly pronounced hip, the other clutching a bag I wouldn't be able to afford if I saved for a year. Did she never eat at home?

"Move on, Katrina," I said, turning back. I was so acutely aware of Tara's questioning gaze I could feel my blood rising to the surface.

"Move *on*?" Katrina barked. "After what you and your so-called husband did yesterday?"

I frowned and swung my stool back around. "What *we* did?" I hurled. *Dial it back. Dial it back.* "Let's replay, shall we?" I wasn't dialing it back. "Whose husband kissed who? Whose husband can't keep his slimy little hands to himself? Nick was just reminding Alan that I'm not a free-for-all."

She stepped forward, the challenge sparking in her overly lined eyes. "Who can't keep her tits under wraps?"

I stood up, nearly nose to nose with her. "You started that one, chica, when you invited my husband in the house for a little slap and tickle."

"Oh, and he loved that tickle too," she said under her breath, an angry smile warping her expression. "Did he tell you about it?"

"Enough," said a male voice harshly behind me, making Tara and I both jump. "You know damn good and well I rejected your pathetic ass, Mrs. Bowman. You and your husband *both* need a lesson in boundaries."

My head and face were so hot I had to be glowing, and my heartbeat in my ears was deafening. Tara's eyes were huge as she looked from Nick to me.

"Yeah well your little lesson is going to cost you our dental bills," Katrina spat. "You knocked two teeth loose."

"He was charging *me*," Nick said. "Like a wild animal. He's lucky that's all that got knocked loose."

"Okay," Allie said as she walked up behind Nick. "Let's all go to our corners, shall we?" She patted Nick's shoulder. "I believe you have an order or two back there. Mrs. Bowman--"

"He insulted me," Katrina said. "Your employee insulted a customer. I want him fired."

"Mrs. Bowman," Allie repeated slowly. "As I was saying, there are plenty of empty tables on the other side. Why don't you find one?"

Katrina scoffed and adjusted the bag on her shoulder. "I spend a ton of money here every week, but if you won't respect a paying customer, then I'll bring my business elsewhere."

Allie nodded. "I'm sorry to hear that, but it's your choice."

Huffing, Katrina turned on her heel and marched out, and Nick's jaw set as his eyes glazed over and he walked back to the kitchen without a word or a look to us.

Conversations started back up around us, making me realize how quiet it had gotten. I sat back down on my stool and stared unseeingly at the menu.

"Boring and no action, huh?" Tara said, perusing hers.

My ears felt like they might self-ignite.

"Usually."

Allie came back with a towel on her arm and two glasses of ice water. "I'm sorry about that, y'all."

I gave her a what-the-hell look. "Allie, I'm sorry. She did all that because of me and Nick. You didn't have to do what you did."

Allie waved a hand toward the wake Katrina left behind. "The Bowmans are blowhard assholes."

"Blowhard assholes with major cash flow," I said.

She leaned forward. "I do just fine, don't worry about it. Your husband makes sure the whole town keeps coming back."

Allie took our orders and walked off, and Tara stayed unusually quiet. I sucked down my water like it was the last I'd ever get as I tried to cool my blood. The silence was eventually more than I could stand, and I grabbed a nearby cardboard coaster to have something in my hands.

"Still think small towns are quaint and cute?" I said.

She shrugged. "I guess you're right. Everyone knows everything you do, even the stuff you try to hide."

Nick's words about not trusting Tara rang in my ears. How she'd sell us out if it worked for her agenda.

"Yep. Pretty much," I said.

"This deal with you and Nick," she said, finally looking at me. "It's not pretend anymore, is it?"

Words left me. Thoughts crashed and tumbled against each other. I was barely coming to terms with that myself, much less being able to talk to his ex about it. She wasn't to be trusted. But she was too smart to accept a lie too.

I stared at the printed ads on the coaster, not seeing the words.

"No," I said finally. "Or at least not fully. It's—complicated. We don't even talk about it."

"Oh I get that," she said. "Nick's not a talker. He's not big on feelings, either."

"And neither am I, which made this perfect!" I said. "No strings, no ties. And yet somewhere along the way--"

"Things got tied?"

I blew out a breath, willing myself to shut up. "A little bit."

"You fell in love with him."

"I—what?" I said, nearly choking on my water. "What? No! No!"

"That's what you said," she said.

"No I didn't," I countered. "I can assure you that I most definitely did not say that. I said it got complicated, or different or something. I mean living, with someone day in and day out makes lines blurry after a while, that's all."

She gave me a long look and then smiled as our food landed in front of us.

"He's easy to love, Lanie," she said, buttering a tall stack of pancakes and reaching for the syrup and the local raw honey provided on the side. "And hard to get over. Be careful."

I laughed uncomfortably, looking at my eggs and bacon that he'd cooked for me and losing my appetite completely.

"It's not like that," I said. "I told you, it's just—maybe a step above just friends."

"Uh-huh, and I'm guessing that woman's husband kissed you, and Nick punched him for it?" she said, licking syrup from her fingers.

She was too observant.

"How are those pancakes drenched in butter and syrup living a healthy lifestyle?" I asked, needing a diversion.

"Pffft, I made that shit up," she said, fluttering her fingers. "I started running, and as long as I keep doing that I can eat whatever the hell I want."

"You're lucky," I said. "If I ate that, I might as well glue them to my thighs."

"Then you wouldn't get the joy of this," she said, taking my fork and stabbing a steaming dripping forkful of pancakes and shoving them into my mouth. "You don't pass up Nick's pancakes."

"Ohmehgrrdd," I mumbled around the lightest, fluffiest most amazing buttermilk pancakes I'd ever tasted.

"Yep."

I glanced sideways at her. "Okay since we're doing true confessions, it's your turn."

She chuckled. "No thanks."

"Only fair."

"I don't play fair, didn't he tell you that?"

I met her eyes. "Yes he did. But for some reason I think you will with me."

Tara blinked a couple of times and went back to her food. "Yes."

"Yes, what?"

"Yes, I'm still in love with the man you're married to," she said. "But I always will be. He was my first love, my everything. And I'm just not good at that."

What did I say to that? What possible words on this earth were an appropriate response for that?

"But I know we aren't good for each other," she said, a frown creasing the skin over her nose. "And I will deny ever saying that if you repeat it, but I'm admitting it to you. We had our time, and now—now we are just parents."

"You didn't come here because you're parents together," I said. "Come on."

"No, I came here because I'm me and I'm twisted and I needed to see what had my Nick so distracted," she said. "You know, that *one step above friends* thing you swear by?" She winked at me. But honestly, I just want to see him happy."

"And why are you telling me this?" I asked.

"I have no idea," she said. "Are you a witch or something?"

No, but I do have an Aunt Ruby in my pocket. "I must just be easy to talk to.".

"Maybe," she said. "Or maybe finding out that the new Mrs. McKane isn't out to screw him over, but actually has his best interests in mind puts my manipulative little heart at ease." She leaned sideways. "I'm not the total self-centered privileged bitch he makes me out to be."

Tara definitely had more substance than Nick made out, but I still felt I had to be wary. Their daughter didn't trust her either, and that had to mean something, right?

"Just be good to him," she said, mopping up the last of her pancakes while I was still stabbing around at my eggs. I did eat the bacon. Because—bacon. "He deserves someone like you. That will put him first and defend him to the end. That will love him without all the baggage we have weighing things down."

I shook my head. "It's not—"

"Not like that, I know," Tara said with a small grin. "I hear you."

* * *

The next day at work was an exercise in squirrel tactics. As in my every thought was a new one. I couldn't focus to save my life; I gave one man back the check he was cashing along with the cash, I put money into the wrong account of another man, and while counting out a thousand dollars, I nearly gave one woman an extra six hundred dollars.

I was toast. I hadn't slept well again, thank you Nick and now thank you Tara too. Her words kept circling me like buzzards. In fact I think the buzzards were laughing at me when I did doze off. Laughing and pointing and telling me that I would never get laid with my clothes on and when I told them I'd take them off when the time came they all flew off because I didn't know how to say I love you.

Now seriously, what kind of jacked-up shit was that?

Buzzards, no less.

When I parked myself in the break room for lunch, my phone rang. With what I'd come to recognize as a California area code. After grabbing my turkey sandwich and Coke, I scurried out the back door to the smoke break chair. Luckily, it was vacant.

"Hello?" I answered.

"Lanie Barrett?" a female voice asked. A different one.

McKane.

"Yes, can I help you?" I asked.

"Well, this is Nancy Tanner from Cali Dynamics," she said. "Is this a good time to talk?

I chuckled. "As good a time as any."

"Good, good," Nancy said. "Well, I'm happy to tell you that you've been chosen for the ad copy block. Congratulations!"

I got the job.

Chills went on top of goose bumps. I got the damn job. Oh my God.

Oh my God.

What the hell did I do now?

"Oh my goodness, wow!" I said, tossing the sandwich into the nearby garbage. Eating was suddenly the furthest thing from my mind. "Thank you!"

"You're very welcome," Nancy said. "Now should you choose to accept the position, we can arrange to take care of the paperwork online until you can get here."

"Um," I said, feeling the panic rise in my throat. "How long do I have? Before the job starts, I mean?"

"Well, we like to get people here as soon as possible.".

"Because I'm on a very important project right now," I said. "Kind of hush-hush. And as I mentioned in the phone interview, I won't be able to leave for two more months."

There was a pause. "That's quite an extended wait."

"I know," I said. "In fact, I really thought it lost me the position when I told them about it. I could totally understand if that is a deal breaker."

"No, it's not," she said. "It's actually in the notes in your file." I had a file. "We were just hoping that perhaps the situation had changed since then."

I closed my eyes. "No, unfortunately not."

"Well then, that's that," Nancy said. "I'll pop this paperwork over to the e-mail address you listed on your application, and you can look it over. It includes all the pertinent information regarding salary, benefits, job duties, and so forth. If it suits you, and you're still interested in becoming part of the Cali Dynamic team, my number will be on the e-mail. We'll get you set up for whatever date you need."

"Sounds good," I said. "Thank you for calling me."

I hung up and sat there, wondering who decided when life got to be so smart aleck and cold. When a month ago, I would be dancing out the door that very day, now I just sat in stunned silence. Because one, Aunt Ruby's house. And two, the fact that there was a number two. Nick. He wasn't supposed to figure in, but it sure as hell felt like he did.

I stayed out there, sipping my Coke till a smoker came out, needing a fix.

When I forgot how to log back into my machine after lunch, my boss came and suggested I take a half day and go home and take some aspirin and go to bed.

I almost hugged her. And when I couldn't stop rambling and told her that I had so much on my mind—old stuff, new stuff, random stuff—she said to look at what I thought of first thing each morning and my last thoughts every night, and throw everything else away. All the rest was just noise, but those two things were worth diving off a cliff for.

So as I thanked her for her wisdom and walked out the back door of the bank, I thought about what my two things would be. It wasn't the job. It wasn't any of my jobs. What did I wake up thinking about? Where did I go every night as I closed my eyes?

Goose bumps covered my whole body.

I couldn't get to my car fast enough.

* * *

I wasn't even bothered by the extra car in the driveway. Tara was okay. She was more than okay, actually. She was the one to show me my feelings, and essentially tell me it was okay to feel them. That giving a shit was a good thing. Okay, she didn't actually say that, that was my interjection, but she insinuated it.

I could thank her. If I were a writer, I'd put her in the acknowledgments. As it was, maybe I'd just send her a three-month supply of honey. It would make her feel all homey and remember the gooey moments.

Nick had made her out to be such a bitch. And in truth that was more show than reality. Then again, I also hadn't lived with her or tried to raise a child with her, so probably my sense of reality was slightly skewed.

My heart skittered in my chest as the thought of looking Nick in the eye and saying what I needed to say swirled around me. That face, those eyes, the slow lazy smile that warmed my thoughts every morning and wrapped me up safely at night.

I needed to find him, to touch him, to say the words before I chickened out. A glimpse of movement outside the back patio doors caught my attention and I headed that way, my heart speeding up to double time. *Breathe.* Having a heart attack in the middle of a monumental moment wasn't sexy.

Then there he was, smiling, talking to Tara, but that was okay. She'd see my face and know, and make herself scarce. As I reached the window-paned doors and touched the knob, however, my nerves up in my throat, something wasn't right. Tara's hands went up to his face, his came up to hold her head, and—no.

No.

I froze in that spot as Nick kissed her.

The sound of my heartbeat was overtaken by the sound of my breaths. I could hear them one by one, proof that I was still alive in a body that had gone numb.

It wasn't a sexual passionate kiss, but I'd kissed him enough now to recognize intimacy. The lingering of mouths, the touching of faces, the— oh my God, the thing I was going to say.

I was so stupid.

I'd done it. I'd gone there. The thing I swore I'd never do, never say, never act upon because it turned sane people into idiots. I'd channeled my weak mother and done it. I felt the hot tears trekking down my cheeks before I registered that I was crying.

I was crying. Over—sweet Jesus, I was pathetic too. A little squeak escaped my throat and the knob made a metallic sound as I removed my hand and backed up a step.

Nick looked up. He looked up from kissing his ex-wife, his first love, the love of his life, the woman who played me like a needy fucking fiddle. He looked up, her head still in his hands, the perfect hair spilling over his fingers, and looked at me.

"Lanie."

I couldn't hear it, but I saw my name on his lips. The lips he'd just kissed her with. His eyes registered alarm in the last second before I turned and walked away. I didn't care. Let him be alarmed. Let them both burn in hell. They deserved each other.

Blindly, tears distorting my vision blink after blink, I made it to the door and out into the sunshine. Stumbling down the steps, I skipped the car and just kept walking. Circling around the property, I headed down the rock path. I needed clarity. I needed home.

My name was being yelled in the background but that was meaningless. That went with the guy that made the girl a stupid fawning give-a-shit-way-too-much idiot. I was even about to turn down the perfect job for him. I'd become my mother, minus the booze and the pain pills. And something mentally slapped me upside the head on that thought and said that was overkill, but I wasn't thinking straight. I wasn't thinking straight because I'd let myself believe—just for a minute—that the thing I'd avoided my whole life could maybe be for me after all.

"Lanie!" he called out from the house. I was most of the way hidden into the path, protected by the trees, but he might know me well enough to—fuck that. He knew nothing.

Keep walking. I blinked new tears free as the image of them holding each other stabbed at me repeatedly.

"Lanie!"

He was closer. Damn it, he figured it out. He must be jogging. Maybe she donned her cute little blue sweatband real quick and came with him.

"Go home, Nick," I called out, passing the old fireplace, needing the soothing trickle of the water over the pebbles. *Home.* How fucking ironic. "Go back to *my* home, actually, and tell *your woman* to get her lying, conniving fucking ass out of my house, and then I don't give a shit what you do." The irony of those particular words was not lost on me. Even in my churned up state. "Go, stay. Do whatever the hell you want to do as long as I don't have to see—"

"Stop," he said, swinging me around by the arm.

"Don't touch me," I said, yanking my arm free.

He stepped back when he saw my face. "You're crying."

"Gold star," I said, swiping angrily at my face.

"Lanie."

"Your woman is waiting," I said. "Get her out of there before—"

"My *what?*"

"Don't insult me, Nick," I muttered, turning on my heel.

"My—" He stopped when I took up speed-walking again, and took three long strides to cut me off. "Excuse me. My woman?"

"I didn't stutter."

I was trembling like a leaf, though. He shook his head like I wore *him* out. Really?

"My *woman* is the crazy chick I'm chasing down right now," he said. "The one that drives me fucking mad and makes me laugh and want to pull my hair out all at once. The one I can't figure out to save my life. Who'll do anything to save an old house but nothing to save herself. My *woman* is the one I'm supposed to be faking it with, and yet I'm at a loss for what to do because there's nothing fake about it anymore."

Good words. Excellent words, actually, but they didn't take away the visual I'd seen. Nothing could purge that intimacy from my brain.

"Stop," I choked.

"Because she's the one who I can't wait to tell a funny story to, or see at the end of the day," he continued. "And then I do see her and my first thought is *She's mine*, and then my second thought is *Wait, what the fuck?* And then damn if my third thought isn't *God, yes. She's really mine*."

He stopped and took a long breath, locking his gaze in on me with something I understood too well. Fear.

"I love you, Lanie McKane."

Chapter Seventeen

"Don't say anything you'll have to apologize for later. Crow tastes like shit."

What did he just say to me?

Nick's expression looked like he was asking himself the same question. He took a deep breath and blew it out slowly like it was keeping him balanced.

"You—" I began. "I saw—"

Complete sentences weren't happening.

"You saw good-bye," he said.

Breathe. "What?"

"She was leaving," he said. "Tara was leaving. She probably left as I ran out the door. And she had some things to—I don't know, get closure on I guess. I told her." He paused, his eyes boring into mine like the second time took more strength. "I told her I loved you."

All my blood rose to the surface.

"She knew," he said softly. "She said she saw it on me. She recognized it. And yeah, I kissed her good-bye," he said, as if he'd said they threw a football around. "We have eighteen years and a kid between us. It seemed right." He wiped a tear off my cheek with his thumb. "But not if it made you cry."

All the rage and the hurt and the anger and the retribution of five minutes ago tumbled around inside me like lottery balls in a cage at his touch.

"I'm fine," I said, blinking free the rest and wiping them away. God, I couldn't think.

"Why did you come home early?" he asked. "What did you come

to tell me?"

What had I come to say? *What he'd already said twice.*

"I got the job in California," I blurted.

He tilted his head as if he hadn't quite heard right. He'd just spilled his guts. And I said—that.

I deserved to rot somewhere really bad.

No-the-hell-wonder I sucked at this.

"You—what?" he asked.

"They just called me," I said, crossing my arms over my chest, letting them drop, crossing them again. "Offered me the job."

Nick just nodded. His eyes started to glaze over; he was shutting down the portal he'd just blasted wide open. The one that exposed his heart and soul and everything he was afraid, like me, to do. The one that trusted me for about two-point-five seconds. Well, I'd trusted him too.

"So," he began, crossing his own arms. "What does that mean?"

"I—I don't know," I said. "I mean, once upon a time, it was all I wanted, it was everything I thought I'd never get, but—"

"But what?" he said, his tone flat. "Now a rickety old house with bad plumbing means more? Or were you coming to tell me you were leaving? That the gig was up?"

I shook my head. Everything was happening too fast. Nick was jumping to conclusions before I even fully grasped what the questions were.

"No," I said.

"And if that was the case, why the hell would you care who I was kissing?" he said, his voice low. He turned to walk back to the house.

It was going south for the second time and I hadn't even caught up to the north part.

"No, Nick," I said, pushing my legs forward to catch up to him now. My hands were on his arms. "I came to tell you that I—" Say it. *Say it!* The words that felt so ready just minutes ago stuck in my throat, cowering behind hurt and fear and justification. "They're giving me the two months, so—"

"Good for you," he said, just above a whisper. His eyes weren't blinking. They were angry. And hurt.

"No," I said. Again. It seems that was the only word I could keep saying without reservation. "I can't imagine any of it. Going, staying, *anything*—without you now. I—give a shit." I gave a weak smile. "A lot."

"We're past give a shit," he said.

"Wasn't that just yesterday?"

"This isn't a game anymore, Lanie," he said, pulling free of my hands

"It's real. I don't know when or how it got that way, but it is. And if you're not there with me, then okay. I get that." He raked his fingers through his hair. "I don't get why you just stormed off crying and spouting all that crap if you're not, but okay. There are so many things about you I don't understand, I could—"

I pulled his face down to mine and kissed him with all I had. There was only a second's pause where he inhaled sharply, and then he groaned into it. My hands shook as I slowed us down, kissing him softer, deeper. With my heart. Five seconds later, hands cradling my face, he pulled back and gave me a leery look.

"Don't play," he said, his voice scratchy.

I didn't realize my eyes were full of tears again until I opened them. Kissing him like that, with every emotion and intimate feeling I had—it was gut-wrenching. It was exposing and revealing and felt like my heart was being laid wide open. I wasn't familiar with that. It was terrifying. But I felt like I would self-combust if I didn't have more of it.

"Does this feel like play to you?" I asked, my voice not more than a whisper and wobbly as two tears fell over his hands. I pulled him back to me, needing to feel his lips against mine. "I don't know what the future brings, Nick," I said, kissing his lips again and again, tasting the salt from my tears. "But I know I can't imagine one without you."

Covering my mouth with his, he dove deep, one hand fisted in my hair and the other traveling my body, pressing me hard against him as he went. I wrapped both arms around his head and let it take me. God, kissing him was like leaving the planet and going to Disneyworld and the best food and the best wine and the best of everything all in one. I wanted to keep it loving, to show him my feelings that my mouth wouldn't spill, but my body was on fire for him.

All the foreplay from two days ago hadn't been forgotten. It was like it just lay dormant, waiting to take up where we left off, except there were suddenly all these clothes in the way and my God I needed them gone.

Nick responded the same way, his breathing going erratic as his hands traveled me, pushing up my breasts and meeting my cleavage with his mouth, kissing, tasting, swiping under the fabric with his thumbs to find my nipples and making me arch against him. He reached around to unzip but there wasn't one, and I could feel the need buzzing off him.

"You kill me in this dress," he moaned against the inside of my right breast.

I lifted his head, lightheaded with desire. "Sit against the fireplace," I breathed.

He backed up the step to the bench and sat, his hands running up the outsides of my thighs to grip my ass and pull me against his face.

"Lift your dress for me," he said, his voice thick with desire and his eyes so deadly hot I could have come right there.

I let go of him to lift my dress up and took it all the way over my head before tossing it on the ground, bra too, as he gazed heatedly at my body and curled two fingers into my panties without hesitation.

"Please," he groaned, his lips grazing the tender skin as he lowered them.

Words left me as his mouth followed them down, lingering where I needed him most. He let the panties drop as he gently picked up one of my legs at the knee and held me as he hooked it around his neck.

"Oh God, Nick," I mouthed without sound as he kissed me there the same way he kissed my mouth. Without boundaries. With abandon. Teasing, tasting, making me tremble in ways I hadn't in a really long time. His fingers joined the party and I had to let go of his head and grab the rusty metal handle on the side of the fireplace. My legs weren't going to hold me. Nothing was going to hold me. My bones were going liquid as heat and everything molten built up, taking my words away, my breath away. I bucked against his mouth as the earth shook under me and the world as I knew it exploded in light and waves, and if fireworks were a good thing for me, they'd have been there too.

Nick held me as I came down from on high, and looked up at me unblinkingly as he slowly wiped his lips on my thigh and unwrapped my leg from his neck. Breathing hard, I lowered on very shaky knees to the ground in front of him.

"That was the hottest thing I've ever seen in my life," he said, his voice strained.

"You're damn lucky I didn't snap your neck," I said, bringing a chuckle from his throat.

"What a way to die."

"Your turn," I said, running my hands up the legs of his jeans to the boulder residing at the top.

Nick shook his head. "I doubt that."

"And why is that?" I asked, kissing his stomach as I unbuttoned his jeans and unzipped very slowly, letting him out inch by excruciating inch. I looked up to see his jaws flex and his eyes shut tight as he sprang forward. Commando. God help me. "Mmmm," I sighed, running my tongue up the length.

He started as if given an electric shock, and grabbed my head.

"Fuck, that's why," he said, tangling his fingers in my hair as I dropped wet sloppy kisses on it, working my way up, and when I took him in my mouth and made love to it the way he had, Nick moaned. "God, that's so good." Then he pulled me off. "Too good," he breathed. "Keep that up and I'll never make it inside you."

"Tell me what you need, baby," I said, repeating his words from last time. His eyes, heavy-lidded with need, winked at me.

"You," he said. "All I need is you."

Everything wrapped around my heart and squeezed. It was the perfect time to say the words. To tell him everything that was beating down the walls of my heart.

"How do you want me?" I asked instead. Because—me.

In one move, he had his shirt off and on the ground, and his jeans followed when he stood. Sweet Jesus.

"Lie down," he said. I didn't move, standing across from him. "What?" he asked.

"You are—breathtaking," I said, drinking him in.

He crossed the inches and touched my face with one hand, kissing me slowly, maddeningly, letting our bodies melt together without groping. We fit. We fit so well. By the time we broke the kiss, we were both shaking.

"Please lie down," he said against my ear. "I need you so fucking bad."

I dropped slowly, kissing my way down until his cursing sounded painful, and then I lay on his clothes and he came with me, kissing my nipples one by one. He raised my leg as he kissed his way up my neck.

"This the position you want?" I whispered, my whole body on thrumming mode.

"I want all of them, Lanie," he said against my lips. "But right now I just need deep."

Fuck balls, he was going to kill me yet. All the blood left my brain on his words, and anything that was left departed when his fingers found me. When the head of his dick played at the opening. And when he sank so deeply inside me that I couldn't tell where one of us began and the other ended.

"Nick!" I exclaimed on an inhale, arching off the ground as if I could get closer, be a part of him somehow.

The primal growl that shook his whole body emanated through me. His fingertips dug into my thigh and he raised my leg higher, over his shoulder, giving my thigh a playful nip with his teeth.

Nick sank into me again, closing his eyes as he started a rhythm.

"Jesus, you feel so good, Lanie," he breathed, barely forming the words. "So fucking tight."

I wrapped my free leg around him and used my hands on the ground as leverage, moving with him. He hit everything, filling me so completely there was no way to say anything back. I had no words that would do it justice. He was everything I'd never experienced. Including the burning look in his eyes as he watched me. Watched me as he made love to me, because that's what it was. I knew that's what it was because I'd never done it.

"Are you okay?" he asked as we moved faster, exertion popping the muscles in his neck. "Are you comfortable?"

I could have done this on a bed of nails and been just fine. I was riding a wave. A beautiful, building, crescendo of a wave. When he put my other leg over his shoulder and increased the pounding, the wave took steroids and began to lose its mind.

I arched off the ground, fisting handfuls of grass in my hands. "Oh God, Nick, keep doing that, I'm—"

I couldn't breathe; I couldn't talk. I could only feel my mouth wide open, and if I was dead, then hallelujah.

"Fuck, Lanie," he forced through his teeth. "I can't stop, I'm gonna fucking blow."

Freaky sounds came from my throat at the same time the most majestic roar came from him. Loud and feral and branding. He was marking his woman. And I liked it. As the second mind-blowing orgasm of my day shattered me into a million pieces, I liked being marked as his. That had never been me. What did that say about me now?

That I'd just been truly and thoroughly fucked for one thing.

And that I was head over heels in love.

Holy hell.

We came down in a tangle of limbs, heaving oxygen into our lungs and holding each other for dear life. It didn't get more basic than that. Two naked creatures mating in the woods. There was something weirdly comforting about that.

When we could breathe, I felt it, and I knew he did too. That moment. The awkward thing after first time sex when the adrenaline calms down and you don't know what direction to go.

Nick lifted his head from my shoulder and looked into my eyes, and warmth spread throughout my insides. It was still there. Sex hadn't changed it. He was going to say something profound, and this time I was going to say it back. Because I could now.

"Marry me again," he said. "For real."

Chapter Eighteen

"There's gonna come a time when beauty fades and senses go. Your body goes to shit and all you've got is what comes out of your mouth. Make it amazing."

My hands went to his face and my eyes burned. That went past profound right into taking breath away.

"What?" I said. "We don't have to Nick, we're there." I wiggled my left hand. "We have rings, we have a license—"

"We have signatures on a paper, and your ring is glass," he said, smoothing my hair back. "I meant what I said. I love you, Lanie. I want to look in your eyes and say those words for real."

Two tears trickled back into my hair. I felt like the Grinch when his heart grew ten sizes that day. I was overcome with so much everything.

"I I—"

"Lanie, you back here?" came a male voice in the distance.

Nick and I both stiffened in a fight or flight moment of *oh shit*. He instantly spread out his body to cover mine.

"Who is that?" he whispered.

"I don't know," I whispered back.

"We used to wander around back here when we were kids," said a then familiar voice. "Both their cars are here so I'm thinking—"

"Alan?" I hissed. "What the living hell?"

"Scramble over there and pull your dress on," Nick said, rolling off me. He grabbed his jeans as I crawled to the relative shelter of the fireplace, rolling onto his back to yank them on.

I, of course had an inside-out, fitted sundress with no damn zipper that was difficult to get on standing up, in air conditioning, with all the time in the world. I pulled it right-side out—I hoped—and struggled wrangling it over my head, while Nick pulled down on it. No bra. No panties. He tugged his own shirt on, it twisting around his shoulder.

"Your underwear," Nick whispered hurriedly.

I kicked them under a pile of leaves and sat on the bench, still hidden from view.

"Lanie!" Alan called again.

"What?" I asked, standing again and stepping out from behind the fireplace, putting on a very perplexed look.

I had no idea what my hair looked like, whether I was covered in dirt or not, or if I had anything on my face. I didn't care. I wanted him to leave so I could get back to my conversation. It only took me a lifetime to get there. I felt a tug on my backside as Nick pulled down a section of my dress that didn't make the trip.

Alan and Bryce were halfway down the path with their backs turned as if they were about to give up and head back. Damn, we should have waited them out. Both their heads swiveled back my direction.

"You *are* here," Alan said. "What are you doing back there?" Nick rose up behind me, and Alan physically stepped back, dislike morphing his features.

"Whatever I want to do on my own property," I said. "What are *you* doing here?"

"Nick," Alan said, ignoring my question and saying his name like it tasted rotten. "How appropriate to find you here."

Nick looked around. "Well, I live here right now, so I guess it is."

"Right now is the key part of that sentence," Alan said.

Nick nodded, eyes wide. "Yes, right now," he emphasized slowly. "We live in California. We're being forced to do *this*," he said, circling with his hands. "By Lanie's aunt."

"You're not being forced to do anything," Bryce said, his oily voice making my skin crawl. "But you're sure as hell going all out."

"And what are you babbling about?" I asked, hands on my hips.

Bryce held out a bent and dog eared piece of paper. It had some sort of stain in one corner.

"Your fake marriage," he said.

"I can assure it's very much real," Nick said, speaking up. "So if that's all you came to harass us about—"

"It may be technically real," Alan said. "But not for the five years you claimed."

Nick looked at me, a mock frown dipping his eyebrows. "Did we claim five years?"

"You live in Sage," Bryce said. "Lanie's in Louisiana. Where the hell is all this California crap coming from?"

Okay, we were running out of bluffs.

"What are you so busy and concerned with, that you have time to worry about me?" I asked. Either of them, really.

"I'm concerned that you got hitched for the sole purpose of defrauding a will."

"We did not," I said.

"Last month," Bryce said.

"Okay, so what if we just got married," I said. "What difference does it make?"

"It's a lie," Alan said. "You lied under oath."

I lifted an eyebrow, pretending to think. "Nope. There was no oath."

"For all intents and purposes, you got married under false pretenses," Bryce said. "Under duress from Ruby's will instructions. Making your stay of three months here invalid."

I walked up to bald and bulbous Bryce.

"No, my aunt said that my husband and I needed to stay here," I said. "So I obtained a husband and we're staying here."

"Jesus, it sounds like you bought him at Walmart," Alan sneered.

"No, I picked him up in a parking lot for a steal," I said, listening to Nick chuckle behind me.

"You got married for the purpose of keeping this house," Alan said. "Plain and simple. It's no different from when people get married for green cards. It's fraudulent."

"What are y'all doing back here?" All heads turned to where Carmen was picking her way down the rock path on heels that had no business there. "Shit, I'm switching to flats. I don't care who says they're unprofessional."

"Oh good," I said, pointing dramatically. "A lawyer! Aunt Ruby always said where's a lawyer when you need one?"

Carmen snickered. "Yeah, right."

"This is a private conversation about family," Alan said, as Bryce's head started to glow.

Carmen stopped picking and looked at him. "And you're family?"

"Well, we are all God's children," I said. "So come on, Carmen, let's hold hands."

Alan huffed out a breath. "So were you in on it too?" he directed at her.

"You could be disbarred."

My heart stuttered a bit on that. He was actually right, and bluffing I hoped. Because I would die right there if Carmen lost her license because of me.

"I'm not sure what you're talking about, but it doesn't matter," Carmen said, then turning to me. "Do you want to retain my services?"

I blinked. "Sure."

"What do you have on you?"

I reached in the little pocket of the dress and my fingers closed on a dime. I held it up like it was hidden treasure. "Perfect," she said, plucking it from my fingers. "I'm Lanie's attorney and with that goes confidentiality."

Oh, I loved her.

"You're full of shit," Alan said. "And she's a fraud."

"And she's about to lose everything," Bryce blustered.

"No, actually, she's not," Carmen said, pulling an envelope from her bag. She wiggled it at me. "Got some interesting mail today."

"From?"

"Aunt Ruby."

* * *

We all went back to the house, to the front porch. I for one, needed to sit, as my rope-climbing-then-suddenly-used-for-crazy-sex muscles were starting to whine. I couldn't care less if Dumb and Dumbassery stayed, but they seemed hell bent. Bryce kept eyeing everything like he was appraising property, and I really wanted one of my missing shoes to drop on his head out of nowhere. *Come on, Aunt Ruby, show me some skills.*

"Evidently your aunt wrote another letter, to be mailed to me after month one of the arrangement," Carmen said. "It came today." She handed it to me and then held up her hands. "This, I honestly knew nothing about," she said. "This was entirely on her."

I paused, the envelope suddenly heavy in my hand. I wasn't sure if it was good or bad. I wasn't sure about anything. I looked at Nick, who was watching me from the porch rail, leaned back against it, his arms crossed over his chest. His wedding ring glinted at me. *Mine.*

I was sure about him.

I pried up the metal prongs holding the flap and opened it, peering inside. One piece of paper. Notebook paper. Pulling it out, I glanced at Carmen and then Nick again. His eyes burned into me with something that kept echoing in my head.

I love you, Lanie McKane.

No one had ever said that.

I swallowed against a shaky breath and blinked the carefully scrawled handwriting into focus.

> *My Lanie girl,*

My heart squeezed.

> *You're probably mad at me still, and that's okay. I couldn't have asked for a better daughter if I'd birthed you myself. You've been the joy of my life, and my only regret has been that my sister didn't live to appreciate the gift she had in you. You are so full of life, Lanie, and have so much love inside you. So much to offer. But you keep it all locked down tight for fear of becoming something you'll never be.*
> *You're not your mom, honey. Relax.*

The words swam in front of me and I blinked tears free.

> *I know I pissed you off with the house and all. But my girl, your lying skills haven't gotten any better with age. I forgive you for just trying to make a daffy old woman happy, but it just had to be done. And because I know you and how stubborn-assed you can be, I'm gambling that you finagled some way of coming up with a husband to keep this drafty old house. I'm also gambling that maybe something real happened along the way. If I'm wrong, I'm wrong. But I feel that I'm right. And you know how I get about my feelings.*

Carmen chuckled, and I did too through my tears.

> *So since I'm feeling good about things, you should know that there's no three-month deal. There never was.* I stopped and read that part again. *There never was.*

"What?"

"Keep going," Carmen said.

I took a deep breath and let it out.

And don't fuss at Carmen because I didn't tell her, either. The money's yours, the house is yours; it's already deeded over to you.

"Oh my God," I breathed, gripping the arm rest of the rocker.
"Wait, what?" Bryce asked.

Tell the Clarks I'm sorry, but they're all greedy blowhards and they can consider it payback for making me use the Porta-Potty that day when I came to visit their dad and the construction guys were doing the upgrade on that ridiculous house he couldn't afford.

"Are you *kidding* me?" Bryce said, his shiny head, neck, and face going red.

They did come by all that entitled greed honestly, so I can't blame them too much. My brother, rest his soul, was a son-of-a-bitch. Damn, I might have to deal with him again now.

"Are you gonna say something?" Bryce asked Alan, nudging him.
"Say what?" Alan said, disgust all over his face. "It's done."
"But she can't do that," Bryce said.
Alan raised his eyebrows. "She just did."

Anyway, I did it all for a reason, Lanie girl. Remember me by living life instead of going through the motions. Quit being afraid. Life is messy. Love is messier. It's what makes it all the more glorious when you get it right.

Everything in me wanted to look at Nick. To see if we got it right. But I couldn't.

Now go enjoy your house. Live in it, rent it, sell it, do whatever you want with it, but don't let the Bowmans get their sticky little hands on it.

"Hey!"
Alan's face turned three shades of purple, and Bryce stormed down the stairs, headed back toward Alan's house.

I don't trust them. They smile too much. And you know how I feel about people who play with bees. Just not right in the head.

"Amen to that," Carmen said under her breath.

So do what you want to do, but do it with purpose and passion. And love, baby girl. Love with all you have.
Big crazy hugs and finger wiggles,
Aunt Ruby

I suddenly felt drained as I set the paper and the envelope on the small table next to me. The one with the chipped vase and the wooden bowl with the painted on flowers. That belonged to me. Free and clear.

"I think this was a rigged piece of bullshit," Alan said, headed down the steps. He turned around and pointed at me. "Congratulations, Lanie. You won by out-conniving me."

I met his eyes and swiped at mine. "There was nothing rigged, Alan. I'm hearing this for the first time just like you." He waved me off and started walking away.

"It was survival," Nick said, turning in Alan's direction. His voice, silent till then, cut through the air. "Doing what she could to hold on to what was hers. That's not conniving. Or anything whatsoever to do with *you*."

Alan stopped and gave a sleazy grin that didn't reach his eyes.

"How cute, taking up for the little missus. What did you get out of it?" Alan's eyes narrowed. Somehow I felt the next three moves like a chess player, and I couldn't move quickly enough. "Money? A piece of that ass? Free blow jobs every—"

"Nick!" I cried, as he was past the steps before I could blink.

Alan was off his feet and shoved up against Nick's truck before anyone could fully exhale.

"I'm so done with you," Nick seethed. "Talk like that about her again, and I won't give a shit how long I spend in jail for it, I'll enjoy beating you to a pulp."

"Nick, he's not worth it," I said, finding myself at his side. I pulled at his arm. "C'mon, just let him and his jealousy slither away."

Nick slung him sideways, and Alan barely got his feet under him in time to avoid hitting the ground. Still, always the mouthy scrapper, he had to turn around and get another dig in.

"You think I'm jealous?" Alan threw back. "Of being used and tossed away?" He pointed at Nick, and I swear if I weren't a grown-up, I would have picked up a handful of gravel and thrown it at him. "She has no more use for you, buddy. You've outlasted your purpose."

"Walk away, Alan," Carmen called out.

"Oh, shut the hell up, Frosty," Alan said, his face contorting. "You're no better than she is. Throw men away when you're done with them. You would've done the same to your little nomad boy-toy if he hadn't thrown you away first."

"Leave, Alan," I said, noting Carmen's expression at the mention of Sully Hart.

"Speaking of cheap rides," Alan continued, a sneer on his face. "Did any of you hear about the new deal for Bailey's Pond?"

"What deal?" Carmen hissed.

"It was in yesterday's news, don't you read the paper?" Alan asked. "No, of course you don't. You're all too busy fucking strangers."

I grabbed Nick's hand and felt him tense.

"Charmed is building a mini-theme park at the pond," Alan said. "No more carnival after this year after all, Frosty. So I guess this will be your last chance for a redo." He grinned. "Last opportunity to remake *Carmen and the Carny do Charmed.* Or maybe *Trailer Trash Delight?*"

"This is your last chance to get out of my sight," Nick growled.

"Go home," I said, shooing Alan like an unwelcome bug. "My property," I added, pointing at the ground. "Go play on yours."

"Gladly," he said, walking off.

"Have a good day."

"Kiss my ass," he called over his shoulder, disappearing around the curve.

I waited a full count of five, tapping my foot.

"No thanks!"

I caught Nick's eye and he shook his head. "How did you ever end a date?"

I ignored that, and focused on Carmen. "Are you okay?"

She pasted on a smile, but the hands rubbing up and down her arms said more.

"Just never gets fucking old," she said, visibly shaking it off. "So now how about you?" She ran down the steps and hugged me. "Oh my God, just when I think that woman couldn't surprise me again."

"No shit."

"Congratulations!" Carmen said. "No more hiding. No more pretending. Y'all can get on with your lives! And if California—"

"Oh my God, I didn't get a chance to tell you," I said. "Cali Dynamics called today and offered me the job."

Carmen squealed. "Holy shit!"

"I know!" I exclaimed, her excitement ramping me up. "I told them I needed two more months."

"And now you don't have to!" she said, grabbing my hands. "I mean, I'll miss you, but *girl*, you've got to grab this! I'll take care of the legalities here."

The legalities. For the first time since I read Aunt Ruby's letter, I looked to Nick. Really looked. He had backed up to lean against his truck, thumbs hooked in his pockets, watching us. Like a bystander.

Words flew by like a ticker sign. My boss's words about what's important in life. I had left work to tell him I wasn't taking it. Then Nick's words. The *I love you's* and the *marry me for real* and Aunt Ruby's *quit being afraid, love with all you have*—a hell of a lot of significant words in the span of maybe an hour.

Words that I never got to respond to, and that was all over him.

I licked my suddenly dry lips. "We definitely have some things to talk about."

He nodded and his gaze dropped to some point on the ground between us, and then he pushed off and walked toward the house.

"Where are you going?"

"In."

"In?"

"Thanks, Carmen," he said, stopping on a half turn. "I appreciate all you did to help us."

"No problem," she said. "The money should be free and clear in a few days."

Nick gave a thumbs-up and kept walking. I had an odd sense of not-rightness. A disconnect. He was ticked off that I hadn't said anything back, and that I was excited about the job again, I got that. But the game was just turned on its ear, and we needed to talk about the new parameters. We didn't have to play it out for two more months. We—could go back to our lives, or no. That was in no way appealing. And he didn't have a job there, and his daughter was about to leave for college. We could stay here and work the jobs we have, which wasn't appealing to me, but would be wonderful for him and we'd be together. *Marry me for real.* Or I could go to California, and he could stay here in Charmed and make a life. Without me. That one made my stomach hurt. *I love you, Lanie McKane.*

"I wonder if he'd come with me."

Chapter Nineteen

"When you've been kicked in the gut, doll yourself up and paint your toes bright red to spite the devil himself."

Carmen turned back to look at me, and I realized that had been out loud. "Seriously?" she said.

"We *are* married."

Her eyebrows shot up. "So has the blind-to-what's-right-in-front-of-them duo finally seen some clarity?"

"My underwear is currently under a pile of leaves in the woods," I said. She nodded. "Okay then."

"And he asked me to marry him again," I rambled like I was reading a grocery list. Or like I was numb. Or like I'd just been fucked and proposed to, declared love to, and then given a house and eight hundred thousand dollars.

I mean, that would throw a person a little off balance, right?

"Oh my God." Carmen turned to square off in front of me, bringing my foggy focus back to her. "Lanie, what did you say?"

I blinked. "Nothing yet." At her incredulous look I continued. "That was right when the peanut gallery showed up and I never got the chance."

"Do you love him?"

I blew out a breath. "Oy with the L word."

"Really?" she said. "How old are you? Did you hear your aunt? Quit being a pussy!"

"I'm pretty sure that word never came out of her mouth or her pen."

Carmen sighed. "Okay look, let's talk more later, I gotta run. I'll text you with the money details, and I'll go pick up the deed from the mortgage company and get it to you next time I'm this way."

I watched her drive away and I glanced back at the house where my husband was inside somewhere sulking. I'd fix that. First, I had to make another trip down that—down *my* little rocky path, to *my* old stone fireplace, to where my underwear and bra were communing with nature. I wasn't wired for commando. Open plumbing with a dress was just weird.

I made it down there and retrieved my treasure, then sat on the bench and leaned back against the stone, closing my eyes. It really was magic there. I'd just experienced it. And it was like the stress of a million weights were off my shoulders, but they'd moved to my stomach.

Why was I so friggin anal when it came to love? My mother, okay, but I was a grown woman, not a child. I was fully capable of deciding my own actions and not being governed by some myth that her story would become mine. Where were my big girl panties? I looked down at the pair in my hand. Well maybe I should start with wearing them instead of carrying them.

It was when I was almost back up the path, emerging from the trees, that I felt it. Maybe I heard it, too, a faraway rumble or something down the road. But it was more of a *knowledge*. Intuition? Whatever it was named, it was bad.

I jogged the rest of the way, noting the absence of his truck. The weights in my stomach swelled to something more like water balloons when they're filled too full. I couldn't catch a good solid breath. And when I went inside, nothing so and cluttered and lived in had ever felt emptier.

"Nick?" I called out, already knowing there wouldn't be an answer. Not a human one, anyway. Ralph jumped down from the couch and wagged his way over to me, stretching from a nap.

My eyes burned, and I dropped the bra on the floor as I ran upstairs.

"Nick!" I cried anyway, running to his room.

All the air left me as I saw his closet door open and empty. His suitcase gone. His pictures of Addison—gone. I whirled around and ducked into his bathroom. Cleaned out. He didn't have much with him, and taking his leave wouldn't have been difficult, but still—I was down there for all of ten fucking minutes!

"How dare you," I sobbed, not even aware I'd been crying till then. "How could you just—leave? Not say good-bye?"

Something made me turn around and go to my room, and there it was. A piece of notebook paper with handwriting on it. My second one of the day. With his wedding ring on top.

"You son of a bitch," I breathed.

Lanie,

I'm sorry. It's easier this way. Telling you bye face to face would be too much after today. But I love you enough to let you go. Go get what you're looking for. It isn't me. If it was, then you could have said you loved me. And you could have said yes. Even through the fear. I know because I was scared too.

It stopped being about the money for me and I wouldn't even take it if Addison didn't need it, so if that's still on the table, please wire it to the account below.

Hope you kick ass in Cali.

Love,

Nick

* * *

I felt sweaty. I felt sick. Driving around town knowing damn good and well he wasn't in Charmed anymore, but having to look, anyway. Just in case. I'd run to my car to retrieve my phone and texted him. Nothing. Called—went to voicemail.

Hey, this is Nick. Talk.

"Why the hell would you do this?" I said. "You don't even know what I was coming in to say. You just assume you know the score and make the decision for both of us." My breaths skipped with my sobs. "Well that was an asshole thing to do, Nick."

Now I was driving in circles and considering chasing him back to Sage, but I was too pissed and proud for that.

"The Blue Banana," I muttered, doing a U-turn in the middle of Main. He wouldn't leave his job high and dry, would he? He loved it there. He loved being Chef Nick.

My eyes scanned the parking lot as I pulled in and parked crooked. I didn't care. I wouldn't be there long. No truck. My heart sank a little lower. I got out and swiped at my face as I went in, hoping I didn't look as deranged as I felt. I'd gone from sex in the woods to ditched to panic attack in a short time, with no assistance from a mirror to see what affect that might have. I glanced at my reflection in the window and decided not knowing was better.

A couple of people nodded in my direction, a few more looked at me funny, and more just pretended I wasn't there. I was good with that.

I went to the lunch counter and tried peering through the order window, but all I could see was Dave, the fry cook.

"Is Allie here?" I asked a younger waitress who looked terrified.

"Um, Miss Greene?" she said, clutching her pad. "Am I in trouble?"

"Not at all," I said. "Just need to talk to her."

"Can I tell her what it's about?" she asked. "Get you a free drink on the house?"

My head started to pound out a rhythm. I looked down at her nametag. Brianna.

"Brianna, there's no problem. Allie's a friend of mine and I need to talk to her if she's here," I said. "Kind of quickly. And do you know if Nick—if Chef Nick was here?"

Her eyes lit up. Even the young ones appreciated beauty.

"For a minute, yes," she said. "He was talking to Dave—or Chef Dave now," she said, chuckling.

I gripped a nearby chair. There was someone sitting in it, so I had to apologize.

"Sorry," I whispered to them. "I might be having a nervous breakdown." I turned back to Brianna. "Can you get Allie now?"

The waitress scurried off, and I caught sight of a more accurate reflection. Good God, I was a mess. I smoothed my hair down and pulled a leaf out of it. Jesus Christ. My eyes teared up again thinking of where that would have come from, and then another thought chilled me. In this kind of old-fashioned dress, if I squinted just right, I looked a lot like my mother.

Including the part about being a mess. Over a man.

You aren't your mother, honey.

Then why was I acting like her?

"Lanie?"

I jumped and smiled to cover it as Allie walked up, a concerned look in her dark eyes.

"Hey, Allie."

She gave me a once-over. "I'm gonna guess this has something to do with Nick quitting."

My bottom lip quivered. "I was hoping that wasn't the case."

Her eyebrows lifted. "I wish that, too, but he said he had to go." She nodded back toward the order window. "He said Dave was up to speed, that he'd been teaching him as he went when there was time, so we'll see. We're gonna miss him around here, though. I told him he had a job if he ever decided to come back."

I nodded, a hand against my sternum as if everything might disintegrate if I didn't hold it in.

She tilted her head. "Did y'all break up or something?"

"Or something," I breathed. "Thank you, Allie." I squeezed her shoulder as I passed. "Talk to you later."

"Mrs. McKane?"

Stab.

I turned to see Nick's protégé, Dave. coming from the kitchen.

"Yes?"

"Ma'am, Nick gave me his motorcycle and trailer, and—"

"I'm sorry, what?" I clutched at my throat before my heart could escape out of it. His motorcycle? "He—he gave it away?"

Dave looked unsure as his gaze darted from Allie to me. "Yes, ma'am," he said. "We always talked bikes and stuff while we worked. I've always wanted one, and I kind of know what I'm doing around an engine—"

He thought I needed to know it was going to a good home. No. It wasn't a dog. But it was Nick's pride and joy.

"I'm sure you'll be great with it," I said, holding out a hand. "I just didn't know he was—getting rid of it." Of me. If he handed that thing off, he wasn't coming back. He was handing me off too.

"So—I was wondering when a good time would be for me to come pick it up?" Dave asked, his words having a weird echoey quality.

"Anytime," I said, turning. "Doesn't matter."

"Hey, you want a coffee to go?" Allie asked. "You look like you might need one."

"No thanks," I said. "I have a feeling I might just want to go to sleep."

I wandered back out into the sunlight and caught the glint off my fake diamond. The "glass" he wanted to replace with the real thing only hours ago. I'd have to get divorce papers drawn up with Carmen.

I got back into my car, turned it on, and cranked up the air conditioner to full blast. Let it blow on me while the world broke around me. His smile, his eyes, the way he laughed at the silly things I'd do, the way he'd look at me when I was all he saw in the world. The way his eyes darkened when he wanted me and the way his hands felt on my skin. The way it felt to be wrapped up in his arms.

The way the words *I love you, Lanie McKane* sounded on his lips. He'd waited for me to say it back. To say anything even close. Instead, I said, *We definitely have some things to talk about.*

I laid my head on the steering wheel and came apart.

"I love you too, Nick," I sobbed.

Sure, *now* I could say it.

I didn't care who walked by or wondered. I let myself shatter.

* * *

Ralph and I had to make a trip back home. The real home. In Louisiana. I met with movers and packed up the rest of what I was bringing. At least what I was bringing to Texas. I could have left him back in Charmed and had Carmen come stay with him that night, but truth be told I liked his company. And I was about to be leaving him for a couple of days anyway to go for my initial orientation in California.

California.

What I always wanted. And what the rest of town expected. That's the story we had sold them, after all. The story we'd sold ourselves.

I kept having to tell myself that more and more. It had been two weeks.

"How you doing back there, boy?" The tail thump told me what I needed to know. His mom left him behind, he got a new mom and dad, and then the dad left. As long as he could see me, he was good. "We'll be home to your backyard in a couple of hours."

I'd get back and get unloaded, leave on Monday for my orientation, look for a dog-friendly apartment, fly back, and start the second round of packing for California. Only what would fit in my car. Around Ralph. That was all I needed.

One person didn't need a lot. Granted, my old place didn't reflect that. I had accumulated a lot of worthless crap. But I'd thrown out a lot of it while I was there, left the furniture behind for my coworker's niece (she'd decided to take it over), and kept what needed keeping.

It all just seemed…trivial.

And the closer I got to Sage, the magnets started pulling at me.

On the way there, I was able to ignore the tug. I was on a mission and I knew I'd be coming back by. Now—God, it was killing me. I saw the diner, scanned the parking lot with the eye of a professional stalker (no Nick truck), and passed the turnoff road with no less than three punches to the steering wheel, a ten-mile-an-hour slow down, and I lost count of the curse words.

"Keep going," I muttered.

My chest burned and my knuckles whitened on the wheel, but I kept going. Then Ralph whined like he needed to do his business, and I turned that baby around. Turned down the road I'd followed Nick down nearly two months earlier, and took the curves with an increasingly loud pounding in my ears.

What if he got mad that I was there? What if he didn't want to hear what I had to say and told me to leave? Or worse—what if he took me into his arms and told me he never wanted to let me go again? My breathing got erratic just thinking about that. What would I do? No question. I wouldn't make the same mistake twice.

I'd sent his money to the account number he left for me, but I still hadn't filed for divorce. I couldn't do it. Not yet. If that's what he wanted, he could take care of that.

The final turn came into view, and my palms started to sweat like crazy with anticipation. I swallowed hard and tried to take a deep calming breath, blowing it out as I rounded the clearing.

And stopped.

I clapped a hand over my mouth.

A large FOR SALE sign decorated the front yard. No lawn chair. No fern. No truck. No Nick. No anything. It was like he was never there. The hot tears streamed down my face for the five hundredth time in the last two weeks, as I realized this was it. It had been my last ace in the hole. If nothing else, if I could just get up the nerve to come here, that's where he would be.

And I was too late.

Again.

I got out and let Ralph out to do his thing, staring at the home that I never knew him in, except for one fifteen-minute stretch and the first time I ever saw him in a towel.

We got back in and I turned around, refusing to look in the rearview mirror. I wouldn't do it. I wouldn't say good-bye—

I stopped, sucking in a deep breath. No. I wouldn't do that to him. Even though he did it to me. Even though he wasn't there to hear it or see us or know I was doing it. I looked at the house in the mirror.

"Good-bye, Nick," I whispered. "I love you."

And then I rounded the bend back to the highway.

* * *

Houston Intercontinental Airport was a beast. Highway construction nearly made me miss my exit, and then I couldn't find the damn parking garage for nearly thirty minutes. Once I did, the little machine that spits out your ticket wasn't working, and the guard who wasn't expecting to do anything other than occupy space in the booth that day looked at me like I needed to fix it.

Fifteen minutes and several irritated drivers behind me later, I was parked and shouldering my two carry-ons. It was only two days, so I'd managed to pack professional but easy clothes and not need to check a suitcase. For some reason, that was important to me. Like a suitcase meant I'd get stuck there forever or something. Which was an odd issue to have, considering I was moving there. It didn't get more stuck than that.

Luckily I'd planned in a ridiculously large buffer of time, because an hour in security, another twenty minutes by walk and tram to my gate, and I felt like I'd already been traveling for a full damn day. My shoulders ached from the carry-ons, my feet were already tired, and as I settled in to wait for boarding, I cursed the fact that I hadn't included a bottle of Tylenol in my bag.

"We will begin boarding for Continental flight 1506 to Los Angeles shortly," said a disembodied female voice over the speaker that wasn't either of the chicks standing at the gate kiosk. "Beginning with first class and those with special needs or traveling with small children. Please have your boarding passes in hand."

Of course I wasn't first class. I was nowhere near first class. Back in the old steamship days, I would have been considered "steerage." As in where the cows would ride. In the belly. I would have been one of the first to die on the Titanic.

Small children weren't in my wheelhouse, but special needs? Maybe not, but if they really knew me right now, they'd make me a poster child.

I stared at the sign announcing IAH to LAX.

California. I'd been Googling the state since—well, since Nick left and there was nothing on TV and getting my laptop out was the next thing to do. I'd looked up things to do in Los Angeles, San Francisco, San Diego. Of course I'd need to go to Disneyland. And the Lego place. Because.

Cali Dynamics was evidently on the outskirts of Los Angeles, so I mapped it and looked up apartments nearby. It would be nice to be close. I mean, I knew I wouldn't get as lucky as the two-minute commute to work I currently enjoyed, but I didn't want to spend hours in my car every day. My life was already depressing enough.

Just me, my dog, and—nope that was it.

Only months ago, that was fine. In fact, there wasn't even the dog in that scenario. Ralph hadn't entered the picture to pee on me yet, and my life consisted of me, myself, and I. Going to work, coming home, meeting up with friends occasionally, dating guys who only found me cute occasionally, and I'd been fine with that. Totally fine with that. Why did it now fall into the look-how-sad-this-is category?

Because I'd had more. I'd had a taste of coming home to someone. Grocery shopping for two. Going out to eat with a date. Having someone cook for me and letting me help. Sharing my work day antics with another person and listening to his. Hanging out and feeling that other person's presence and knowing that a simple reach out would find me a warm hand.

Looking across the room at the other person reading, and feeling so comfortable in that silence that it fills you up.

Not being alone.

My eyes burned as the simple funny memories played in my head. I couldn't do that. Sit and dwell. That had been fun, and sometimes not fun, and sometimes dramatic like life tends to be, but it was over. Nick was gone. He'd moved on.

Just like I was about to move on. Me and Ralph. I'd find us a little apartment that would be easy to take him out, figure out my work hours that I already knew would probably run late, and get on with it.

The job would certainly be better and more interesting than counting money out to people at the bank. Although even through its humdrumness, it had its charms. Old Mrs. Brewster who brought me the change she collected every few days from combing the park and the pond area with a metal detector. Dee Dee, the little girl whose mom worked at the donut shop two doors down, and her daily deliveries of donut holes to get us to buy stuff. Mr. Masoneaux from the candy shop down the block, who always threw in homemade lemon drops or freshly minted peppermints with his daily proceeds because he used to have a crush on Aunt Ruby. The other ladies were fun, even if one was a bit of a diva. There were plans in place to bring me out for Mexican food and margaritas next week before I left for good.

I just realized how many of those things involved food. Well, food is love. Especially when your husband is a chef.

Bam.

Those thoughts still kept coming. The zingers that poked their little stabbing prongs into me as reality dawned. I wondered if Nick experienced them. If I had gotten under his skin like Tara had.

A family of three sat down across from me, the mom and dad looking harried and preoccupied, but still holding hands while the little boy ran his matchbox car along all the chairs. Another single woman sat two over from them, and I smiled at her thinking she was more like me. We *aloners* needed to stick together. And then her eye caught something off to the right, and her whole face lit up. Her guy approached, looking at her the same way.

They had the *more*.

I blew out a breath and fidgeted, wishing the boarding would get going. The people watching wasn't cutting it for me. Too many of them had friggin lives, and it was pissing me off. Then a lone guy walked up and took up a piece of wall, scrolling on his phone. An old lady said something next to him and he smiled politely and went back to scrolling. A good-looking girl asked if anyone was sitting in the chair nearby—something clearly unnecessary to ask, given the proximity, so it was an obvious flirt—and he just shook his head and went back to his phone.

Seriously dude, this chick was hot. And maybe he had a girlfriend, or maybe he was a jerk, or maybe he was just stupid. But the hot girl sat down and shook her head and looked around the room. She caught my eye for a second and smiled and probably thought, *we aloners need to stick together.*

Nothing was going to change. It was going to be the same life, just in a different place.

"Attention passengers," the phantom voice said over the loud speaker. "We are now boarding Continental flight 1506 to Los Angeles out of Gate 45. Beginning with first class and those with special needs or ..."

I stood.

Chapter Twenty

"When you need me, Lanie girl, close your eyes. I might not be upward. But I'll be there."

"How do you want your bills?" I asked Mrs. O'Hara. An adorable elderly lady who wore wigs in a different shade of red every time I saw her. "Are twenties okay, or do you want them smaller?"

"Twenties are fine, sweetheart," she said, patting my hand. "I'm not going to a strip club or anything."

I laughed, realizing how good it felt to do that. I hadn't done much of it in a while.

"Well, you never know."

Mrs. O'Hara chuckled. "Your aunt was so proud of you," she said. "Every time we played Bunko, she bragged about how good her Lanie was doing."

"Aunt Ruby played Bunko?" I asked. "Blind?"

"We had to tell her the rolls, but she managed," Mrs. O'Hara said, shrugging.

"And it stayed honest?"

She shrugged. "Mostly."

I chuckled and shook my head. I was coming back. Coming back to me again. Slowly but surely, one baby step at a time my broken heart was healing. Like normal. *I wasn't my mother.*

I'd fallen with all my heart, and it was amazing, and then it was gone, and I was broken for a bit. But not beaten. Like all the other normal people in the world who didn't avoid love, I got hurt, and probably did the hurting as well. I know I hurt Nick, and thinking that he felt like I did killed me. But neither of us would curl up in a ball and quit. Heartbreak was part of life; it meant you'd been blessed enough to feel something.

I was good with that.

I was good with a lot of things. Like never getting on that plane to California, for one. I got up to get in line and walked the other way instead. Right out of the airport. Back to Charmed, to my house, to my dog, to my friend, to my lame-ass bank job, with people so non-lame that they still took me out to lunch after I told them I wasn't going (back) to California. That I'd decided to stay.

Stay in the town that hadn't always been kind to me but then again I hadn't always stroked it nicely, either. It was time to change that.

Aunt Ruby was less ornery too. I'd only had one thing come up missing in the past week, and that was my favorite sunglasses. They'd been hers, too, so I liked to think maybe she was wearing them up there, sporting a little fashion, Barrett style.

I was okay.

And then I heard it.

That distinctive, incredibly familiar voice, low and commanding at the same time. It wasn't possible, and yet all my spidey-senses turned on full blast. Mrs. O'Hara left, and another lady took her place. The bank lobby was pretty full for a Wednesday afternoon, and all the bodies I could see were not what went with the voice. I craned my neck to see who my cohorts might be talking to, but I couldn't see.

Then there it was again. A chuckle and a full sentence about a deposit. My stomach felt like jet fighters were zooming around in there. I had to be imagining it.

"Ma'am?" said the lady in front of me.

I jerked back to reality, staring at the young woman in front of me.

"I'm sorry," I said, shaking my head free of the insanity.

I was crazy after all. I'd just comforted myself with the thought that I wasn't. I was a loon. Certifiable, I believe he once called me. Yep. That was the case, because now I was hearing his—

The two people in the next line cleared away, and all coherent thought went out the door.

Nick.

Two lines down.

He was here. In my town. In my bank. In my line of vision. Talking to Tracey, the new teller that was transferred over. He—he was here. And he couldn't even come to my kiosk? Then he looked my way, and our eyes locked, and I was pretty sure I was having a stroke.

"Ma'am?" the young woman repeated, louder.

"One moment," I mumbled.

I got to my feet without stumbling, miraculously, so okay maybe no stroke, but what I was doing definitely qualified as not in my right mind. I pulled my badge from the keyboard reader, left the back of my area, and walked straight to Tracey's, not giving him a single look.

"Trade with me," I said.

She looked up from typing. "What?"

"Trade places with me," I repeated. "Go take care of my customer. I'll finish here."

She looked at me like I was nuts. I was. Certifiable.

"I—We can't," she said. "You know that. I'm logged in. I can't—"

I pulled out her card and handed it to her. "You aren't anymore."

"Hey!" she said. "I was in the middle of the transaction."

"So he'll have to start over," I said, seeing too many shades of red for any of this to make sense. "Oh well. Please go take care of my customer, she's waiting."

"Lanie," Nick said.

I gripped the cold marble that made up our workstations, willing the icy cold to chill what his saying my name just did to me.

"It's her husband," Lynn whispered from the next kiosk. "It's okay."

"Even less so," Tracey argued. "We aren't supposed to handle family—"

"Tracey," I said, feeling the edge coming on. As in the edge of the cliff that I was about to tumble over. "Please."

Something in my voice finally made an impression, thank God, because Tracey finally huffed over to my area.

And then I had to look at him.

Balls.

Shock, gut kick, and exhaustion emanated off him.

"Why are you here?" I managed, blinking away from the dark eyes that I was trying to forget.

"Why are *you*?"

I met his gaze again. "I work here."

"You're supposed to be in California?" he said. "I'm pretty sure that was the plan—"

"The plan?" I said, laughing bitterly. "How would you know anything about any plan? You didn't stick around long enough to know of one."

He inhaled like he was counting. "Okay. I'm the devil here, I get it. I was trying to get out of your way, Lanie."

"My—" My air left me in a big rush. I shook my head. "My *way*?

Don't fool yourself. I'd just told you I couldn't imagine life without you, and then I get blindsided with my aunt's shit and you just couldn't give me a minute. You had to make the decision for me, and leave me before I might leave you."

The physical reaction in his face couldn't have been more real if I'd slapped him myself. He gave me a long look and then picked up his wallet, moved out of the way of another customer, and walked out.

Again.

"Shit," I breathed, feeling the burn take over my chest, my eyes, my everything.

"I'll take you over here, ma'am," Lynn said to the customer, nodding for me to go.

Go where? After him? No.

I refused.

To the bathroom? No, it would just get worse.

Home to wallow?

Hell no.

I got up and went to the breakroom fridge before pulling out a water bottle and downing most of it at once. I laid the cold bottle against the back of my neck and let it cool my blood. I had three hours left of my shift, and I wasn't going to bail on it because of a man. Not even *that* man. I was okay ten minutes ago, and I'd be okay again.

I blew out a slow breath.

I'd be okay again.

* * *

It was the longest three hours ever, in the history of time.

I went through the motions, dealing with customers, concentrating really hard on monetary transactions, but all that kept playing on long loop was that Nick was back.

Or—maybe. The look on his face when he left didn't give much reason to think he'd stay. He might have bolted again. I didn't know and I shouldn't care. But I was also human and female and still married and heart-clenchingly in love with the guy, so I figured I could cut myself a little slack on the independent female *I am woman* mantra.

I felt like I'd done one of those events where you run a marathon and then ride a bike and then swim an ocean or something. I was drained. I just wanted to get home, curl up on the couch with Ralph, and watch something brainless that didn't require thought. With ice cream.

The little tingle on the back of my neck when I rounded the corner wasn't fast enough. I'd already seen it. Nick's truck in my driveway.

My heart slammed against my ribs and just fell down. Spent. I didn't have the energy to even get excited that he was there. Not if he was just going to give me some spiel about things working out as they should have or that he was moving back to town and we could coexist peacefully. Or if he came to serve me papers.

My stomach lurched. All things that I'd thought of all afternoon. All possibilities. Now he was here and—on my porch, I noticed when I got out. On my porch, with my dog. Sitting back in a rocker like it was the most normal thing in the world.

Ralph bounded down the steps to me, jumping up for his afternoon love-fest.

"I see how you are," I said under my breath as I scratched his chest. "Traitor."

When I could get my breathing stable, I stood back up.

"It's been a day, Nick," I said. "I don't have the energy to fight with you. So whatever you came here to tell me, can you just do it and go?"

"What happened with California?" he asked.

I closed my eyes and blew out a breath. "I didn't go."

"Why? It's what you wanted."

"Well, I changed my mind," I said. "It didn't feel right. I just—" I shook my head, wanting him to understand without me explaining it.

Kind of like wanting him to know I loved him without me saying it. Jesus.

"You were right," he said.

I crossed my arms protectively. "About what?"

"About leaving before you could," he said.

I nodded. "Okay. I knew that."

"I didn't." He got up and held onto the railing. "I never saw it that way. But that's exactly what I did. What we both did."

I frowned. "I didn't go anywhere."

"Yeah, you did," he said, walking down the steps. "You and I both are terrified of being victims. Mine's trust. Yours is love. You will walk this whole earth alone if it keeps you from doing what your mother did, and I refuse to let another person walk out on me like my brother did. Like Tara did. I'm always looking twenty steps ahead, and you just avoid completely."

I blinked and held my arms crossed tighter, lifting my chin.

"Well, there you go," I said. "Baggage met baggage. We sunk. Game, set, match." My voice caught on the end, and I swallowed hard to stem it.

"I was wrong, Lanie," he said, his voice low, his eyes piercing me. *Oh fuck.*

"What?"

"You heard me," he said, stepping closer. "This thing we stepped into—"

"A pile of crap?" I said.

Amusement pulled at his lips. "A pile of crap that we flipped. We did this. We made this crazy thing work. We made it real."

"And I got scared," I breathed, wanting to cross the feet between us so badly it hurt.

"I know."

"I wanted to say things," I said, hearing the wobble in my voice, feeling the burn that would bring the tears I hated. "They were there, in my head, and I couldn't say them out loud."

"And so I walked away," he said, taking a step closer. "Before you could."

"I wasn't going to," I said, two hot tears streaming down my cheeks. "I couldn't imagine—I was going to ask you to come with me, because I couldn't not have you in my life." The sobs turned on the words like a faucet and I couldn't stop. "But then you were just—gone, and you wouldn't take my calls or my texts and—" I pressed my hands to my heart. "I went to your house and it was vacant."

"You went to my house?"

"I was beside myself, Nick," I said, laughing through the sobs. "I was so afraid to become my mother, that I ruined us and was *still* becoming her. I was miserable without you. I mean, I'm pulling things together now—" I held up my hands. "Not that I really look like it at the moment."

"You look beautiful," he said.

"That's such a load of shit."

"No shit," he said, one step closer again, so close I could feel him. Smell him. Touch him if I wanted to.

God, I wanted to.

"You gave up on us," I whispered through my tears. "You gave your bike away. I knew then that you weren't coming back for me. And I still couldn't file the fucking papers." Heavy sobs shook my body. "How could I sign a paper saying I wanted a divorce from the man I love? The person I wanted to spend the rest of my life with?"

Through my tears, I saw his. I'd never seen him cry. Never seen him even well up.

"What did you say?"

"I said I don't want a divorce."

"I don't, either," he said, his voice rough. "But you know that's not what I'm talking about."

My fingers found the bottom of his shirt and his hands moved up my arms.

"The man I love," I whispered through a hiccup.

I felt the rush of air from his exhale as his hands went into my hair.

"Lanie."

He tilted my head.

"I love you, Nick."

When his mouth covered mine, there was nothing better. Nothing sweeter, not a better fit in the world than this one man's body against mine. His kiss mingled with mine. The way our arms fit around each other, the easy way my legs wrapped around him when he lifted me. It was perfect. Diving into his mouth, my fingers tangled in his hair as he palmed my ass—it was perfect.

I have no idea how we made it up the porch steps and all the way up the stairs like that without bodily injury, but when he laid me on my bed and looked into my eyes with no walls, no barriers—I knew I was home for real.

"Thank you for coming home, Nick," I said, his face in my hands. "I love you so much."

He kissed my lips, my eyes, and worked his way down to the sensitive spot below my ear.

"You are my home, Lanie McKane."

* * *

I'd never felt so thoroughly sexed in my life. Every inch and muscle in my entire body whined with exhaustion and yet felt so incredibly loved. I stretched like a cat, spooning in his arms, loving the feel of his limbs entangled with mine.

I craned around to see him blinking awake and smiling at me.

"We fell asleep," I said.

"We earned it," he said, sliding his hand up from my belly to palm a breast, and he sighed happily against my shoulder. "I love these so much."

I giggled.

"I'm glad I can provide."

"We should probably eat something. What time is it?" he asked, leaning forward to see, stopping as he did.

"What?" I asked, looking at him and then following his gaze.

His wedding ring still sat on my nightstand. Not the letter. I'd put that away, unable to keep reading it, but his ring—that meant something to me. Even though it stood for an arranged marriage and not for love, it had turned out that way and I kept it sitting there by the clock.

I guess I hadn't totally moved on, after all.

"Yeah," I said.

Nick looked down at me with a look so full of everything I couldn't have responded if I tried. Thank God I wasn't expected to.

He pushed up and off the bed, and I instantly missed him.

"Where are you going?"

"To take care of something that I should have already done," he said, retrieving his jeans and digging in the pockets. Satisfied with whatever he was looking for, he walked back to the edge of the bed. "Sit up please."

"Sit up? What are we—"

He lowered to one knee. Completely naked. Dear God in Heaven.

"What—" There was no sound to the word. More like a slow exhalation around the thought of it.

"Lanie Barrett McKane," he began.

Oh. My. God.

I pulled my pillow into my arms and pressed fingers to my mouth so I couldn't squeal or say something completely wrong or inadequate like I was prone to do. *Don't mess this up, Lanie.*

"I was going to plan this out for some big night, but—you and I don't work that way. Our best moments have been unexpected."

Understatement of the century.

"I never expected you," he said, emotion catching his voice. "But God tossed you right in the middle of a jacked-up day and said 'This is a gift, boy. It's up to you to realize that.'"

Tears filled my eyes for the ninety-ninth time that day.

"I love you," he said. "I love the way you mess things up without even trying."

A laugh bubbled up through my fingers.

"I love how your favorite time of day is getting up and stumbling to the coffeepot when you could just sleep longer," he said. "I love how you hide behind a pillow and peek out and cry during sad movies, and how your laugh can turn my day around."

He pulled my hand from my lips and held it.

"Most of all, I love the way you look at me, the way you touch me, the way you can walk in a room and take my breath away and not even know it," he said, his voice so full of fire it made *my* breath catch in my chest. "The way you fight to the death to protect what's yours." One corner of his lips tugged upward. "Using any means necessary."

"A girl's gotta do what a girl's gotta do," I said.

"I never expected you," he repeated. "I never saw you coming. But I'm damn glad you did." He opened his other hand, and sparkles caught the light, making me suck in a breath. Holy mother of bling. He bought me a ring. *He bought me a ring!* "I put a fake ring on your finger the first time," he said. "But that isn't us anymore. We deserve the real deal."

Nick slipped it onto my finger, and my throat felt like it would close up.

"Oops," he said, starting to slide it back off. "I forgot to ask first."

"You take that off, Mr. McKane, and you'll be pooping it out tomorrow," I said through happy tears, making him laugh.

"So you'd marry me again?" he asked.

I wrapped my arms around his neck and pulled him to me.

"I'd marry you a hundred times over, Nick," I said, my lips against his.

"I only need one more," he whispered.

"Did you hear that?" I called, casting my eyes upward to Heaven. "You can relax now!"

Ralph barked downstairs as if on cue, getting progressively louder.

Nick dragged his lips from mine. "That dog needs to learn timing."

"He doesn't bark at much," I said.

"I know, that's why I'm not ignoring it," he said, pushing to his feet and bringing me with him. "Throw something on."

"I'll blind them with my ring," I said, grabbing my white fluffy robe. He pulled on his jeans commando again. Good God, my husband was hot. "When did you buy a ring?"

"Today," he said. "When I left the bank." He dropped a kiss on my nose. "There was no question. Now stay here, please."

"What?"

"You heard me," he said, pointing before he headed down the hall.

"Mm-hmm, they get bossy when they put a ring on it."

I heard a chuckle over Ralph's hullabaloo, and I sank back onto the bed, wrapping the robe and the covers around me. Life had a way of flipping on a dime lately. Good one second, bad the next. Phenomenal the next.

I was riding the phenomenal wave at the moment, and really *really* hoping it was a long one. Nothing had ever felt this good or this right, and while that *feelings* thing scared the shit out of me, I was learning. It was worth it. Nick was worth it.

I held my new bling up and just stared.

"I wish you could see this, Aunt Ruby," I said softly. "I wish you could see *me*. I'm happy," I whispered to the ceiling.

"Lanie, come here, babe," Nick called up, his tone sounding odd.

"Oh *balls*." I swung my legs down. "Here we go." The downhill slide. "Who's here this time? All your ex-girlfriends?"

Ralph was still making a ruckus when I landed on the bottom step, but not at the front door. I rounded the stairs and headed toward the noise when I smelled it. Baked apples.

Baked friggin apples.

"Oh my God," I said, my hand on my chest as the aroma brought tears to my eyes. "Do you smell that? Did I ever tell you—"

I stopped short.

There under the shelf holding the wooden spools, where Nick stood holding a cabinet door open and Ralph was now turning in circles in lieu of barking, was a collection of things. Our things. Even from a few feet away, I knew exactly what things they were.

Goose bumps covered my body as my gaze rested on neat stacks of shoes, shirts, a couple pairs of socks I'd blamed on Ralph, my favorite sunglasses, and Nick's ratty black ball cap.

"Sweet Jesus," I whispered, walking close enough to touch them. "My phone charger?"

"I thought you threw my hat away," Nick said.

I picked up one of his shirts and held it to my nose. It still smelled like him. *She was baking apples.*

She was happy.

Because I was.

"I love you," I said.

He did a double take. "Your house just upped the spook factor by a mile and that's where your head goes?"

I nodded. "That's what it's about."

Nick shook his head and pulled me in for a hug. "Will I ever understand you?"

"Do you need to?" I asked. "Because that could get boring."

He laughed. "True," he said against my hair. "And I have the feeling that life with you will never be that."

"You have feelings?" I asked, tilting my head in a tease.

Nick's chuckle vibrated against the sensitive skin of my neck as he slipped the robe from my shoulders.

"Let me show you one of them."

Aunt Ruby's Hot Baked Cinnamon Apples

WHAT YOU NEED:

10 apples, cored, peeled and sliced thinly (I like Granny Smith or Jazz)
2 teaspoons of cinnamon
1 cup of brown sugar
2 teaspoons lemon juice
1 pinch of salt
1 pinch of nutmeg
Finely chopped pecans (optional or as many as you like)
Whipped cream (optional) or ice cream (optional) (like either of these is really optional?)

DIRECTIONS:

Preheat oven to 375°F. Place cut and peeled apples in a mixing bowl (or if you mix everything in the baking dish, there is less to clean up. Just saying…) Gently mix all the ingredients together except the pecans.

Put apples in a non-stick pan if you mixed in another bowl, cover and place in the oven. Bake for 45 minutes, stirring at least once every 15 minutes.

Once they are soft, sprinkle with the pecans if you are using them, and cook for another few minutes to thicken the sauce.

Enjoy alone or with just about anything. I love it with ice cream, personally, but I'm an ice cream addict.

Keep reading for a sneak peek at Sharla Lovelace's

second book in the Charmed Texas series

LUCKY CHARMED

Chapter One

"C'mon people," I muttered, traversing the grocery parking lot for the third time. "The sales aren't that good this week. It's time to wrap it up."

I could go to the bigger supermarket in Charmed, but I preferred this smaller one in Goldworth, near my office. Less people. Less judgment.

Less parking space.

Spotting a mom shouldering two reusable canvas shopping bags with two kids in tow, I cranked the wheel in her direction. She smiled quickly and pushed her kids in front of her as she approached an SUV, as if she was used to being stalked. As anyone who shopped here should be.

I groaned under my breath at the big cartoonish honey bee sticker on her back window that sported a dialogue bubble saying, "It's sweeter in Charmed!"

I was so tired of honey. I despise it, honestly. I know that sounds like a random and insignificant fact, but when you live in a town like Charmed, Texas, that lives and breathes by the stuff, it can become a thing. Not that I'm averse to sweet. Chocolate, for instance, could easily run from my tap and I'd celebrate, but I have issues with a substance made by one insect throwing up on another, then party number two spending the next couple of days playing with vomit.

There's a disclaimer to living in a town that breeds bees and brags of World Famous Honey on its welcome sign. You know a little too much about the process.

Summer was the hardest to stomach—no pun intended—with the annual Honey Festival kicking off right after school kicked out. It was even more everywhere than usual. Every retailer sports a stash of jars from whatever apiary hits them up first. Every restaurant sells them at the checkout. Hell, even the Quik-Serve convenience store had a supply on the counter last time I was in. I couldn't pop in for a coffee and a package of chocolate donuts without being accosted by honey jars.

This summer was a little better. My best friend, Lanie, was back in town with her new hubby (wink, wink) and so the consummate honey frenzy was overshadowed by a tinge of gossipy drama. The festival's annual dance had all eyes on her, and no one noticed that I showed up to help her out. I don't usually go. Most of the good townspeople of Charmed don't care much for me, and that's okay. I gave up on that fight a long time ago. Small towns are good at holding on to ancient grudges or still living through their high school days. I get it.

Once upon a time, my eighteen-year-old self was scandalous. Heaven forbid. My sins then evidently tainted the next decade, the perfect sainted (cough) man I married, and my mother, who apparently could never again hold down a job. (Side note: she wasn't holding down a job the previous decade, either.)

So anyway, there was the festival, including the ridiculous Honey Wars, with crazy people hawking their self-labeled jars on every sidewalk, and then the Lucky Hart carnival a month later. It's not honey-driven, but it's crazy too. Or it was, anyway. I haven't stepped foot inside that carnival in six years, since my divorce from said saint, now-the-mayor, Dean Crestwell.

As honey-bee-reusable-bag-mom drove away, I pulled into the spot and got out, ready to go load up on chocolate anything in those evil plastic grocery bags that I'm gonna go to hell for. My cell buzzed from my wristlet and I pulled it out and laughed as I answered, entering the store.

"Just couldn't stand it, could you?"

"I know, I'm worse than a mom."

It was Lanie. Calling from Vegas, where she and Nick were vacationing after renewing their vows. With real rings. That's a story for another time.

"Are you kidding me?" I said. "You are a mom. You fawn more over that dog now than anyone I've ever seen."

I was house-slash-dogsitting while they were gone. Lanie kind of inherited a Rottweiler when her old neighbor skipped out, and while it was a little iffy at the beginning, Ralph had won her over. The jury was still out for me in that regard, but I had to admit, Ralph was kind of sweet. When he wasn't licking himself.

"He's family," Lanie said.

"Well, he's fine," I said. "I shared my blueberry muffin with him this morning, and gave him a bacon treat before I left."

"See, you're a softie, too," she said.

"Don't ever say that out loud." I stopped in front of an end cap of chocolate syrup. I'd seen some vanilla bean ice cream in Lanie's freezer and that would be a great compliment. I kept walking, though. It was a maybe. I could always come back. "How's Vegas?"

"I'm down $100 already today," she said, "So I'm playing the penny slots and waiting on my handsome hubby to finish his game and come whisk me off upstairs for naked room service."

I was hit as always with that mix of being so damn happy for her, fighting through her baggage to find her soul mate. And feeling so damn envious.

"So you're calling me why?" I asked.

"I saw a slot machine themed with pancakes and I thought of Ralph," she said.

I nodded. "Of course you did."

"Did we miss anything interesting at the carnival?" she asked. "Or did you go?"

I snorted. "What do you think?" I picked up a bag of peanuts and then put it back down. Salty wasn't the thing tonight. It had been a long day at the office, and besides, celebrations were all about the chocolate.

It was over. As of yesterday, that damned infernal beast that descended upon the little town of Charmed every year was over. Forever. Not everyone shared my view or saw the summer carnival as beastly. Kids loved it, of course. A lot of the adults still rolled out for it in spades, probably grabbing the one last chance to mingle and see who was doing what—or who—since the Honey Festival the month before.

I always looked at it as one more year in the bag. One more summer of successful absenteeism. That festival would probably go on till the end of time, but now, with Charmed taking on a new entity—a planned outdoor entertainment area that everyone was buzzing about—the carnival itself would stop here no more.

The Charmed city council had voted in a bid to build a permanent mini-theme park, boardwalk, and restaurant-and-retail row on Bailey's pond near my mother's trailer park. Lots of sales tax dollars from surrounding towns, more local jobs, something for people to get excited about besides flying insects and honey (thank God). And an end to the yearly nomadic reach of Lucky Hart Carnivals.

It was a win-win, and I was so friggin excited, I couldn't stand it.

I'd forced myself to go out there with Dean for years, just to prove a silly point. Smiling, flirting, overly doting over my husband every time a certain hooded gaze landed my way. A gaze that was once the most intense and mind-altering drug I could ever know.

Prove a point to whom? To Dean? To myself? To the man behind the eyes?

Yep. Absolutely. And now I never had to think about it, demean myself, or avoid an event again. Not that I ever should have in the first place. I should have been above it all. But hey, small towns have big memories and every time I tried to forget about the very public Carmen Frost Public Humiliation of Summer 2001, someone was always around to remind me.

I breathed in deeply, savoring the satisfaction as I rounded the cookie aisle at the grocery store. Chocolate-covered graham crackers were just the ticket to celebrate.

"I know," Lanie said. "I just thought maybe you'd surprise me. Where are you?"

"The grocery store," I said. "Getting some party food."

"You having a party without me?"

"Can't help you had to go honeymooning," I said. "I filed two briefs today, settled a divorce case in mediation, and spent most of the afternoon avoiding Judge Constantine and his unibrow." And Lucky Hart Carnivals was trucking along their merry way. "I'm having a comfort food extravaganza to celebrate."

Lanie chuckled. "Comfort food meaning three batches of brownies?"

I laughed out loud and then held up a hand to a woman who took a break from studying various Oreo flavors to give me a double-take.

"Sorry, I'm having a moment," I said. "Don't mind me."

I grabbed my package of bad-for-me and turned back. Smack into a broad chest with a set of arms that felt just as solid. One of the hands attached to them gripped my upper arms as the chocolate grahams crushed between us.

"Oh! I'm so—"

Then my eyes panned upward. Into the eyes of the drug I thought I'd never see again. Eyes that had gotten older and wary. That were supposed to be gone. They flashed with as much surprise as I'm sure mine did, in the two-second span we both stood there frozen with cell phones to our ears.

"Shit," I exclaimed.

"Carmen?" Lanie voice called in my ear from somewhere far far away.

Backing up a full step so that he had to let go of me, my mind went on a roller coaster ride. Ha. Roller coaster. That was ironic. Or delusional. Or perhaps I was just having a stroke and my life was flashing by as the man I'd spent fifteen years trying to forget stared down at me. Regardless, I got a five-second speed reel in my head of all of it. All of us. Me and Sullivan Hart.

"Sully," I managed finally.

"Su—Sully?" Lanie said, her voice tilting up at the end. "As in Sully?"

It was like a bird chirping in my ear, as I held up my chin and tried not to notice the rest of him. The thick dark hair, not as long as it once was, maybe shoulder length, but enough to be pulled back with what looked like a leather strap, a pair of Ray-Bans shoved up on top. The light scruff on his face. His smell, the heady mix of something woodsy and adrenaline that I'd still know if I were struck deaf, dumb, and blind. The way he ran a hand over his face, inhaled deeply and made his gaze go guarded like he used to do when he felt anxious.

He was anxious?

He mumbled something into his phone and put it in his pocket.

Suddenly, I was eighteen again. Standing in the second empty parking lot of the day and sweating through my clothes. Clutching a duffle bag to my body as the wretched sickly sweet smell of melted cotton candy baking on the asphalt stung my nose. I'd seen him since then, of course. From a distance. Years ago. I was so over it.

So why was the sudden one-on-one giving me chest pains? Why were his eyes so friggin intense? Ignore it! So what that your fingers are going numb! Maybe it was a stroke. He was supposed to be gone, damn it. Gone with that cursed carnival.

"Let me call you back, Lanie," I mumbled, the phone already lowering before the words were out of my mouth.

"Hey," he said, clearing his throat.

I willed my face to go neutral and unaffected, but I couldn't really feel it anymore, so it was kind of a crap shoot. I would have given anything at that moment for a speed superpower so that I could flash out of there the next time he blinked. Assuming he blinked. He hadn't yet.

"Hey."

"How've you been?" he asked.

No. We weren't doing that. We weren't catching up like old buddies.

"I thought—you—" I gestured something with my hands that I hoped demonstrated awayness.

His eyes narrowed, however. Crap. He didn't understand the universal sign language for Why the living hell are you still here?

"You thought what?" he asked.

"The carnival left," I said. "I assumed you were with it."

He nodded. "You don't know."

"Know?" I echoed, crossing my arms over my chest and backing up another step.

No, I clearly didn't know. Was I supposed to? Were there people that knew and left me out of all the things to know? My heart thundered so loudly in my ears, it was all I could do not to clamp my palms over them.

Why was he here?

"About the Bailey's Pond project?" he prompted, crossing his own arms.

A tattoo peeked out from his muscle, under a shirt sleeve. The tattoo. Shit. It was all I could do not to run my thumb across my left breast where its clone resided.

My mouth went dry as all kinds of confusion exploded in my head. Keep it together. Don't show weakness. He left you.

He left you.

A calm washed over me and all my strength as a professional business woman, as just a woman who'd been through and seen a few things, came back and held me up. What did it matter that the love of my life, the man that shattered me into a million pieces in a stadium parking lot was standing in front of me fifteen years later looking good enough to lick from head to toe?

I was better than that.

"What about it?" I asked. "Your carnival won't be coming through here anymore."

An eyebrow shot up, and the hazel flecks in his eyes danced. "That's right. Shaw will bypass all of Cedar County from now on."

Something familiar and yet not knocked on my skull. Something I should know. Seems there were quite a few things I should know.

"Shaw?"

"My brother," he said, gesturing to his phone like that would clear it up. Bingo. Shaw Hart. I had a vague recollection of a sulky pre-teen boy hanging on the outskirts. Sully's half brother. "He's running the road show now."

I blinked, and the warning bells started to ding. Shaw was on the road? Sully wasn't on the road? Hell no, he wasn't on the road, he was standing in my grocery store. My grocery store. The small one in Goldworth near my office that I frequented instead of the Charmed supermarket for the sole purpose of running into less people.

"And so you are--?" I prompted, a sick acidic burn starting low in my belly.

Somewhere deep in my psyche I knew the answer before he could tell me.

"The major investor in the development," he said, his voice smooth. The tone deep and the words slightly lazy as they rolled off his tongue, just as I remembered it. Why did I remember it? "The park will be named The Lucky Charm, but that's not public knowledge yet."

I just nodded. "Good for you," I said, as my lawyer brain started ticking away.

Being an investor—especially one getting the name of his corporation included in the project—meant bringing major capital to the table. Investing that kind of money would mean sticking around long enough to watch the progress. Or it would if it were me. An accountant would probably set up a per diem for his stay. And seeing as nothing had even started yet—dear God he could be there in Charmed for months.

"So you're here for a while, then?" I added, digging my nails into my upper arms.

Sully blinked a couple of times, giving me a studying look like he was contemplating his words. That was bad.

"I bought a house, Carmen," he said. "In Charmed. I'm not leaving."

There was one of those moments where things spin around and lights look funny. I blinked it clear and just breathed in lieu of words. There were none. He bought—

"You—" I shook my head and forced a smile. "You what?"

Sully gave me a long look followed by a glance toward the Oreo lady. She's not gonna save you, buddy.

"I assumed you'd probably heard."

I chuckled. "Why?" I asked. "Why would I hear about random people buying houses?"

Like how I did that? Making him a nobody to me to lessen the tension and maybe slow my heart rate? But now why didn't I fucking hear about him buying a house? I went to Chamber breakfasts. Occasionally. Wasn't there someone there that would have known? I couldn't pump gas without someone telling me about my ex-husband's latest hilarious Facebook post. Or my mother's most current medical issues. But let the hot carny that made me an overnight sensation come back and buy a house in Charmed, and nobody has anything to say?

Sully held up a hand. "I don't know. Never mind." He laid the hand against his chest, and my eyes fell to it of their own accord.

Damn it, I'd loved his hands. The long, roughened fingers of a working guy, even back then. My mind flashed to what they looked like—what they'd felt like on my skin a hundred years ago, and I felt the heat rush to my face.

"I mean, what do you think? I hang out with realtors?" I said, hearing how stupid that sounded.

"Sorry," he said, backing up, looking like he'd rather be anywhere else. "I guess I figured—small town. You're a lawyer—"

"How'd you know that?" I asked.

The tired expression went focused as he tilted his jaw just slightly. I saw the spark. The challenge. The grin that pulled at his lips. He grabbed a new package of chocolate grahams from the shelf without breaking eye contact with me, and switched them out with the one in my hand.

"Well, people do talk to me."

Oh. Hell. No.

No he didn't.

I lifted my chin, and refused to look away. No matter what was liquefying in my chest as his gaze burned through me. No matter what images flashed like a movie reel in my head. I wouldn't give him that satisfaction.

"Good for you," I said, placing the package back on the shelf. I needed them more than ever but I would not need them in front of him. "Welcome back to Charmed."

I made to walk around him, but the heat from his hand on my arm stopped me.

"Carmen, wait."

His voice was like hot honey over my body.

I hate honey.

I was proud of myself. My acting ability to not suck my tongue down my throat, or choke on my own spit, or jerk my arm free like I'd been bitten by a rabid squirrel—was Oscar-worthy. Instead, I patted his hand and smiled up at him, slowly stepping to the side until his fingers slid free.

"We're grown-ups now, Sully," I said, wondering where the hell the words were coming from. "It's all good. Have a great day."

And I walked away. And out. And to my car. The pains stabbing through my middle stealing my breath. Damn grateful for nothing else in my hand because being chased down for shoplifting cookies while in a blind haze of what-the-fuckery would have been the final icing on a messed up cake.

Fumbling for my keys, I hit the button and got in as quickly as possible. I had to leave. Now. Before he came out. Before I could see what he was driving and then obsess over every other that vehicle I saw in every other parking lot in Charmed. Before I could succumb to the temptation of watching to see where he went. Where he lived, what his home looked like.

"Leave," I whispered, my voice sounding vaguely desperate. I felt the burn behind my eyes and I shook my head and tilted my head back. "No. You will not cry, damn it."

I blinked at the roof. I was thirty-three. Eighteen was a long time ago.

Suck it up, Carmen.

I took a deep breath and faced forward, just in time to see him walk out of the store. He'd slid the sunglasses down over his eyes, causing a stray lock of dark hair to fall next to his face. He was probably twenty-five feet away, and I could feel that strand of hair on my fingertips.

Without another look, I pulled out and drove away.

About the Author

Photo: Leo Weeks Photographers

Sharla Lovelace is the bestselling, award-winning author of sexy small-town love stories. Being a Texas girl through and through, she's proud to say she lives in Southeast Texas with her retired husband, a tricked-out golf cart, and two crazy dogs. She is the author of five stand-alone novels including the bestselling *Don't Let Go*, the exciting Heart Of The Storm series, and the fun and sexy new Charmed in Texas series. For more about Sharla's books, visit www.sharlalovelace.com, and keep up with all her new book releases easily by subscribing to her newsletter. She loves keeping up with her readers, and you can connect with her on Facebook, Twitter, and Instagram as @sharlalovelace.